Grant Stockbridge

Carroll & Graf Publishers, Inc.
New York

First Carroll & Graf edition 1991

Carroll & Graf Publishers, Inc.
260 Fifth Avenue
New York, NY 10001

ISBN: 0-88184-730-5

Manufactured in the United States of America

This volume is dedicated to
the memory of Harry Steeger,
whose love of justice, adventure,
and action inspired him to create
The Spider.

Secret City of Crime

CHAPTER ONE

The Spider's Suicide

In four months, there had been twenty bank robberies and twenty murders. All of them were perfect crimes. In each raid, the bandits deliberately shot down one person, usually an inoffensive bystander.

They were perfect crimes because the police could not solve them.

Richard Wentworth had been working on those crimes, too. And for four months, those twenty robberies remained perfect crimes—even to the *Spider!* That was why he planned the action that his associates said was absolute and certain suicide.

There were lines of pain etched about Wentworth's mouth these days and a bitter flash to his gray-blue eyes. He explained very carefully to Nita van Sloan:

"All police methods have failed, Nita. All my efforts have failed. It is certain that all these robberies are the work of one brain—and yet every robbery is different. The men are different and the methods are different—except for one thing. In each robbery, one person is wantonly slaughtered. It is almost as if the brain that planned these robberies wanted to make sure his signature was on them.''

Nita's hands were small white fists. ''You can't do what you're planning!'' she cried. ''I won't let you throw yourself away. It's suicide! Please, Dick—don't do it!''

Wentworth brushed that aside. ''In the last month I have kidnaped seven known bank bandits. I have questioned them under the truth drug. None of them knew anything . . . Until I hit Killer Gordon.''

Nita shuddered. ''He must have killed a dozen people in his life!''

''He won't kill any more,'' Wentworth said shortly. ''He let drop one thing, one little thing—and then he died from an overdose of the truth drug.''

Nita was listening, but also she was tapping her fingers together. Behind Wentworth was his Sikh comrade-at-arms, Ram Singh. The man's shoulders and build were those of a giant. His eyes, as they rested on his master, were idolatrous. His lips were grim beneath his beard. Nita was signaling to Ram Singh with her fingertips, tapping in Morse code.

''D-o-n-t l-e-t h-i-m g-o. H-e w-i-l-l b-e k-i-l-l-e-d. K-n-o-c-k h-i-m o-u-t b-u-t d-o-n-t l-e-t h-i-m g-o!''

Ram Singh scowled and began to pay closer attention to what his master was saying. He had never disobeyed the master, but then Nita van Sloan had never before suggested such a thing. It was a danger that even a warrior of the Sikhs hesitated to face!

''Killer Gordon told us,'' Wentworth went on, ''that crooks can *buy* their plans now, and buy full protection through a central office. I know where that office is. I was trying to learn more about it when he died.''

Nita asked sharply, ''Do you have to do it in this wild and reckless way? Oh, Dick, it's certain death!''

Wentworth put his arms around her. "You're adorable when you're angry," he whispered.

And Nita knew he would go through with his plan, in spite of her, in spite of anything. Behind his back, her fingers signaled to Ram Singh.

"*K-n-o-c-k h-i-m o-u-t. L-e-t i-t b-e o-n m-y h-e-a-d.*"

Nita's heart ached, but she felt she was justified in taking this step. It was dangerous at any time for Richard Wentworth to appear in the robes of the *Spider*. For any member of the Underworld and any policeman would shoot the *Spider* on sight!

And this time Richard Wentworth was going to wear the robes of the *Spider* in broad daylight, in fact, during the noon rush hour. He was not going to move secretly, he was going to show himself to thousands of people—in crowded Times Square! As if that danger were not enough, he was going to make sure that a policeman was looking at him—then he was going to kill a man!

No wonder Nita called it suicide!

"It's the only way," Wentworth explained eagerly, as he went over his plan again. "The only way I can make sure of getting behind the scenes of these perfect crimes."

Ram Singh's face was set in a scowl. *Wah!* The *missie sahib* was right! This was not bravery—it was madness. There would not even be anybody to fight! Ram Singh lifted his mighty fist. Nita swung onto Richard Wentworth's arms.

Suddenly Wentworth moved, set her aside and dodged past Ram Singh. He stood at the door of the room, and his eyes were sorrowful but there was grim determination on his lips.

Ram Singh dropped to one knee. "*Sahib*, master, do not do this mad thing!"

Nita sobbed, "Oh, Dick, please. . . ."

Wentworth said shortly, "I must."

He was gone. Those who loved him were sure it was to his certain death!

It was one of those rare days of bright sunshine that drops sometimes into mid-winter in New York, and the sun-starved people thronged the streets. They stood thickly in the central triangles where the thin warmth could reach them; they packed the sidewalks, milling into restaurants, jamming in and out of the subways. Autos and street cars crawled among pedestrians who preempted roadways. Horns blatted, the police at the intersections worked furiously but above it all was the hum of voices, the shuffle of shoe-leather. The scene had a certain peace.

The World Brotherhood Building had been newly completed on Times Square before priorities shut down on steel and metals. It was a glistening tower of white tile laced with brilliant chromium and it had a gilt dome topped by a sixty-foot metal statue of the Redeemer of Man, hands extended in blessing, head bowed toward the teeming square.

The building had been built by the man the newspapers called the "eccentric" millionaire philanthropist, Donaldson Gust. On the first floor was an auditorium where noonday lectures were delivered. Foreign language schools thronged the lower floors. Preference was given to men of other nations in the rentals, and there was a perpetually changing exhibition of the products of other continents. There was also a radio station that specialized in "culture." Station WBB broadcast in 12 languages.

It was a lavishly constructed building with many useless columns inside and out. The walls were said to be completely bomb-proof. And the offices were laid out on the plans of the palaces, chateaux, villas of foreign countries. The architects and workmen, too, had been a mixture from all lands, so that the newspapers had dubbed it the "Tower of Babel." They wrote that the workers had to use sign language to communicate with each other. And that plans were always being changed during its construction. There had been seventeen architects, with a special division of labor. Not even the famous secret Norden bombsight was constructed in more parts by more men who did not know what others were doing.

It was in this confused labyrinth that Perfect Crimes, Inc., had its headquarters office. The name on the door read:
Self-Help to Greatness, Inc.

The building stood on a corner, and men drifted idly into the auditorium within, where a lecture was going on about Esperanto, the "universal language." Scores stood against the outer walls, half-blocked the doorway. One man, square of jaw, military in bearing, stood against a column and watched the traffic with alert, intelligent eyes. He spotted a coupé that was crawling toward him down Broadway. The windows reflected the sun, and he could see nothing of the interior. He smiled faintly, unbuttoned his overcoat and rolled his shoulders. It freed the butt of the revolver under his arm.

The coupé trundled on, then suddenly as it reached a spot in front of the World Brotherhood Building, it swung broadside across the street.

Traffic was instantly blocked in all lanes. Horns started blaring, and in an instant the autos were checked for an entire block. They stopped cross-traffic on Forty-second street and Forty-third. A policeman started striding angrily toward the stalled car. He lifted a white-gloved hand and gestured urgently.

The car door swung open and the people, staring from the sidewalks, saw a curiously lithe crouched figure slide to the pavement. A broad-brimmed black hat hid half his face. From his shoulders swirled a long black cape. He stood there for an instant and the traffic officer, squeezing between stalled autos and taxis, saw him. The cop's face went blank with amazement, then he began to claw for the fastened flap of his revolver.

The man who had leaned against the base of the building column scooped a hand under the lapel of his coat and whipped out a revolver. He sprang up on the pediment of the column, where he had a clear view over the heads of the people on the street—and started shooting! He held the gun at arm length, sighted deliberately and fired accurately at the *Spider!*

People screamed in sudden panic and began to run. The crashing echoes of the shots ran along the canyon of buildings. The policeman was shouting now. He had not got his revolver out yet. He tucked a whistle between his lips and started screaming through it.

The *Spider,* after that initial moment of pause against his car, was in constant motion. He darted toward the curb, toward the man who was shooting at him. As he ran, he suddenly had two revolvers in his hands. They blasted out a furious thunder of gunpowder. The man on the column winced and seemed to shrink against the column. He fired twice more, slowly, while the *Spider* was rolling out ten shots. The man opened his mouth and screamed. He leaned out from the column, twisted slowly and pitched limply to the sidewalk!

The policeman was charging along the sidewalk.

He loosed a bullet high over the heads of the people and shouted. The *Spider* seemed to see him for the first time. In two tremendous bounds, he reached the entrance of the World Brotherhood Building and popped inside. A path through the crowd opened in terror. He went through the people, hit the steps, and vanished upward.

The traffic policeman reached the door, and an elevator starter with an angry face pointed toward the steps. The policeman stood in the doorway and kept blowing his whistle. He slammed shut the doors, started locking them.

"Nobody leaves this building!" he shouted harshly. "Get back, damn you!"

He still had the whistle in his mouth and it kept making piercing noises as he tried to speak. When he wasn't speaking, he was blowing it furiously. He gestured at the elevator attendant.

"You there!" he ordered. "Call police headquarters and tell them I've got the *Spider* sewn up in this building!"

On the sidewalk outside, people stood back timorously from where the gunman lay. Suddenly, the man got to his feet, and sprinted! People screamed and dodged. He spun around the corner and vanished.

But the police had the building sewn up in a space of minutes. They were certain this time that they had the *Spider*.

CHAPTER TWO

Self-Help to Death

When the shooting started in the street outside, a buzzer whirred in the offices of "Self-Help to Greatness, Inc." The girl at the reception desk pressed a button in the floor and in every office the electric clocks on the various desks briefly glowed with a crimson alarm light.

In one of the offices, two men came sharply to their feet. One of them crossed over to a big pier mirror in the wall (it was on the French floor) and standing in front of the mirror, he twice jumped up with both feet. The mirror slid aside and he stepped out of the office. The other man scooped up a small rubber-bladed fan and pulled it close to his mouth.

"What's up?" he asked shortly.

The voice that came out of the fan was faint but distinct. "*Spider's* in the building. Took stairs to second floor. Police have closed all doors."

The man smiled at the fan-microphone. "Stay on duty," he said calmly. "If you sight the *Spider* again, shoot him with *0-0-3*. That won't make any noise and your hideout won't be discovered."

He pressed one of the screws in the fan base and said, "Report."

"Second floor," the voice answered. *"Spider* ran up steps. Gone third floor."

The man repeated his orders, and kept on the quest, checking with each hidden watchman on each floor. He traced the *Spider* to the eighth floor, and he was reported starting for the ninth. The ninth-floor watchman had not seen him.

The man frowned and sat waiting, tautly. His office was on the sixth floor. The *Spider* had gone past him, apparently, and yet. . . . The man leaped to his feet. A gun sprang into his hand, and he reached the window in a single long stride. He flung it up and peered out, scanning the wall of the building. The *Spider's* favorite entry was by way of a window, using his famous silken rope that was called the Web.

The man saw nothing. There was a light tap at his door, and he whipped about. His gun went into his pocket, but he kept his hand on it.

"Well?" he said coldly.

The girl from the outer office slipped in and closed the door behind her. She was quietly dressed, and her makeup was of the slightest, as was her hairdress, but there was something flamboyant about her. She was a little excited now; her eyes glistened. She stood with one knee bent, a hip turned a little to one side, provocative.

"Well, May?" said the man.

The girl jerked her head toward the outer office. "Guy out there, Sam," she said. "Claims he wants to learn how to make himself great. He says he's pretty good already, but he wants to get into big-time stuff. Says his name is Gordon."

"Is that all?" Sam Martin asked.

The girl smiled, still excited. "No. He said, 'If this Sam Martin is the guy I think he is, my dibs will mean something to him.'"

"Do they?"

The girl smiled and took a hand out from behind her. She held a pack of cigarettes by two diagonal corners. She placed it carefully on Sam Martin's desk. She opened a cigarette humidor, dropped it inside. She pressed the hinges on the box, bent her head over it and said, "Right away, please!"

She looked up, while still bent over, and her lips were parted. "Boy, is he handsome!" she said.

Sam Martin grinned. "Not in office hours, May." He picked up the fan again, and the ninth floor still hadn't any report on the *Spider* and neither had the eighth. The police had the building sewn up and were questioning everybody. They thought the *Spider* was wounded.

There was a click in the cigarette humidor, and May opened it to withdraw a new pack of cigarettes. The fan reported, "Those fingerprints belong to Killer Gordon. Want his record?"

Sam Martin said, "I know his record." To May, he said, "Send him in. He's a phony. Flash that word ahead."

The girl's lips still smiled. "Okay, but how do you know?"

Sam Martin said shortly, "Killer Gordon is dead."

The girl's eyes widened, "But the fingerprints—"

Martin's lips were thin, and his eyes narrow. *"He* was the one who mentioned fingerprints. He could have been prepared!"

As the girl moved toward the door, Sam Martin stepped to the wall opposite the mirror, and there was another mirror there. He reached up and beat out a slow rhythm on the gilded gable above it. The mirror slid to one side and showed an ordinary door. Sam Martin went back to his desk.

"Killer Gordon" came into the office.

Sam Martin stood up and stretched out his hand. "How'd you find me, Gordon?" he asked.

The man who took his hand with a slow and affected languor was handsome in a flashy way. His teeth were big and very white when he smiled. His eyebrows were coal black, and his regular features were damaged by a selfishly arrogant mouth. Also, his eyes pulled down a little at the outer corners with an effect of leering.

There was nothing about either the face or the manner to indicate that this man was not really Killer Gordon. That was the perfection of the *Spider's* disguise. He not only altered his appearance; he changed his manner of thinking. He *was* Killer Gordon. But Sam Martin wasn't that good at dissembling.

There was a tension in Martin's hand when it shook the *Spider's*. And he moved his hand back quickly and put it in his side pocket, which had the bulge of a gun. Moreover, Martin's eyes had a fixed and watching steadiness.

The *Spider* smiled broadly, and drawled, "Oh, I get around." He looked about the office. "Nice racket you got here. Why leave that babe outside. She rates a private room with a fence around it."

The *Spider's* casual glance took in the entire office. The mirror had a certain quality of opaqueness that is characteristic of mirrors made of Argus glass. A person behind such a mirror can see through it, without being seen. In the elaborate molding just to the right of the mirror, there was one rosette from whose central shadow came a glint of metal. It was a gun port.

His voice turned suddenly short and cold. "You're just in front, Martin," he said. "You always were just a front, even before they caught up with you in Chicago and disbarred you. Suppose you pass me on to whoever is higher up in this racket. I got hold of a whisper on the grapevine that sounds like straight stuff to me. There's a new brain in the bank-heist business, and you're fronting for him. I want to sign up with that brain."

Martin could wear an oily smile, and he put it on now like a hat. "You always were a smart one, Gordon. I'm sure you could attain 'Greatness.' But the course costs money."

The *Spider* smiled back at him. "Show me you got the goods and I'll pay," he said.

Martin crossed to the door which he had uncovered and pulled it open. It revealed a small automatic elevator.

The *Spider* grinned. "Ain't that sweet?" If he had not been suspicious before, he would have been now. This was entirely too easy for the smooth criminal organization which functioned behind this front.

As he started past Martin, he suddenly knotted his fist into the man's coat lapels and slammed him into the elevator. He went in after him, and his charging shoulder drove Martin's head solidly against the steel side of the elevator. Martin shivered and sagged, unconscious.

The *Spider* did not loosen his grip. He took the man's gun, pocketed it. Then, one-handed, he whipped a thin rubber mask out of an inside pocket and drew it over his face and head. There was a tube that ran under his coat and connected with a filter and a small oxygen tank.

As the door closed, the elevator started to move smoothly. It was completely closed in and except for the brief sag at the beginning, there was no way of telling that it was descending rather than rising. Then, behind his mask, the *Spider* smiled faintly. Right overhead, there was a small opening and his keen ears caught a faint hissing sound there. He had guessed right. Gas was being released into the elevator!

He need only pretend to be overcome and, at the last moment, rip off the mask, and he would discover, at least, the next step in this intricate pattern of crime and murder. The *Spider* deliberately settled on the floor in a collapsed limpness that simulated unconsciousness. Then he heard a faint *pop* as of discharged air-pressure. Something stung him on the back of the right hand.

He saw a splinter of some transparent substance had penetrated his skin. Was it *poisoned?* He snatched it out and jerked up the gas mask, clapped his lips to the wound to suck at it. He had to hold his breath, create the necessary vacuum with cheeks and tongue. He realized that he could not feel, on his hand, the contact of his lips. It was numb. His arm was numb. His brain. . . . Blackness swept down over him like thick black smoke. He was suffocating. He was— nothing.

It wasn't possible to tell, of course, how long he had been unconscious. The *Spider* wondered vaguely about the police. He had deliberately started them searching the building so that there would be plenty of help on hand when he blew the crime racket up from inside. It was an old trick of the *Spider* to put on police pressure by a trick, and then start the fireworks. Under that double pressure, many criminal headquarters had been smashed.

Wentworth slitted his eyes to look about him. The light was dim. He moved a hand slightly. He was not bound in any way, and he was alone. Beneath him

21

was a hard cot. The *Spider* rose cautiously to his feet—and he was staring at the inside of a door of steel with a small steel-barred window. The room in which he was imprisoned was just double the width of the cot and only three feet longer. Good Lord! *He was in jail!*

CHAPTER THREE

Frame-Up

The shock of that discovery drove the ultimate shadows of unconsciousness from Richard Wentworth's brain. He peered out the narrow grating and saw a row of similar doors across the hallway. There was a man at one of them, and he looked at Wentworth with steady suspicion, finally grunted and turned away from the door.

Presently, he heard the slow authoritative tread of a guard moving down the corridor. The man had a dully cruel face.

"So you slept off your jag, did you, Killer?" he asked, harshly.

Wentworth gave him Killer Gordon's brazen grin and said nothing. He sniffed the odor of alcohol on his clothing. A suspicion worked in Wentworth's brain, and he put it instantly to a test.

"I want a mouthpiece," he said. "You ain't gotta thing in the world on me."

The guard spat. "Just a little matter of bank robbery and murder, that's all," he said. "You pulled a

hell of a stunt, getting drunk after a job like that."
He turned and paced away up the corridor.

Wentworth laughed silently. Now he knew the truth! This whole thing was an elaborate fake! He inspected the lock on the door. Then he found an old envelope in his pocket, part of Killer Gordon's equipment. He proceeded to chew it to a pulp, and then stuffed the resulting mash into the keyhole. When the lock was turned, it would jam open, and could not be locked again. It was a spring lock and he would have no difficulty in leaving the cell, once it had been unlocked and closed. That done, he threw himself down on his cot.

He knew now that this cell was part of the most elaborate lay-out for crime he had ever known. It *might* be a part of the way in which criminals were tested.

Or they might have discovered that Killer Gordon was really the *Spider!*

Wentworth had made his own arrangements concerning that. The man with whom he had swapped blank cartridge shots in Times Square was his comrade, Ronald Jackson. If the thing had not blown up in a half hour, Jackson was to understand that he was playing a quiet game instead of forcing the issue—and at the end of half an hour, Jackson would have put on the *Spider's* robes, and shown himself to the police in such a way that they would believe he had escaped from the World Brotherhood Building.

Wentworth laughed at the irony of that name!

There would, then, be no interruption by the police; and the probability was that the criminals did not even suspect he might be the *Spider*. The guard had addressed him as "Killer." He fingered his face lightly, and knew that the disguise was intact. Then he looked at his fingertips, which he had covered by undetectable replicas in a flexible plastic of Killer Gordon's prints.

The *Spider* came sharply to his feet. Those fake fingerprints had been stripped off, and he was looking at his own, undisguised prints! *They knew that he was not Killer Gordon!*

It was while he stood there, trying to probe the purposes of the criminals—to understand why, when they discovered he was not Killer Gordon, they had allowed him to live—that he heard the footsteps of men tramping down the corridor.

The guard peered in through the door-window. He grinned, unlocked the door. Behind him were three men in police uniforms, big men, heavy in the shoulders, tough of jaw.

"Come along, Gordon," the leader said. "We want to have a little talk with you."

Wentworth laughed at him in Gordon's sneering way. If they wanted to continue the game, it was his cue to continue it. They were going to pretend that they still believed him to be Killer Gordon.

"Okay, copper!" Wentworth spat out. "But I ain't talking till I get a mouthpiece. You ain't gotta thing on me!"

As he swaggered across the sill, the big man hit him on the nape of the neck with a blackjack. It sent agony through his skull, loosened his knees. He swore and swung about as Gordon would. The other two "cops" caught him by the arms, twisted them violently behind him and heaved him that way along the cell-lined corridor.

"A nice little talk," said the leader and chuckled.

Wentworth held himself in tight control. He knew that these men were criminals, but there were things he wanted to find out before the *Spider* gave them

25

their deserts. He was pushed into a square thick-walled room, for all the world like a room at police headquarters where they questioned prisoners.

They slammed him down into a big chair, and turned a hot, blinding light into his face. They began to hurl questions about why he had been in the World Brotherhood Building; to what office he had gone. They told him they had him framed for the last bank holdup and murder, but that they could crack that frame and throw it away if he would talk.

The "sergeant" tapped his blackjack against his palm and drove questions at him. His voice was sweetly reasonable. "We've got you dead to rights, Gordon, but we're not really gunning for you. You're just a cheap yellow punk. But there's a crooked organization that works out of that building. We think they're the brains behind the bank robberies. You know something about those crooks and you're going to squeal!"

Wentworth pretended to be nervous. "You can't prove a thing on me!"

The sergeant grabbed a fist full of hair and tapped Wentworth above the ear with the blackjack. He did that for emphasis every three or four words. "We won't bother to prove it, Gordon," he said. "We'll just shoot you and say you tried to escape. Now talk, damn you, or—" He jerked back the blackjack for a blow that would have crushed Wentworth's skull. His face was ugly, gloating. He was a man who liked to kill.

Wentworth made his voice a whine. "Listen, you are nuts. Your boss sent me there to pull that stall. He told me everything I know."

The man said stupidly, "Our boss?"

He stepped back behind the light, and the other two men drew toward him. Wentworth wasn't bound.

26

With three of them, all powerful men and armed, they hadn't thought it necessary.

The sergeant said, "Damn you, Gordon, you're lying!"

Wentworth just grinned at him wolfishly. "You can find out, can't you?" he said. "Just call him up. I tell you he told me everything I know, and sent me there. How in hell would I know why?"

The sergeant growled, "I'll find out. If you're lying—I'll club you to death!"

He turned and stalked across the room then, but his feet didn't make much noise. Like many big, powerful men, he was extraordinarily light in his movements. The door closed—and without a preliminary movement to betray him, Wentworth surged to the attack!

As he went past the standard of the glaring light, he caught it up in his left hand. The lamp was five feet high and Wentworth held it near the top. Its speed was tremendous.

The two men were caught completely off guard. One of them leaped toward him, whipping up a blackjack. The other man clawed for his gun. It was at the second man that Wentworth swung the lamp's base.

The edge of the disc caught the man just back of the jaw. His head snapped over at an impossible angle; his body wrenched about and his feet were whipped off the floor. He sailed six feet through the air and landed with a crashing thud. His body had the meal-sack limpness of death. The lamp swept on, caught the shoulder of the blackjack artist, drove him sprawling on his face. At the same moment, the long wire of the lamp jerked taut and snapped the plug out of the socket. There was a small flare of blue-white light and darkness swept on the room.

Wentworth took a short step forward, rigid fingers outthrust, and struck the man's throat a paralyzing blow. There was no sound at all in the room now.

Then Wentworth laughed the soft, mocking laughter of the *Spider!*

And in a crouch, the *Spider* silently glided toward the door through which the sergeant had gone. He could hear the man's shout, hear the swift beat of his feet. There wasn't time to search for a gun or another weapon. He was only halfway to the door, when it burst open and the sergeant plunged into the room.

The sergeant had a gun in his hand. There was light at his back. He checked just beyond the threshold so suddenly that he took an off-balance step forward, his big body bent at the waist.

The *Spider* stepped lightly to meet him. His left hand caught the sergeant's gun wrist and yanked. As the man reeled forward, the *Spider's* right came up like a pile-driver to his jaw. The gun came loose in the *Spider's* hand; the sergeant slumped to his knees. But as the *Spider* sprang past him, his heavy arm circled the *Spider's* legs and almost spilled him to the floor. The sergeant heaved up to his feet and charged.

The *Spider* had the gun in his fist, but though this man was a criminal, he was unarmed—and the *Spider* was no killer. He had never done more than execute justice against criminals. He dodged aside from the man's charge, drove his left fist savagely against the jaw. The man wheeled toward him, shook his head, and waded in.

The bull-like sergeant was not trying to hit. He had his arms outstretched to wrap around the *Spider,* and two more blows into his face did not stop him. There was blood on his mouth. He shook his head, whined like a hurt animal, like an eager, hungry animal. He came forward, shuffling his feet, arms arched for a crushing grip.

The *Spider* found himself in a corridor, which the man's reach easily spanned. Behind him were doorways, but the *Spider* had no thought of flight. For one thing, it would be dangerous to leave this man to give an alarm. The *Spider* pocketed the gun, grinned into the sergeant's face.

"I don't like you, sergeant," he said. "I don't like the way you question prisoners. I don't like the way you use a blackjack."

The sergeant lunged for him. The *Spider* drove his left straight into the man's face, and then his whole body, from heel to fist, straightened and snapped taut as he hammered his right up under the big man's jaw! The man stopped, went back on his heels, and twice more the *Spider* slammed in those blows that sounded like an axe biting into an oak log. The man shook his head. He was out on his feet, walking flatly, solidly. He came in again, pawing, reaching for the *Spider!*

His left hand brushed the *Spider's* shoulder, fastened on the bicep. He tried to shred the muscle from his arm, haul him close for a bear-hug that would snap his spine! The *Spider* stepped close and hit three trip-hammer blows to the belly that actually lifted the giant's heels off the floor. But the man got his arms around the *Spider* and, with a whimper of eagerness, knotted his fists together in the small of his back. Then, using his skull as a lever, he began to force the *Spider's* chin backward!

At that moment, Wentworth heard a door slammed open behind him, and heard a shout!

"Nice work, Hugo!" a man yelled. "Just hold him like that while I blow a hole through his backbone!"

CHAPTER FOUR

Easy Street

There was death threatening the *Spider* from two sides, and that knowledge would have been enough to paralyze a lesser man. But the *Spider* was accustomed to death, and the risk of death. He knew that when his end came, it would find him fighting.

Hugo, straining to snap his backbone, had his weight planted solidly on both feet, but he was leaning forward. The *Spider* took advantage of that meager fact. He had been straining his muscles against the killer; now he made himself as limp as a rag. The sudden drag of his weight tipped Hugo forward. Falling, the *Spider* tucked his knees up to his belly and thrust them violently against the giant's body!

Their double weight crashed down on Hugo's locked wrists. They bruised into the *Spider's* loins, drove his breath out, but that impact numbed the giant's grip. The knees, thrusting powerfully against his body, and the momentum of their fall accomplished the rest. His hands broke loose and he was heaved in a somersault over the *Spider's* head. He fell flat on his back, was instantly staggering to his feet. The *Spider* sprang up. He was not free, but now the giant was between him and the gunmen, and his great breadth filled the corridor from wall to wall.

The *Spider* attacked. His breath came in fierce dryness, and his left arm had been hurt in the struggle. There were strains in his back. He drove at the man, and took off in a feet-first leap. Hugo was up again, flung out his arms.

The *Spider* slid through them. He clamped a scissors grip about the man above the waist. His lithe arms wrapped behind his shoulders, and his palms locked under the giant's chin! With all the resurgent vitality of his whipcord body, the *Spider* forced the man's head back between his shoulders!

Hugo's whimper of pain and anger came out thinly through his throat, strained by that pressure. His beam-like arms reached out and locked about the *Spider's* back. Wentworth had calculated the man perfectly. For Hugo's mind was set upon one purpose, to snap the *Spider's* backbone. But now the giant, squeezing his powerful arms against the locked and rigid form of the *Spider*, was actually putting more strength into the *Spider's* destructive grip upon himself! The more Hugo compressed the *Spider's* body toward him, the more strain he put upon his own backward-wrenched neck!

Hugo howled out his desperation and his rage and, with a final convulsive effort, dragged the *Spider's* body toward him! The end came suddenly. That double force accomplished what even the *Spider's* whipcord strength could not have achieved against the man's iron muscles. Hugo's neck snapped!

As Hugo's body went limp, Wentworth dropped his feet to the floor and, with all his strength, heaved the carcass of the giant upon the two gunmen behind him. The two men had waited, with drawn guns, for a chance to shoot while they shouted encouragement to Hugo. The end had come so suddenly that the catapult-heave of the giant's body caught them unprepared. Their guns blasted, but the slugs only slashed into the already dead Hugo. And behind that battering ram, the *Spider* charged!

These were lesser men. They tried to get a clear shot at the *Spider;* they tried twice. But they were shaken with a superstitious terror. The impossible had happened. Their champion had been overcome in hand-to-hand conflict. It was David destroying Goliath, and the consequences were disastrous. Their shots were crazy wild. As Hugo's body crashed into them, drove one against the wall, struck the other glancingly, the *Spider* was upon them.

These men had guns, and the alarm of gunfire had gone through the hideout now. There no longer was any need for secrecy. The *Spider* fired once, and the reeling killer was driven in death to the floor. The second man reeled out from behind Hugo as he fell. He had a gun but he stared stupidly at Wentworth.

The *Spider* was ready. "You have your gun, use it!" he ordered coldly. It was the incisive tone of the axeman telling his client to stretch out his neck.

The man looked into the *Spider's* blazing eyes, and the man screamed and turned and ran.

"Halt!" the *Spider's* voice sliced at him. "Halt and fire, or I'll drill you between the shoulders!"

The man winced. He turned and began firing wildly. He fired three times. One bullet flicked past the *Spider's* temple and snagged at his hair. Another plucked at his coat sleeve. It was only as the man fired the fourth time that the *Spider* considered he had been given his chance. He did not bother to lift his captured revolver. He fired it as a man points his finger. The bullet smacked between the killer's eyes. It kicked him backward, knees and back curving. He scarcely stirred after he hit.

The *Spider* straightened out of his fighting crouch. There were pains and aches here and there. He was in the midst of the enemy stronghold and already he could hear their shouts, and the beat of their running feet. But it had been a good fight. The *Spider* smiled slowly.

He had been stripped of the implements and tools of the *Spider* but he could make shift. He stooped over and, with blood, scrawled on the forehead of the dead Hugo—*the seal of the Spider!*

Then, as footsteps hammered toward him, he scooped up the fallen revolver of the assassin he had destroyed. He turned and sent his challenge toward the foe, and that challenge was characteristic of this great warrior, this great crusader—it was the laughter of the *Spider!*

It was a cold and chilling sound, metallic, sinister, mocking—and as its flat echoes reached the ears of the men who raced to the kill, they stopped suddenly. There was an immediate grave-like silence throughout these grim corridors, like the silence of scampering rats when the master's footstep falls suddenly in the room.

It was not for nothing that the *Spider* bore the title: The Master of Men! He was master also of death!

After the silence, there were whispers and furtive creepings as the men gathered their forces together for the attack. They made a concerted action, flung wide the three doors at one instant, blasted through the openings with dazzling light, with blazing guns. It stopped an instant later, for they were shooting down an empty hallway. On the floor were four bodies, and on the foreheads of two of them, the *Spider* had scrawled his crimson signature!

They looked down at the dead in awe; not in respect for the fact of death, but for the man who had slain so many, including the gigantic Hugo. They crept past them, and it was as the last man went by that one of those on whose forehead was the *Spider's* death sign rose up and struck! His blow was short, violent. As the faint sound reached ahead, he swore harshly.

"Stumbled, damn it!" he said.

No man turned his head. He eased the body to the floor—and as the hunters crept on cautiously, the hunted followed in their rear, was one of them. Presently the leader called out, "All right, scatter and search! Go quietly, and don't attempt to fight it out single-handed, but if you see him, fire a couple of shots and we'll all come running!"

Then the *Spider* slid into a doorway and when there was an opportunity, he went back to where he had knocked out the hunter and changed clothes with the man, did what little he could to make himself into a likeness of his victim. He knew how the man walked, and the sound of his voice; he wore his clothes. Those things would suffice—unless someone grew suspicious, or looked at him closely in good light.

There was a grim set to the lips of the *Spider*. At last he was free within the headquarters of the criminals!

Swiftly, Wentworth hurried back along the corridors and caught up with the six other members of the killer-gang who had just completed their fruitless search for the *Spider*.

The leader had a hatchet-face, a straight up and down profile with a nose that had been mashed flat.

Seen from the front it tapered to a jagged edge, like an axe that had been used carelessly for years. His voice was muffled by his flattened nose.

"Okay, okay," he snuffled. "We searched everywhere between the doors and he ain't here." The way he said "doors" underlined the word. He plainly didn't mean any of these various doors about them, but some special doors.

Wentworth's eyes narrowed as he analyzed the man's speech. The Doors. . . . That could mean only one thing. This secret group of rooms and corridors was shut off, either from the outside world, or from another section of the maze, by certain special Doors— like the bulkhead doors of a ship's watertight compartments. And the reason was the same. If a "leak" developed in one compartment, it could be closed off from the rest!

The man on Wentworth's right growled, "He didn't come out *our* Door, ain't that right, Jenks?"

Wentworth was Jenks. He rumbled, "He sure as hell didn't."

The leader's hatchet face sharpened. "Then, by hell, he is on Easy Street!"

There were uneasy grunts from the other men before him. Hatchet-face turned and stalked down the corridor that led toward the cells. He stopped in front of the cell where Wentworth had seen a man peer out of the grating, and he stuck his face against the opening.

"It's Furkin," he said to the man inside. "Open up."

The man inside unlocked the cell door and Furkin stood on the threshold, fists on his hips. "You been out of your cell!" he snapped.

The man glowered at Furkin. "Think you're the boss now, do you?"

Furkin made a short movement with his right hand, and a blackjack was in his palm. The man backed away from him. "All right, all right," he said hurriedly. "Yeah, I went out for a while in Easy Street. Hell, a man would get stir-crazy in this cell. It's a hell of an idea!"

Furkin rasped, "Damn you! You let the *Spider* into Easy Street!"

The man's face went pasty yellow. "I ain't *seen* no *Spider!*"

Furkin's nose pulled down even flatter when he smiled. His grin was like an axe cut. "The boss is going to love this," he said with relish. He sat down on the cot and bounced three times. Then he walked to the back wall of the cell and, with his two fists, he beat on certain spots in the wall.

The guard said, anxiously, "Hell, Furkin, he couldn't have figured how to open the door!"

Furkin just laughed, nastily. "He's the *Spider*, ain't he? Maybe he wouldn't need to open the door!"

The back wall of the cell pivoted outward. The men trooped through, and the *Spider* was the last. As he stepped out, he swung his fist to the jaw of the guard and, as the man fell, he jabbed stiffened fingers into certain nerve centers in the throat. He would be out for at least a half hour—in case the *Spider* wanted to return this way!

The heavy door swung shut, and they were in a compartment ten feet square. It had completely blank walls. Furkin moved to one corner of the room and three other men moved to other corners. Wentworth stood in the center with the remaining man. When they were all in place, Furkin jumped up with both feet and thudded down. The man diagonally across from him did the same. Furkin repeated, and the man on his right jumped; Furkin repeated, and the man on his left jumped. The floor of the room moved downward, an elevator.

Wentworth swore inwardly. If it took four men to operate this elevator, how did they think that the *Spider* had gone down alone? Of course, a swiftly moving agile man might duplicate these maneuvers, alone. It *might* work.

That thought dropped a shred of caution into Wentworth's thinking. Nita van Sloan accused him of being reckless, of taking no account of danger. Where he himself was concerned, that was true; but when the crusade might be imperiled by his love of battle, that was another matter. And right now, the *Spider* was the only living mortal who could turn this efficient organization of crime inside out.

The floor-elevator stopped and Furkin opened an ordinary elevator door. Beyond it was a glass paneled door such as those by which office buildings open upon the street. On the transom was a number, *7-11,* and under it, reversed as Wentworth saw it, was the legend, *Easy Street.* The Door opened under "luck" numbers, at *7-11 Easy Street!*

Wentworth walked out with the others onto Easy Street, and he caught his breath in amazement. It was an actual street like an arcade, and there were shops along it and advertising signs. Each shop bore the address *Easy Street* upon its door transom. There were apartments above the shops. Girls were at some of the windows. The street was several blocks long and at the far end, an electric advertising sign flashed on and off; on and off. It showed a shower of golden coins pouring from a hand, and when that flashed off, these words appeared:

"We make crime pay!"

Just opposite the Door was a school that bore the

legend: *"Self-helps to Greatness."* A placard beside the door advertised courses: *Safe-cracking; Locks and vaults; Explosives,* how to make and use them; *Gunnery; How to be tough,* commando murder methods; *Poisons,* their manufacture and use; *Sabotage methods; Automobiles,* their theft and conversion. There were courses in *Gang Leadership* and in *Arson; How to Plan a Perfect Crime,* including murder, intimidation and robberies of all sorts; *How to organize a racket,* with suggestions as to new fields.

Above the door was a big placard: *Don't envy the G-men! Be a G-man of crime! A complete course in G-man and police methods. Know their secrets and beat them at their own game! Testimonials on request.*

As the six men under Furkin's leadership stood in front of the Door and looked keenly about the street, a "conducted tour" passed by. There were five criminals in the group, and a uniformed guide.

"The membership fee," he was saying, "is the only cost. All the rest comes out of profits. We accept your 'hot' money or whatever you steal in our Brotherhood Bank. We deduct our fee. There is compulsory saving, so you always have get-away money, if you want to run for it. But we have splendid 'cooling off' apartments here—and you'll have money in the bank to pay for it. No more hiding out, afraid to go out for cigarettes! No more answering the door with a gun in your hand! This is tough guys' paradise; you live on Easy Street while you cool off! Take a new course while you're cooling; learn new techniques! Be a G-man of crime!"

Wentworth felt a coldness that was rage eating at him, but there was a part of him that gave ungrudging respect to the brain that had conceived and exe-

38

cuted this secret city of crime. His glance ran carefully along the line of shops, the signs on the windows:

BURGLARY TOOLS, *safe drills and torches rented.*

EXPLOSIVES, *bombs up to 1000 pounds, grenades, soup, dynamite.*

GUNS, *revolvers, rifles, shot-guns, machine guns rented.*

JEWELRY FENCED, *highest prices in the city.*

EASY STREET BANK, *hot money exchanged, hot bonds and stocks redeemed; special rates on kidnap ransom money.*

ART GALLERY, *high prices for old masters, cash for art treasures. We advise you what to steal and where to steal it.*

CRIME CONSULTANT, *lists of likely banks, private homes, payroll schedules, with complete floor plans, suggested methods and get-away routes; cream of world's crimes skimmed for these methods. No two crimes alike; no failures. We plan perfect crimes. Testimonials on request.*

KIDNAP SPECIALISTS, *snatch methods, how to collect safely, how to dispose of bodies permanently, hideouts arranged.*

QUICK CHANGE ARTISTS, *facial surgery by experts, new fingerprints, new identities complete, live the way you want to live without fear of detection; perfect to birth certificates and past history. Strictly confidential.*

There was, Wentworth saw, a Rehearsal Hall, where "complete floor plans are constructed for big crimes so that you can practice and make yourself letter perfect." And there was a motion picture show with "educational shorts on crime" and first-run movies. "Bill changed daily."

It was an almost incredible display. Everything that a criminal could need or use.

Furkin turned with a grin, "Cheez, I still get a bang out of this," he said. "By Golly, they do just what they said they do, too. They make crime pay, and they make crime happy."

Wentworth saw then the electric advertising sign at the opposite end of the street, and there the lights spelled out:

"Everything for the successful criminal. We make crime happy!"

This was truly an empire of crime in the making. There was no way of knowing how long this had been operating, but at least four months. Give them a year, and the city would be completely at their mercy; give them five years, and the nation would be ruled by crime!

"Okay," Furkin snuffled through his masked nose. "You know the routine. When we came in, I signaled and every Door has been sealed. It won't be opened for nobody except me. Every guy and dame in Easy Street is locked in, now, and can't leave until we get through. We're going to take every one of them apart. A squad is coming to help us, and . . ." His eyes fastened suddenly on Wentworth. "Jeez!" he gasped. "By Jeez, *you aren't Jenks!*"

The men pivoted, and their hands raked toward their guns. Furkin's hand was a streak of light as he drew.

"You!" he yelled, his voice rising, perilous, deadly. *"You're not Jenks! You gotta be . . . the Spider!"*

His recognition caught Wentworth for once unprepared. His mind had been busy with the facts that Jenks had given; every man and woman locked in his room, no one except the searchers allowed to move about, and the Doors sealed against everyone but Furkin! Even if they weren't, those Doors were

40

intricate, secret, and there were series of them between him and the outside world.

He was locked in a trap from which the only escape would be as one of the men and he could be sure that tests of identity and secret signals would be a part of getting out! And now, suddenly, his masquerade was penetrated!

Death confronted him at the muzzles of the guns of five men, and all of them within ten feet of him!

At point blank range, Furkin opened fire!

CHAPTER FIVE

Murder Street

It was noon when Ronald Jackson staged his fake gun-duel with the *Spider* in front of the World Brotherhood Building. Promptly at twelve-thirty, when there had been no shooting within the building, Jackson crawled out of the auto trunk in which he had hidden himself and where he had dragged on the cape and hat and mask of the *Spider*. He spotted a policeman and then he sprawled on the pavement as if he had just jumped from the window above and landed on his hands and knees.

The policeman saw him, and Jackson dodged between automobiles and, dodging police bullets, he fled across the street and into another building. There was a shop that had two entrances, which he had picked out previously. He went in one door, out of the other and, seconds later, the disguise discarded, he walked into a nearby hotel, flopped in a chair, picked up a discarded newspaper and sat quietly while the police search raged around the neighborhood.

It was one o'clock before Jackson left the hotel and went directly to the Fifth Avenue apartment of

Richard Wentworth to report. Ram Singh was prowling about the place like a caged panther; Nita van Sloan sat very still, but very tense beside a telephone. Her eyes lighted as she saw Jackson and she sprang from her chair to meet him.

"I've heard the news reports," she said. "You must have been the man that he 'killed' in front of the building."

Jackson nodded. He had a broad frank face, honest eyes, and his carriage was that of the soldier that he had been; still secretly was. Jackson still employed Wentworth's military rank when he spoke of him.

"The major didn't tell me a thing, Miss Nita," Jackson said steadily. "He went into that building and left orders that if the shooting didn't start in half an hour, it would mean he was successfully inside, and he would want the police drawn off. So I put on a *Spider* robe and drew them off. That's all I know."

"But what office did he go to? What part of the building?" It was not like Nita, and not in accordance with her rigid self-discipline to be frantic, but the tension of her control sharpened her voice.

Jackson shook his head. "The major didn't say, Miss Nita," he said and his steady tone was a rebuke. "I carried out orders."

Nita bit her lip and swung away from Jackson, walked to the doors that opened on the terrace. The doors were tightly closed, and through them she looked out upon an ice and snow sheathed city, smudged with smoke, thinly washed with winter sunlight. It was desolate, and Nita's heart was desolate, too. She forced herself to relax.

"If anything—serious—had happened, I would know," she said, softly. She swung about. "You accept orders," she said, crisply, "and that is well,

43

but there is a time to use initiative, too. If we have no news by five o'clock . . ."

"The building will close then, Miss Nita."

"Not to me!" Nita's voice was fierce. "Not to us!"

Jackson's face was stubborn. "The major said I wasn't to interfere no matter what happened."

Nita's face grew firm, the round line of her chin was strong, and her usually soft lips were a straight line. Her violet eyes were almost black.

"When the major is away," she said, quietly, "*I command!*"

Ram Singh's towering figure was suddenly in the doorway. "*Wah, missie sahib!*" he jeered. "Why expect a mouse to play the part of a man!" He struck his chest resonantly. "I, I Ram Singh, Singh of Sikhs, I will go into this building and take it apart with my hands! I will kill all that I find! I will bring back the *sahib* to safety!"

Jackson grinned sourly, "You damned clay pigeon," he growled, "all you do is get shot!"

Ram Singh took a stride forward, and the two men scowled at each other. "Weakling! Girl-child! Mouse with the courage of a mouse!"

Jackson grunted, "Bag of wind! You think with your muscles!"

Nita laughed. Her heart warmed to their loyalty. These two would die for each other, but their quarrel over their service was never ended. "That will do," she said, quietly, and her tones carried authority. The two men swung toward her, still bristling at each other.

"I have decided," Nita said crisply. "At five o'clock, if no word has come from or about—*him,* I will enter the building! You shall both play your parts. It is enough!"

44

*   *   *

It was half-past one in Wentworth's apartment; in the secret city of crime it was half-past dying time for the *Spider!* Nita van Sloan could not know that. She could only know that there was pain and doubt in her heart and that anxiety tortured all her thinking. She could only school herself to patience, so often woman's role, and wait for the hour she had appointed.

She told herself, "Dick is always going on these madcap single-handed raids. He always comes out all right. He always wins."

But at the instant Furkin accused him and opened fire, Wentworth was close to despair. From the ramifications of this underworld city, which he had learned, it scarcely seemed possible to force a way out. He had no choice now, but to make the effort. With characteristic keenness and immediate decision, he hurled himself into action an instant after he had spotted that amazed look upon Furkin's face. The man's accusation found him already hurtling forward!

There was a door behind him that led to the secret elevator, to the cell in which lay a guard Wentworth had knocked out. But he had no intention of retreating to that barren segment of the underworld city. It offered no chance of concealment, and no opportunity to learn more, or to exploit what he learned.

Wentworth attacked empty-handed. Five men, a distance of ten feet, made the odds too heavy for even the *Spider*. One thing was in his favor. The men were bunched, instead of scattered. Furkin recognized that fact almost as soon as the *Spider*, but he did not have the bodily training, or the swift decisiveness of Richard Wentworth. Such ability comes only from self-discipline. Criminals are rebels against all discipline except their unrestricted desires.

Wentworth sprang past the nearest killer. Furkin's

opening shot pierced the spot where the *Spider* had stood. Three men stumbled backward, clawing at their guns. The *Spider* clapped a headlock on the first man as he went past, and with explosive twist and wrench of his body, he hurled the man forward over his hip—straight at Furkin! Furkin's gun fired twice while his companion screamed his way through the air. Both bullets struck the man's writhing body!

The *Spider* struck with the speed of light. His throw did not check his forward leap. He drove his shoulder hard into the chest of a second man. The man's heels lifted from the pavement; his face went sick with the sudden stoppage of his breath. He crashed against the brick wall of the building, and his head snapped back against it. The *Spider* dove between the two remaining men and, behind them, pivoted, guns suddenly in his hands. He shoved the muzzle of each gun hard into their loins.

Furkin alone was left. He was pivoting toward them, far off balance. The *Spider's* two prisoners were jammed close together; their guns hung limply at their sides, and their eyes goggled in terror. Just over their joined shoulders, the cold gray-blue eyes of the *Spider* stared into those of Furkin. There was no fear in the *Spider's* eyes, and no anger; they were passionless, and they were inexorable. Furkin recognized the eyes of justice and knew that he had been judged and that death was closing in upon him!

Criminals rarely faced the *Spider* so. Usually, they started shooting at the first hint of his presence. Furkin had more courage than most, but men who live exclusively for their bodies have a transcendent fear of death. It was the panic wild black fear of death that struck him suddenly as he looked into the *Spider's* eyes. Two of his men lay on the pavement, one slain by his own bullets; the other smashed against the wall by the *Spider*.

Furkin cursed. It was a horrible and dragging sound, rising thin with terror.

"Get out of the way, you fools!" he shouted at his two men, who stood as unwilling shields for the *Spider*.

He shouted at them—and he started shooting!

The impact of his bullets slapped into the two men. They were heavy bullets, low velocity but with terrific impact. The bodies of the two men were driven backward. In his panic, Furkin had done a ruthless, but tactically correct, thing. The squirming bodies of the wounded men trapped the *Spider's* gun. They hampered his movements. Deliberately, he went down under their weight. As he fell, something whined viciously past his ear.

Furkin jerked out of his crouch and slapped at his cheek. Impaled there was one of those slender, translucent rods such as had drugged Wentworth in the elevator. The gun dropped from Furkin's hand. Under the protection of the two dying gunmen, the *Spider* writhed about so that he could look behind him—the direction from which the missile had come. There was no one behind him. The street was clear of all movement, all life. Furkin rasped out a choked oath, and his body thumped down to the pavement.

Once more that vicious, seeking whine sounded. The missile splintered on the pavement within an inch of his head! Instantly, the *Spider* was on his feet. The scattering fragments gave him his cue. Even though he could not see the man, there was no doubt that the missile had come from a section of blank brick wall twenty feet away. There must be a porthole there—and a hidden gunman.

The *Spider* leaped forward. He was bent double, and no two paces were in exactly the same direction, nor at exactly the same speed. He was like a super-skilled football player running in a broken field. He was running across the line of fire of the hidden gunman. That way the man would have only a moving target. If he had charged directly, the man would have an equivalent of a stationary target. Thrice more, he heard the whine of the missiles, but the *Spider's* charge was too confusing. They flew ahead of him or behind him, and then Wentworth was flat against the wall from where the missiles came, and out of range.

He was not still for a heart-beat. If there was one such hidden gunner, there would be others. He sped along the wall, bent over, dodging, changing pace. He whipped into the doorway of the gun-shop, cleared the counter in a leap.

There was a clerk behind the counter, and he had a gun in his hand. He blasted, but the *Spider's* leap was swifter. The man wheeled on one foot, trying to throw the gun into line. The *Spider* threw his own revolver, and it caught the man just above the bridge of the nose. He gasped with pain, reeled backward, blinded. The *Spider's* fist thudded solidly against his jaw, dropped him.

For the first time then since Furkin's eyes had flared in recognition, the *Spider* was wholly motionless. While his mind raced with plans, his eyes skimmed over the shop. High up in a wall, there was a light like a red eye that winked steadily off and on. The *Spider* nodded. That was plainly an alarm. His hands reached out and caught up two heavy automatics from a wall rack; picked out ammunition from boxes below. He dumped a box into his pocket, stuffed cartridges into clips. These were the weapons he preferred.

The street was still deathly silent. One of the wounded men was screaming, but that only accentuated the stillness. Nothing moved. No alarm bells rang; no rush of killers into Easy Street.

Why should there be? The *Spider* was sealed into the secret city like money in a quadruple vault. The doors which, in series, lay between him and the outside world, were sealed and no man could go out through them except Furkin. They could afford to take their time, to plan carefully and destroy him at their leisure.

Wentworth heard a click, and a hum of machinery— and saw a transparent film slide snugly home across the front of the shop! It was nearly silent, but it was swift. Somewhere was a brain that had the whole street under control and under observation. It had been he who had directed the hidden marksman to fire, and now he had sealed the *Spider* into a trap!

Experimentally, the *Spider* fired a bullet at the transparent shield. He sent it through the shop window. A hole was punched in the glass; but not in the shield. There was a bluish mark where the bullet had shattered; that was all.

Up in the corner, the red eye had stopped winking. It shone now with a steady blue light.

The *Spider* turned his back on the street and let his eyes roam deliberately over the shop. There was a door at the back. He reached it in two quick steps, whipped it open. A small bathroom. Water suddenly bubbled *up* from the drain pipe in the washbowl! It was yellow water. As it reached the air, it began to send up a white, fuming vapor. There was an odor. . . .

The *Spider* slapped the door shut. He smiled. His situation was increasingly difficult; not only was he trapped, but a gas that was, at best, anesthetic was

49

being released into his walled prison. But he smiled, and there was a steady, warm happiness in his breast. He liked a fight; he liked to fight against keen enemies. And danger was a sauce to the life of the *Spider*.

He started, pivoted. Then he saw that his super-attuned senses had caught a very slight thing. The blue eye high in the corner had changed to white! The *Spider* looked at it with grim recognition of its meaning. The other two signals had been like the civilian air-raid system; red while there was danger, blue as danger lessened. "The danger is over, but stay where you are." A blackout, in other words. Now white was showing; the all-clear had been sounded!

More clearly than any words, that shining white light told the *Spider* that the enemy counted him as good as dead: helpless!

In the washroom, he could hear the liquid splashing on the floor. Soon the fumes would filter through into the shop. If that failed, they would have other methods. The whole of the secret city had been perfectly planned. They would not neglect a means of killing a prisoner in any one of the shops, since they had provided each shop with a bullet-proof screen.

The *Spider* tipped back his head and laughed without a sound. He swept a bow to an enemy he could not see—but who, he suspected, could hear him!

"Gentlemen," he said lightly, "I accept your challenge!"

CHAPTER SIX

Death Watch

The *Spider* bent over the unconscious clerk and began to massage the man's throat. The forehead was swollen from the gun blow. His eyes were blackening. As he worked on the man, the *Spider* spoke in a monotone.

"You are no longer a free man," he whispered, his every accent a command. "You are a slave. I am your master."

The man's legs, arms jerked. His head rolled and he was swimming back to consciousness. Wentworth bent over so that his eyes bore strongly on the fluttering lids. As the man came back to consciousness, the force of the *Spider's* will struck him.

The *Spider* had a reason for speaking softly. In such an efficiently operated and controlled place, there was reason to think that there might be listening devices hidden here.

"You are my slave," he whispered. "I am your master. You will obey!"

The man yielded swiftly to hypnosis. There were few who resisted the force of the *Spider's* mental powers. This man had already been comatose. It was almost instantaneous.

"Answer," the *Spider* commanded, "but in a whisper."

The man said, dully, "I am your slave. I will obey."

The *Spider* smiled faintly. Criminals were always easy subjects to hypnotism. They knew no discipline, hence no strength of will. The *Spider* said, "There is a secret exit from this shop? Answer."

"Yes."

"Is there an alarm connected with it?"

"Yes."

"You will turn off that alarm, and then you will open that secret exit. At once!"

The man pushed woodenly to his feet and moved across the shop to a gun-rack on the opposite side. He reached up to the topmost shotgun on the rack, and pulled the trigger. Then he took the gun free of its rack, which were two metal contacts. Beside him, a trapdoor slid open in the floor. The *Spider* reached it in a bound.

"You have killed men?" the *Spider* asked. "Answer."

"I have killed three men," the clerk said dully.

The *Spider's* lips drew thin. "For your own profit? Answer."

"Yes."

Wentworth would not condemn a man for causing the death of another, unless the reason for the murder were selfish. But this man had so killed. The *Spider's* voice was cold with command.

"You will forget that I came into your shop," he said, "and everything that has happened since then. You will get down a gun and load it. You will be ready. Listen to me: The first man who enters your

52

shop will be the *Spider!* He will have other men with him, and they are the *Spider's* men. They are coming to kill you. They will kill you, unless you kill them first. Understand?''

The man said dully, ''I understand.''

''In five minutes, you will wake up and you will do as I have commanded!'' the *Spider* ordered.

He dropped out of sight, and slid the trapdoor shut above his head. He found himself in a narrow tunnel that paralleled Easy Street. It was lighted by dim widely-spaced bulbs. From each shop, a steel-runged ladder led down. The tunnel ended with a blank wall at each end of Easy Street, but there were three cross-tunnels to the opposite side: one at each terminus and one in the middle.

The *Spider* heard the echoes of men's feet, and the faint mutter of their voices. The killer squad was on its way to destroy him. The *Spider* made three lightning-swift leaps and reached the corner of the middle crossway. The voices did not come from there. He ducked into the cross-tunnel. On this cross-tunnel there were two steel ladders. The *Spider* smiled thinly. They must lead to the hideouts of the hidden gunmen. Then there were six of them at various parts of the street.

The *Spider* gave that no more than a casual thought. He could hear footsteps overhead now, on the street itself. The all-clear had been sounded, and the business of Easy Street went on while a killer squad moved to destroy the interloper who already had been segregated. It might be possible to escape from this death trap now, for probably the Doors would be less strictly guarded, but the *Spider* did not even consider that.

He was in the headquarters of the enemy—and the *Spider* always attacked!

He wanted to locate the brain that was directing this underworld empire. He had only one clue—the man could see all that happened in the street.

It was possible that the man kept the street under direct observation, but if that were so, it would mean the man must leave his post in order to issue instructions, and Wentworth doubted that anything so inefficient was employed in this systematic secret city. Besides, he had noticed in the center of the vault that housed Easy Street, a large glass hemisphere that looked like a central light, but from which no illumination issued.

At the next juncture with the opposite parallel tunnel, the *Spider* checked for a moment. He closed his eyes and, instantly, he could vision the entire street above. Wentworth's memory was extremely good, but he had trained it until it was practically photographic. His life depended many times upon being able to move in exactly the right direction under any circumstances, without making a false step. The *Spider's* movements were always fast, but many men could equal his speed; it was his economy of effort that made his every action seem dazzling. He never wasted so much as the lifting of a hand.

Now, with the full picture of the street in his mind, he whipped around the corner and sprang up the third steel ladder. It should lead into some part of the motion picture theatre. This time, the ladder instead of leading to a trapdoor continued to the second story of the building, and the door opened out of a wall.

There was also a thoughtfully provided peephole. The *Spider* looked out into a dressing room behind stage. There was a girl in the room, zipping on a scanty costume. She bent toward a mirror, touched up her makeup and then ran out.

The *Spider* opened the door and stepped into the dressing room. It was nice to find what he had come for with so little effort. He made a careful selection from the makeup trays, moved to the exit of the dressing room. There was no one outside. The *Spider* stole out and took the iron stairs that led upward.

He was frowning. There was one hampering quality to these buildings. Aside from those sides that opened on Easy Street, there were no windows because there was no outside source of light, and the circulation of air was by means of conditioning machinery. Hence all movement must be confined to the stairs inside the building—and stairs were dangerous.

The room where the Commander of Easy Street sat was in darkness except for a white screen at the end of the room, and various small lights on a map in front of him. All these lights were white or blue except for the one within the Gun-Shop. That was bloody red. There were six blue lights, and these represented the watchmen who were still under shooting orders.

The man looked at the screen, and on it was a full reproduction of Easy Street. It wasn't a picture. It was composed of moving light, and it looked straight down on Easy Street from above. Men walked along the street, and there were curious glances toward the Gun-shop, but for the most part business went on as usual.

The sightseers and their lecturer were in front of the theatre, and the guide was expatiating upon the advantages of seeing crime in action.

"Motion pictures are taken of every Perfect Crime," the man was saying. "They are shown here, in slow motion and studied for ways to improve technique. Also, if any flaw has occurred; if any one has identified a brother, we will know it and can eliminate the witness.''

The speech came clearly over a loudspeaker arrangement. He could control the directional mike by pressing a button beside the spot on which it should focus. He had it pointed now toward the Gun-shop. There was a hidden microphone inside the shop, too, and he had heard speech, but it was oddly muffled and he had been unable to make out exactly what was said.

He could only conclude that the *Spider* had suspected something of the sort, and had taken appropriate precautions to make sure his voice went unheard, or at least could not be understood. The light that indicated the secret exit of the shop was closed still burned steadily. The man had to be inside the shop.

Abruptly, the secret door light went out. The Commander nodded. His men should be in the tunnel now, ready to attack. The directional mike picked up a heavy burst of gunfire and confused shouts.

His attention was focused on the sounds, on the picture, on the screen. There was a central panel of lights above the screen, and suddenly a light in its midst glowed brilliant red!

The Commander uttered a muffled shout, and his hands rested suddenly on the buttons. He pressed a series of them in sequence, and nothing happened. He leaped to his feet and jerked from its rack beside him an automatic shotgun with a special air-cooled barrel. He glared toward the door. It opened slowly.

The Commander jerked the shotgun to his shoulder and began to blast away as a man plummeted through the door. The Commander was a good shot. Three charges from the sawed-off shotgun took the man before he hit the floor. They smashed and tore the life out of him.

Behind him, the Commander heard a flat mocking laughter—and a gun-muzzle pressed lightly against the nape of his neck. A bullet there would snap out the light of life instantly.

The shotgun dropped from the Commander's hands and made a loud clatter in the room. After it was silent, a voice spoke mockingly:

"Nice shooting, but you should first make sure what you're shooting at. I'll take over command of Easy Street from here on."

The Commander's thin lips were suddenly flabby. There was a scream of terror in his mind, but it did not find utterance. That wouldn't be safe. He screamed, inwardly:

"The Spider!"

CHAPTER SEVEN

Commander of Hell

Wentworth ripped off the man's tie and bound his hands with it. He thrust him into a heavy chair and, with shoe laces, bound his ankles to the legs. He did not bother to gag the man, but took his place at the seat behind the control panel.

"You have a nice system here," he said. "The *camera obscura* works very well, but the big lens which focuses the street scene and by mirrors, focuses it on this screen, should be hidden. For those who have a modicum of knowledge, it is pretty obvious. Also, its location limits the number of places in which you could have the control room. The height of the theatre, plus its proximity to the lens are as clear as if there were arrows pointing the way."

While he talked, he was studying the control pattern before him. One glass panel apparently had three lights beneath it, like the "eye" in the Gun-shop. Some showed white, a few blue; one red. There was a headset and a phone jack by each light. There were other lights, with a button beside each. He could only guess at their meaning, but some of them undoubtedly represented the secret exit of each shop.

"There is one thing," the *Spider* went on conversationally, "that no man can defeat, and that is the pattern of his mind. Since there were two exits to every other place, it was logical that there would be two here. I simply tricked your guard into dashing up the steps, and then came into the backdoor. There is an ingenious variety in your modes of operating the secret doors, but basically all of them are alike. It is a matter of closing or breaking an electrical current."

Wentworth had found what he wanted now, the phone that connected with the watchmen when he plugged into their jacks. "Trouble in Gun-shop," he spoke crisply. "Get over there. Shoot at the slightest suspicion." He repeated that to the six watchmen in the gun towers, and their lights changed to white. He gazed at a scene on the white screen, smiling thinly.

There was a renewed crescendo of shooting from the Gun-shop. It racketed in through the loudspeaker. Wentworth searched out the various shops, and began listening in on them in sequence. It was when he reached the office of Crime Consultants that he paused.

". . . the time will be approximately 5:09," a voice said easily. "It may be a minute one way or the other according to how quickly the wagons respond to the call from the subway. You will wait until they come, until there's a crowd around the subway exit. Then you'll take the bank. There should be between a half and three quarters of a million, cash, quickly available. This is payday for five major plants, most of whose workers bank there. Any questions before we go to rehearsal hall?"

One man said jerkily, "That's fast work. It's after four now, and we take them at five!"

The smooth-voiced man laughed. "This way, there's

no chance of a leak, or a tip-off. The job is already set up in the hall. You'll have a full-scale rehearsal. Of course, we won't show the subway wreck. You'll just hear a sound record of that.''

The jerky voice said, ''Okay. Nobody has ever muffed one of your jobs, but this is big stuff. Lots of people could get killed in that subway wreck—''

The smooth voice was even oilier. ''You can always withdraw, if you're yellow,'' it said.

''Don't get me wrong!'' the man yelped. ''I don't want to withdraw the way guys do down here! We'll take the Big Bank all right!''

There was the sound of footsteps. A green light flashed beside the glass that represented the shop. Wentworth pulled the plug. He had been prepared to maintain his watch here long enough and learn the intricacies of this secret city; now there was no longer time. The killers had never before done anything like this. They were planning to wreck a worker-jammed subway train in the rush hour, in order to loot a bank where people kept their savings. At least a score of persons would be killed in the wreck, and that was conservative. In the rush hour, those trains were suffocatingly packed, seats filled, aisles so crowded it was hard for a man to lift an arm. Smash even one car. . . .

The *Spider's* eyes fastened on his captive and detected there a look of gloating. Nothing moved in the room; there was no alarm either audible, or visual, but the Commander was happy. That could mean only one thing. There was some arbitrary method of talking over the phone, or else when that green light flared, the *Spider* should have made some conventional response—and his failure to do so would set off some sort of inquiry!

Grimly, the *Spider* looked again to the board.

60

There was a central alarm board, and he jabbed the red button there. Instantly, every white light on the entire panel turned red. He glanced at the street scene, and saw the people hurrying into doorways. The big signs at each end of the street had stopped flickering and, instead, spelled out the word:

"Blackout."

He had at least immobilized all the fighting units of the underground city.

The *Spider* rose from his chair and crossed to stand over the Commander. His voice was quiet when he spoke, but it had a ring like tempered steel.

"We're going out of here," he ordered. "At the first hint of treachery, I'll kill you." He freed the man's feet. "You are the Commander. The rules that apply to others do not affect you. Therefore, you will take me first to the hall, where we will *call off* the rehearsal that has just been started there. I am sure that you can take me there secretly."

The Commander's head was tipped back, and there was hatred in his face, but there was also fear.

"I would advise you also *to be sure*," the *Spider* whispered.

The man lurched to his feet and moved toward the secret door by which the *Spider* had entered. He had not been faking his fear. It was fear for his own life. But there was slyness also in his eyes, and a certain satisfaction. For this emergency, too, their shrewd Brain had prepared. By now the Brain knew that something was wrong in the Control Room, and with the previous information that had been sent him, he would have a pretty good idea what was wrong.

This had come about because there was an arbitrary rule of which the *Spider* could not possibly know. When he had caused the blackout signal to be given, he should have plugged the phone into a certain unlabeled jack and made a report as to why the blackout had been commanded. His failure to do that would inform the Brain that there was treachery in the Control Room!

The office of the man whom the Commander knew only as the Brain was not connected by any wires with the Control Room. The whole connection was by means of certain constantly operating and tuned radio circuits. Thus the blackout signal had caused a predetermined sequence of radio impulses to go out over a transmitter. That had actuated a relay in his office, and now an oil painting on the wall, perfectly illuminated by rod-lights, was washed with a reddish glow that turned its previously silvery sky into a fire scene.

The man's eyes focused on a small ship model on his desk, and he waited. His eyes were large and intelligent. His lips were small, very red and smiling. It was a smile of self-satisfaction, of a man sure of himself and of his power. He was not a large man, though when he was seated he seemed to be. His head was beautiful, and the arch of the forehead was strong and high. It might have been the face of a saint, except for that smile and what it did to his mouth: a merry, vicious saint.

There was a sweep second hand in a clock that was set in the side of the ship model, and he watched it while it ticked over the space between three and four. Five seconds—and no phone report. The man's eyes twinkled, and he pulled the dial phone to him, pressed a screw head in its base and spun the numbers 9 and 0. His eyes shifted now to the painting with its rosy glow. He had actuated a sensitive heat-detector in the Commander's chair in the control room. The rosy light remained unchanged. He nodded. This time

when he took the phone, he lifted the talking mechanism and dialed three times. His eyes quested over
his office. In five separate cages were five dogs, pit
fighters. When he wished to amuse himself, he set
two of them upon each other.

There was happiness in his eyes. He was a man
who liked a fight, and loved power for its own sake.
There had been a time when he was one of the
biggest men in the oil industry. The oil industry, in
its inception, had a record of ruthlessness and brib-
ery, sharp practice and even murder. He had come
into the business a little too late for those things, but
he refused to recognize that fact.

He succeeded phenomenally and those who stood
in his way—went under. Some of them died, and
others suffered nervous collapses, and others were
ruined or discredited. There were one or two who
were too strong for that, and those suffered a sudden
sequence of accidents. When that started, they either
quit or died.

And none of those things was ever traced back to
their author, except in a general way. He was fantas-
tically successful; and to those who opposed him—
things happened. So the oil men had drawn their
lines tight, and put on a sudden squeeze. They did it
in such a way that if he had used his customary
tactics, there would have been an F.B.I. investiga-
tion. So he allowed them to buy him out, at virtually
his own price—and looked around for a field in
which his genius would be properly appreciated.

The phone call went through and he spoke in a flat
and undeviating monotone in which each word rang
clearly and with the precision of a machine-aimed
bullet.

"The *Spider* has seized the control room," he
said. "He will go first to the rehearsal hall and then

he will attempt to leave the building. He will have the Commander a prisoner with him. There is no need for alarm. Arrange matters so that he uses the emergency escape elevator. If you send out sound signals *one-two-three* the Commander will understand. Use anesthetic gas and fire anesthetic bullets. The combination should suffice. When you have taken the *Spider* prisoner, report. That is all.''

The man leaned back in his chair and smiled merrily. He lifted a delicate fist and smashed it down on his desk. It hurt and he smiled at his aching hand.

''I have you, *Spider*!'' he said, and all the viciousness that did not show in his face was in his voice. The five caged dogs were fighters, bred for ferocity and courage. At the sound of his voice, they tucked their tails and cringed against the backs of their cages. One of them whimpered in terror.

The man laughed delightedly. *Power!*

CHAPTER EIGHT

The Trap

As the *Spider* accompanied the Commander through the narrow secret passage, he heard a vibra-phone bell sound delicately. It was a soft tone, with a peculiar power of penetration. It sounded once, then twice, then three times.

"What does that signal mean?" the *Spider* demanded shortly.

The Commander said hurriedly, "It means the blackout is complete."

The *Spider* smiled thinly and had his answer. There had been no such signal in the previous blackout, therefore the man lied; therefore it was an alarm. In some way he did not understand, but undoubtedly a mechanical means, his capture of the Commander had been discovered.

"Faster!" he snapped.

The Commander broke into a run, and there was perspiration on his forehead. He stopped abruptly before a door. "This is the rehearsal hall," he said with strain. "It's empty." He pointed to a small green light beside the door.

That checked. There had been a green light when the men left the Crime Consultants office. A grim smile moved the *Spider's* lips. He knew that forces were mustering to destroy him. He reached out and clamped stern fingers upon the nape of the Commander's neck. The man struggled. His mouth flew open, but without sound. He went limp. The *Spider* took from his pockets the makeup articles he had removed from the theatre dressing room.

He set to work with that compact efficiency of movement and skill which made all his activities so swift, yet so effortless in appearance. Within five minutes, he revived the Commander and issued his orders.

"You will take me out of this place by the most direct route," he said flatly. "All Doors will be opened at your command. Remember, my gun is at your spine!"

The Commander stumbled a little at first as he walked, and his head hung. Presently, he walked more erectly. They passed no mirrors. He did not look toward the *Spider*. Once he started to turn his head, and his cheek struck the cold muzzle of a gun. He did not try again.

They came presently to a door and he stepped through it. A small elevator shot them upward swiftly. He opened not the front, but the side of the cage, and the wall was blank. He manipulated the wall with a sequence of pressures on various bricks. The wall slid aside, and they stepped out into a hallway.

There were two guards with drawn guns. The Commander said shortly, "You will open the Door!"

The *Spider* said harshly, "Open it!"

The men stepped backward three paces and solemnly jumped up and down, alternately, three times. The wall in front of the *Spider* slid aside, and there

66

was another elevator. His eyes swept it as he went through the door with the Commander. There were small, almost concealed, apertures about the ceiling. And there was a gun-port in the roof. The *Spider* sucked in a deep breath, held it.

As the elevator started upward, the Commander turned about suddenly. He looked at the *Spider's* face, and his mouth gaped open. He sucked in a deep breath to yell, and his face suddenly flushed, his eyes glazed, his head wobbled on his neck. At the same instant, the gun began to speak through the gunport. It didn't make much noise, but a series of five of the anesthetic needles struck their small fragile points into the flesh of the Commander's face. He pitched forward on the floor.

The *Spider* slumped against the wall, slid down awkwardly. His face was flushed by the compression of his breath. He tipped his head back so that the gunner above would have a good view of his face. He was quite sure the gunner wouldn't have orders to shoot his Commander; as the Commander, in his turn, had been exactly disguised to look like—the *Spider!*

But the *Spider's* senses were reeling now from holding his breath. The time was very close when he must take in air or suffocate. And the elevator was still gliding upward. It had not yet stopped moving. The *Spider* let his head sag forward and slipped sideways. In his left hand he had a handkerchief which he had seized an opportunity to moisten. It would help some. He pressed it over his nostrils and mouth and drew in a shallow breath.

He felt the elevator lurch to a halt, but the door was not opened. The *Spider's* head was reeling; blood pounded in his throat, in his ears, in his temples. He could not afford to lose consciousness. If the killers who would open this elevator got a close look at his face, they could not fail to detect that it was disguised. There had been time only to do a limited job of make-up, and the materials had been theatrical grease-paint, not the substances that the *Spider* had developed for personal use.

Blackness that was unconsciousness clustered in his brain, thickened. He heard only faintly the opening of the elevator door, felt the blessed rush of fresh air. He did not have strength enough to pocket the handkerchief. He pressed it against the floor, smeared it toward the corner. A dirty handkerchief might escape immediate observation. He felt hands seize and lift his body, and he made it completely inert.

A man's voice said, raspingly, "What do we do with the *Spider?*"

Another said, "We report first."

The *Spider* could see a little now. Three men stood with machine guns trained on the unconscious Commander. Wentworth was tossed carelessly on a bench. One of the men stepped to the wall, lifted the receiver of a phone and spun the dial once. As far as the *Spider* could see, it was the number one that he dialed. He waited a moment, and then dialed *one* again.

"We got the *Spider,*" he reported. "Out cold."

He listened and then said, "Okay." He hung up and walked back beside the three men with the machine guns. "This is it," he said. "Empty your guns into him."

"Empty them?" one of the men turned his head, his face strained.

"That's it!"

The three men pointed their machine guns and started firing. It doesn't take long to empty a ma-

68

chine gun that fires at the rate of six hundred a minute—not when the drum holds only fifty cartridges. You can't do it with one pressure of the trigger. The recoil, even though compensated, would jerk the gun off the target. It took probably half a minute for the tearing bursts to empty the guns. The men began to swear. One of them turned his head away from what was in the elevator, and fired the last burst blindly.

The leader had stepped aside. He reached out and set his hand against a panel in the face of the elevator. That was the moment at which the *Spider* struck. He was still weak on his feet, but he counted on his momentum to accomplish what considered action would have done at another time. He charged across the narrow corridor and it was just as the leader set his hand on the panel that he drove into the man, slammed him against his companions, sent them all reeling wildly toward the elevator.

The *Spider* had to reach out and slug one man with his gun butt. The men were screaming. The screams were hollow and they faded downward. The *Spider* had his hand on the edge of the door, and he was staring into the elevator. . . .

He didn't close the door. The bottom had fallen out of the elevator. What was left of the Commander, and the four men who had slaughtered him were hurtling downward through the shaft. Their screams were wild, crazy, frantic.

The *Spider* spoke aloud, thickly. "That's why he pressed on that panel, to release the floor of the elevator."

The screams choked off and from far below, there came a thick multiple splash. There was a dull moment of silence, and then the screams started again. They were beyond all human quality, the sound of

69

animals in incredible pain, hoarse, tearing, fearful. Presently and it was quickly, there was only one man screaming. He kept it up and it grew weaker, but still kept on, hoarse, meaningless, the body of a man already dead that still cried out. It stopped after a while.

The *Spider* turned away from the opening, and his eyes were sick. *What was at the bottom of that shaft?* A strong shudder shook him. He knew the answer, and it was fearful. It must be acid. It could be nothing but acid. Probably such a death pit was at the bottom of every shaft, probably every elevator's bottom could be dropped out any time. He had meant to imprison the men in the elevator, not to destroy them, though it was merited.

He shuddered, and heard the elevator move— downward. He remembered then that there must be a man on its roof; the man who had fired the anesthetic gun! Even as he staggered forward, sick and still dazed from the anesthetic, he heard doors open, two doors. They were at each end of the corridor. Men charged in, with drawn guns!

"What happened?" a man asked, harshly. "What in hell happened?"

Wentworth recalled with difficulty that he was disguised as the Commander. He could stall for an instant, but the elevator was moving downward. When the gunman on the roof spoke, he would reveal the truth. He must have seen Wentworth hurl the gunmen to their deaths!

Wentworth made himself shudder again. "The damned fools!" he said. "The damned fools! All of them got into the elevator, and the catch on the floor came loose! They fell down the shaft!"

He moved toward the men, making himself seem more sick than he was. He had to get past them, or at least among them, before his disguise was penetrated. He was almost upon the men when the cry he had been dreading, the warning that would expose him came from behind.

"Kill that man!" a voice shouted hoarsely. "Kill him! *He's the Spider!*"

CHAPTER NINE

Death's Moment

There were three gunmen just ahead of him, and more behind him; there was also the man atop the elevator who had cried out, who undoubtedly had his gun pointed as he shouted. Wentworth's stumbling pace suddenly became as efficient as a tank. He dove into the nearest killer. His shoulder rammed into the man's stomach, doubled him up. The impetus of Wentworth's leap carried the man backward, between his two companions. They were wedged aside.

As his victim fell, Wentworth hurled himself over the man in a slashing somersault that took him through the open door, landed him on his feet. His outflung left hand speared the edge of the door jamb, and he whipped about on that pivot to the protection of the wall. His hand was numbed by the slam of a bullet close by. The air behind him was torn to shreds by the whipping fury of gun-driven lead.

The *Spider* clapped the door shut, wedged it with a chair—there was time for no more—and raced on along the corridor. The memory of that sickening trap in the elevator's shaft stayed with him. Where there was one such trap, there would be others. He would have to watch for them. Behind him, the door was shivering under the impact of blows.

Wentworth reached a bend in the corridor, whipped around it and flattened against the wall. His chest lifted sharply with rapid breathing. He closed his eyes, listening, thinking swiftly. The corridor came to a blind end a dozen yards around the bend. There would be a secret door there without a doubt. He did not know how it was manipulated. He peered upward at the ceiling. It was fairly high, the corridor was not more than four feet across.

He bridged the corridor, feet against one side, back against the other, and inched swiftly up to the ceiling. When he reached the topmost point, still out of sight around the corner, he partly turned so that his shoulder rested against one wall, his straddled legs against the other, and drew a gun. He then waited, looking down into the corridor.

It was a wild gamble. The men might see him, but they all wore hats, and after their tradition, those hats were dragged down low over their foreheads. It was part of the secretive nature of such men that they should feel more secure with a hat-brim partly hiding their faces. A gamble. . . .

The door crashed, and there was a streaming rush of men along the corridor. Bullets fanned past the edge of the wall. Plaster dust flew. A bullet ricocheted from the floor and dug into the ceiling close to the *Spider*. He waited, gun in hand. A man sprang out past the corner, gun blazing—and cried out:

"He's gone! He worked the Door!"

Men streamed past under him. They were in a close bunch, and then two others trailed more slowly. They were limping and cursing. They were two of those the *Spider* had spilled. An instant after they had passed, the *Spider* released his braced position and fell, soundlessly, on hands and feet to the floor.

He was up instantly, just behind the men. He was careful not to watch them, lest they feel his presence. He kept his eyes on the group ahead. They were manipulating a Door, and presently they jammed through into another elevator. Wentworth crowded in with the last two men.

One of them glanced sourly toward the *Spider* and he struck instantly, a furtive blow with stiffened fingers that instantly compressed heart control nerves and dropped the man to the floor!

Wentworth said, wonderingly, "What the hell's the matter with him?"

He looked down at the fallen man, and other eyes focused on the victim. It was then that Wentworth felt the effects of the gas. He cut off his breathing instantly, but the others did not. They slumped one by one to the floor, and the elevator kept on moving. It was a very slow elevator, and it went upward. Wentworth reached up and fastened his hands into a fretwork near the top of the cage, with the memory of that other awful shaft, and presently his breathing choked him. He had to breathe; he *had* to.

The world reeled around him. He was beginning to understand this system of Doors. At each one, the entire crew that passed through was knocked out automatically by gas. In that way, they were helpless and the guardians of the Doors could make sure there was no unwarranted man present among them! The *Spider's* only chance was that he would revive first; there had been no opportunity for any of these men to communicate to headquarters that the *Spider* was disguised as the Commander.

*　　　*　　　*

74

Wentworth came back to consciousness presently in a big reception room full of comfortable chairs and davenports. Slumped in these chairs were the various members of the gang that had pursued him. There was a single uniformed man in the room on his feet, but his gun was in its holster. There was no restraint upon the *Spider*, he discovered. But how much time had elapsed? How long before the wreck in the subway was scheduled?

Wentworth's eyes focused on a clock across the room and gradually brought it in to clearness. It was five minutes before five. And in fourteen minutes, the wreck would take place! The *Spider* lurched to his feet, moved toward the door, where the guard stood. The man put his hand on his gun, but there was no tension in the movement. It was apparent that this was a routine action. Then he spoke.

He said, *"One for all. . . ."*

Wentworth felt his mind go tight. That was plainly a countersign of some sort. The normal answer would be *"all for one!"* but nothing so obvious would be used. There was another phrase, of course. He stumbled toward the man, lifted his head sluggishly, and said, "What?"

The man repeated the countersign, frowning. His hand was tighter on his gun.

Wentworth said, "Oh? Hell, I must still be groggy. It's 'all for one.' "

By the time he said it, he was almost upon the uniformed man. The guard swore, wrenched at his gun, and the *Spider* swung for his jaw. The man dodged, but was not quite quick enough. He went down, but his dodge had prevented a knockout.

His gun blasted into the air, and the *Spider* went out through the door. He found himself in another office, precisely like the other, except that the chairs and davenports were not occupied, and there were five guards here! Their guns were out!

Wentworth's hands snapped to his holsters, and then for the first time he realized that his guns had been removed! He was unarmed, and the men were beginning to shoot!

Wentworth dived behind an overstuffed chair, and bullets whimpered past him. He braced his shoulders against the wall and, with his feet, he sent the chair rocketing at the nearest of the men. At the same instant, he snatched a pillow from a davenport and hurled it at the head of another guard, and went in behind it. It was deadly dangerous. The man's gun was blasting, but he could not see. The others hesitated to fire for fear of hitting their companion. The *Spider* struck the man, wrenched his gun free, rolled, began shooting.

He dropped two of the men, leaped upon the man who had fallen over the chair. His knees knocked out the man's wind—and the doors batted open and more killers rushed in. They were in overwhelming numbers. There was not even time to count them, and the *Spider's* captured gun was almost empty. Two more shots at most. And time was racing past, the time that was left in which he might hope to avert the subway accident! Already workers were leaving their offices, jamming down the steps to the platforms. They would be wedged in, immovably. A crack-up—a fire!

Desperation goaded Wentworth. He gathered himself to make a charge for the door—and suddenly that door swung open, and three people came through. There were two men and a girl, and they had black hoods drawn down over their heads. The hands of one of those men were huge and brown, and his shoulders were the shoulders of a giant. The other man was square and erect as a soldier, and the girl—Wentworth caught an oath in his throat! There was no doubt about these three. It was Ram Singh, and Jackson—and Nita!

Jackson's guns crashed, one rising and falling in each fist, deadly accurate shooting. Nita had only a single automatic, and he saw that she was shooting low. Nita's nerve had been shaken in their last battle, and she had sworn she would never again kill any man. So she shot low.

Ram Singh was an army in himself. He shouted and ranged across the room in three long strides. He caught up a heavy chair and carried it before him, and bullets thudded into it. He heaved the chair from him like a basketball player shooting for a basket, and men went down like ten-pins under the assault.

Then he was upon the men, and his powerful fists struck about him. His mighty hands seized hold of an arm, and whipped a man off his feet. He used the man's flailing legs as a scythe to cut down two others of the enemy.

In three jumps, the *Spider* was across the room.

"Subway wreck in six minutes," he snapped at Nita. "Got to stop it. Hold them and escape, quickly!"

He plummeted out the door and was gone! He ran with torment inside him. His valiant companions were battling against fearful odds, but he dared not, could not, delay to lead them to safety. They had risked death to rescue him—and he ran away! But innocent lives were at stake, a score, perhaps a hundred persons might die or be frightfully injured in that subway accident. The *Spider* had no choice. His whole life was dedicated to service, and Nita and the others would understand. He must save the innocent—but the *Spider* felt like a coward as he ran away from that battle, sprinting desperately. He had seven blocks to cover; the streets were jammed with people. He was not yet out of the World Brotherhood Building. And he did not know by what means, or exactly where, the subway train was to be wrecked. He knew only that it would be near the nearest station to the Big Bank. Truly, he was racing with death!

Nita caught Wentworth's words as he raced past her. She dodged to her right and had a partial protection in a chair. Jackson was crouched on the left side of the doorway, using his guns terribly. Ram Singh had forgotten about his hood. He was chanting in his native Punjabi, bellowing at the top of his great voice. It shook the walls, and his fighting shook the floors. He had two men by the necks now, and he popped their heads together, kicked the feet out from under a third man. As the man fell, he brought up his knee and caught the man in the jaw. He seemed to have eyes all about him, and where he looked he struck.

"Withdraw!" Nita shouted at him in Punjabi. "Retreat! The *sahib* is safe!"

Ram Singh did not seem to hear, and Nita cried out again, repeated the order to Jackson in French. Jackson began to swear in a low tense voice.

"That damned dumb ox! He's a slaughter machine, and he doesn't *want* to stop!"

He shouted at Ram Singh in his parade-ground voice, the Sikh turned his head. At that instant, one of the killers drew a deliberate bead on Ram Singh's chest! Jackson shouted, flung himself out from behind the chair, and fired all in one swift movement. The killer was driven against the wall by his wild lead, but Jackson felt a punch take him in the side. He was suddenly weak and giddy. He staggered, groped for the wall and didn't find it. He went down to his knees.

Ram Sing's roar of rage was like a lion's. He flung himself upon the man who had fired the shot and seized him by the throat. He whipped the man off his feet, and swung him bodily from the floor, pivoted on his heel.

His hands were locked solidly on the man's head and after that single pivoting on his heel, he stood on planted feet and swung the man through a full circle above his head.

The man's scream gargled into sudden silence. Ram Singh had wrung his neck. He let the man go, flying feet-first into the face of his companions, and then the Sikh charged across to Jackson's side, scooped him up in his arms like a baby.

"Thou clay pigeon!" he growled, and boomed out a sudden laugh. "By Kali, thou art the clay pigeon this time!"

Nita darted out of the doors with Ram Singh. There were only a few men left on their feet in the room, and they crouched, completely cowed by the ferocity of Ram Singh. They went out of the doors— and the hallway that had been open before was shut off now by plates of steel. Nita raced toward the nearest steel plate. It suddenly seemed an intolerable distance away. She tried to think how it might be manipulated, and her thoughts were cloudy and vague. She kept running, and she seemed to be floating. There was, certainly, no sensation of her feet touching the floor.

The steel plate was far off in the distance now. She narrowed her eyes to see better through the sudden blurring of all things about her.

The floor was surging up to meet her. In that last fractional moment before the darkness closed in, she realized that they were trapped.

CHAPTER TEN

Murder Express

The subway gets people where they want to go rapidly. It allows them to sleep a half-hour later in the morning, to add a half-hour to their free time in evenings. For this privilege, men and women consent to being herded together below the surface of the earth, assaulted with storms of sound and thunder, crowded promiscuously with strangers, shaken, jostled and shoved; to having nerves pounded and tempers ruffled. There are those who fear the subways but they are sneered at: nuts and cranks. There are those who take them indifferently, with the stoicism of penned cattle. There are those who endure them.

At the corner of Forty-second and Broadway there is on each side of every street a steel railing that surrounds a flight of concrete steps leading downward. Rarely, these are covered with kiosk whose sides are opaque glass. At the evening rush hour now, it is already dark. A blue light, or a green and white light glows on a standard beside the subway steps, and people swarm toward those lights. Before they reach the steps themselves, they are in the crowd.

The crowd fills the steps from wall to wall and they go down slowly. A few people struggle against this stream, fighting their way up from the depths from which damp wind and the rush and clatter and roar of trains pushes up fitfully.

There are gratings in the pavement and the slashing thunder of the trains is preceded and followed by an upward gush of wind. The smell of it is close and musty. Women, stilting over the gratings, clutch at their skirts, wedge into the downward moving sluggish river of humanity.

It is warmer once the bottom of the steps is reached, but the winds are chill and gusty. Ahead, queues form at the clanking noisy turnstiles. Bursting through those restraining, rotary arms, men break into a run, overcoats flying, caroming indifferently into indignant plodders.

Three boys form a football wedge and go through, shouting. A girl and a man, walking side by side, form an eddy in the hurrying throng and people glare at them. It's all hurry, hurry, hurry. The man who doesn't hurry is an individualist to be looked on with suspicion, a rebel against the order of things.

They clatter down more steps and now they are on a narrow platform on each side of which trains slide in and out, end to end, separated by only the length of the platform. As a train leaves one end, another enters at the far end.

The people jam into compartments formed by steel rails. Guards snap chains across the exits like loaders of a cattle train, setting their shoulders against a press. A door opens, and there is a concerted rush of people, fighting, squeezing, twisting, hats knocked off and crushed, feet stamped on; fighting to board the express.

If they could have known what impended for this

express, they would have fled in screaming panic from its doors. But they did not know that Perfect Crimes, Inc., had designated this particular train the Murder Express! And no one noticed that, amid the rush on the subway platform, there were three men who stood apart from the crush and the slam of the homeward bound crowds. They were down at the far end, near the control house, and no one paid them any heed. Through a window, those three could see the control board where lights flicked on in sequence, marking the movement of trains through safety blocks, and the position of various switches.

It was a gay mystery to most people. But it was no mystery to these three men. That was where Perfect Crimes, Inc., was superior. Thanks to their schooling, they knew just which button to push in order to throw the emergency switch that would derail one of the cars of that chosen train. It was very simple to wrench a car out of the middle of the train by throwing that switch after the leading cars had already crossed it. The front part of the train would go one way, the rear would take a neighboring track—and between those tracks were rows of steel columns that supported the ceiling. It was extremely likely that a car would be broken in half across those beams.

When a steel tube is wrapped around something else of steel, that which is inside the tube is going to be crushed. Especially, something as yielding as the bodies of human beings.

At the doors of the doomed express train, the guards call wearily, "Let them through. Let them off!" But nobody does. The few who want to make their way off the trains are obstructionists, too; rebels. They should be getting on, not off, and the people jam them and jostle them. It is a battle to get off; it is a battle to get on. The cars fill to the doors in a moment. The impatient operators start the doors shutting long before the cars are filled. Let's go! Let's get moving! We've got to make schedule. There's another train coming. Let's close the doors!

The operators press certain control buttons, and there is a hiss of compressed air, and the doors start to slide shut. Someone grabs the edge of the door and pushes it back. A few more crowd on, and then the door starts to shut again, a patient roly-poly: push it back, and it comes to meet you again. Fight the sliding door, get on *this* train, save two minutes. . . .

Down the line, one door finally manages to close. The boy with the girl has let it slip through his fingers. They look at each other, laugh and shrug and stand there. But other people dash for the next door. One of the three boys grabs the door and holds it open, and his two friends jam through before it starts shut.

One more man squeezes in. His derby hat is pushed back off his head; he catches it, and the door starts shut. It closes and he stands, peering out through his glasses, blinking, mildly pleased that he makes it. What determines that this man makes the train; these three boys make the train—and the girl and the boy don't make it? What determines that this car is presently going to jump the track and wrap itself energetically around some steel posts; cruel and implacable steel tube compressing its human contents?

Death is at the doors of this car, whispering, *"You make the train. You stay behind."*

The guards are busy closing the doors now, doing the work of Death. They heave their shoulders against the backs of the mob inside, help compressed air to close the doors. The train can't start until the last door is closed. Gradually, the lights that signal open

83

doors black out, and presently, with a hiss of re-leased brakes, the train lurches heavily into motion.

The crowd inside lurches a little with the movement of the train, lurches and sways as one person. The few people who have seats have elbows wavering before their eyes; their feet are stepped on; their knees bear the weight of those who stand. There is a magic, and it is black magic, that operates on people pressed close together. The scientists call it mob psychology. It is stronger than that. One mind operates them, and it is a mind attuned to the lowest animal emotions: fear.

Men lose their reason in such situations; they become one with the voice, the movement of the mob. Becoming identified with such a mob, they may slaughter, or run wild and, awaking afterward, be completely unable to understand why they behaved as they did. It isn't *like* them. But it is like the primitive animal mob from which they arose, to which they are rejoined when this black magic operates.

In their subconscious minds, there is a feeling of being trapped. They are underground, and other men press in upon them from all sides. Let something happen, and they are trapped. Let the lights go out, and a woman cry out or a man curse hoarsely, and the panic is on. *Let me out of this trap!* Animal fear, the demand for survival. Every man who keeps me from escaping is an enemy! Smash him! Destroy him! Let me out!

Nothing has to happen to start a panic. Let the train stop on the tracks and stand motionless for a while. The people begin to stir and mutter. They crane toward the windows, but there is only darkness outside—the darkness of the trap. Then let the lights go out. . . . So there are emergency lights.

* * *

Perfect Crimes, Inc., makes it a business to know such things. So there are three men at the other end of the platform, to take care of panic; to make sure of panic. Each of them has a large bundle under his arm. It has been difficult to fight their way through the crowd with those bundles. They were scowling, sore at the crowd that has jostled and hampered them—as if unconsciously the crowd were fighting for their lives. Those bundles were fused. They were full of gasoline.

Fire is an excellent begetter of panic, a stimulator of primitive fear. It is especially excellent against crowds that are trapped underground.

The leader of the three men looked at them as the train started heavily past them and nodded. "This is it," his eyes said. "This is the train we wreck."

Their orders were very clear. At regular intervals, the length of the train, they were to toss their three jugs of gasoline in between cars. It would go off in flame a little while before the wreck, but not very long. There would be a very nice "diversion" so that the boys at the bank could have a clear road for their raid.

The leader turned his back toward the platform and prepared to light the fuse of his jug of panic-death.

Down at the other end of the platform, the three men slipped around to the far end of the control house. There was a steel ladder there that led down to the roadbed, and the door would be locked. That didn't matter. They had a key. Perfect Crimes, Inc., took care of everything.

They got out their guns. They could shoot off a machine gun here and nobody would pay any attention. The noise of the trains was a blanket like the thunder of an artillery barrage. The leader looked around at his two companions. They had their guns out. They were ready. He went up the short steel ladder, stood on the ledge outside the door. He slipped the key into the lock, and the two men climbed up behind him. They were ready.

The express train was half-clear of the station. They had about twenty seconds to slide inside, kill the men here and throw the switches. That was plenty of time. They had worked it all out in the rehearsal hall. . . . He shot the man at the board; Janky shot the switch man. Riker pressed the button and threw the switch, as simple as one-two-three.

The leader said, between his teeth, "Okay! Here we go!"

He turned the key in the lock, stepped through the door and lifted his revolver. The man at the board turned a startled head, and the gun blasted in that same instant. It was a deliberate, sighted shot, and it went exactly where it was aimed. It smashed the man in the stomach. He started a scream, and was driven off his chair backward. His legs jutted upward at a silly angle; then his knees bent and he drew into a slow agonized knot. He groaned.

The second shot crashed at the same instant, and the man at the switches took it in the stomach, too. That was the instruction at Perfect Crimes, Inc. When a man was shot through the belly, high up, it did something to his nerve centers, like a *solar plexus* punch. He couldn't do a thing except fold up.

The third gunman reached the board in two quiet steps, looked at it a second, and broke a panel of glass, reached inside and pressed a button. The leader stepped over the switch-man's body and his eyes sought out the emergency lever.

He grabbed it with his right hand, compressing the lock arm with his grip. He glanced at his watch. He grinned. Five seconds to spare, but he had to wait those five seconds. He watched the sweep hand of his watch move across the dial. From just before the eight, until almost the nine, that was the time he had to wait. He kept his eyes on the watch. When he threw the lever, the train would dance a high-land flight. He grinned.

CHAPTER ELEVEN

Perfect Crime

The man had fought his way through the crowd on the kiosk steps. He had not fought savagely, but he squirmed through the crowded ranks of people at incredible speed. He wormed between them, now using a sharp thrust of his hand, now a wriggle with his shoulders. As he reached the bottom, the jam was impossible. He leaped into the air, jerked his feet high. His hands snagged the edge of a steel beam, and he whipped over the heads of the people. He knocked off a man's hat, and a woman screamed. He dropped into a narrow space between two people, and one of them fell.

He did not delay, but raced on at top speed. There was more space now. Somebody yelled experimentally, *"Stop, thief!"*

He was running a broken field now. He went toward the jammed turnstiles at a sprint. He took off when he was a few feet short of the stiles. His hand slapped the top of a coin-box, and his head ducked low under the steel beams. He went over the section between the turnstiles. A woman screamed.

A guard shouted hoarsely, tried to get through the crowd. He was stopped. He turned and ran to a gateway where there was a chain. A crowd of people was coming out that way—and the man had already vanished. He had darted down the steps toward the subway platform. Someone blew a police whistle. The man in the coin booth looked up wearily as a guard started yelling at him through the small round hole in the glass before him. The man looked startled and grabbed a telephone.

The man who had raced through the crowd stopped short on the steps that led downward. He was peering toward the control house. That was the logical place to arrange the wreck. His chest lifted sharply, panting. He paid no heed to the people about him. He crouched and peered between the hanging signs, under the low ceiling toward the window of the control house. He saw a man's feet propped up in the air, slowly sliding down. He saw a man with a hat on reach across the board, break a glass and reach inside.

Then he saw another man move toward the levers on the opposite side of the wall. He could just see this. There was a six-inch space above a sign and a foot between the steel posts on each flank. And it was through this opening that he saw what was happening. He whipped out an automatic and a man cursed and started to run; a woman was jostled aside. She saw the automatic lifted and she screamed.

Then the gun crashed! No other man could have made that shot, angling above the sign, between the steel posts, through a glass window a hundred and fifty feet away. But this man made it; the *Spider* made it!

His gun crashed, and the man who was grasping a long lever down there was whipped about by the impact of the bullet, but he still had hold of the lever that would wreck the train. The *Spider* fired again, and the man's hand was torn loose from the lever. But there were two other men in that small room of the control house. One of them jerked his gun about toward the smashed window and fired blindly. The *Spider* groaned, seeing a man crumple under the impact of that bullet. The *Spider* fired again, and the second man took the bullet in his throat. The range of vision was limited. He had to shoot what he could see. And there was a third man.

The *Spider* remained crouched on the steps, straining his eyes through that narrow slit. People had fled from around him now. There were shouts, and the heavy running feet of guards. A woman reached out and began to beat him over the head with her handbag. The *Spider* reached out blindly with his hand and thrust her away.

He heard a new sound now, and it came from the other end of the platform. It was the sound of a muffled explosion. There was a pause, and then another, and then another. Three muffled explosions, and then a woman screaming, screaming, screaming. But those were not gun blasts. They were not vehement, contained explosions. They were more like the sound of gunpowder ignited in the open: a whooshing roar, a burst of flame.

An agony of fear struck through the *Spider*, but he did not move his eyes from that narrow slit through which he watched the all-important window of the control house. A man yelled behind him and, from the slap of his feet, came charging down the steps.

The *Spider* lifted his gun and fired it into a wooden plank over his head, a sign. It was at that same moment that he saw the third man in the control house leap toward the lever. He leveled his revolver, squeezed the trigger—just as the heavy impact of a man's body landed upon his shoulders!

The *Spider* was driven down the steps under the weight of that body. He twisted to one side, and the man slipped past him, but he was already carried almost to the bottom of the steps. The man reached out and wrapped an arm about his ankles. He wore a uniform. He was a brave man, and he had done his duty as he saw it. But there was no time to argue. The *Spider* had lost sight of that precious square foot of window through which he could view. He reached down and struck his assailant, almost gently. The blow was nicely calculated. It jarred the man's arms loose from the *Spider's* feet, and the *Spider* was racing along the platform.

There was panic now, and the people darted from his path. Suddenly, he had a clear view of the control house window. There was no one on his feet in the room. He had got his man, then, for the door was shut—but he had got his man too late. The lever was pulled out!

The *Spider* looped about and raced back along the length of the train on the express tracks. People shied out of his path. A single guard moved blunderingly to stop him, and the *Spider* whirled him aside and raced to the front of the train. He reached out and shattered the window of the motorman's cab.

"The switch has been thrown ahead," he snapped. "Some men tried to wreck the train ahead. I think they were a half-second too late. Don't move your train out of your place here. Cut off all current. Get in touch with the police and with your officials. Understand?"

The motorman's face was white. "There's fire up there," he said. *"Fire!"*

The *Spider* saw it then, saw the red flare of fire, and the black gush of smoke at the rail tunnel ahead.

He gasped, and the sound of it was a prayer and a curse.

"Kill the current!" he cried. "Pull the switches! Damn it, man, get moving! The control house!"

He leaped to the tracks and began to run. Behind him, a gun crashed and the bullet whined ahead of him, rang on a steel pillar and racketed off into the darkness of the smoke and the flame. Desperation put speed under the *Spider's* heels. He weaved and dodged, racing toward the flame and the fury. He saw the last of three men leap off the opposite side of the express platform. He could see their heads bobbling above the level of the concrete as they raced across tracks toward the local platform beyond.

The *Spider* whipped up his gun. He snapped off a shot as he ran, and the foremost of the men pitched to the earth. There was a flash of blue-white fire as he hit the third rail. The other men screamed, swung about to face the *Spider*. Their guns crashed, and the *Spider* fired twice more as he raced on. His head wrenched back and laughter gusted from his lips. It was the flat and mocking laughter, the battle laughter of the *Spider!* He had not been able to prevent the holocaust entirely, but he had avenged those who were scheduled to die!

Behind him, the gun spoke again—but that would be the police opening fire! There was a strange stillness in the subway now that the trains were stopped. Lights flicked out suddenly as the main switch was pulled. But there was no complete darkness. The red and smoky flame of the gasoline bombs was up here ahead, and it was against that fiery background that the *Spider's* figure showed black and clear.

Through the screams and the cursing panic behind him, the laughter sounded piercingly, and the policeman who had been shooting stared and his mouth gaped; his gun was frozen in his fist. That crouching, dodging figure, that laughter . . . Good Lord! *The Spider!*

Before he could fire again, he saw the figure of the *Spider* leap high into the air and sail clean through that wall of gasoline flame, vanish into darkness beyond!

The policeman realized he was blowing his whistle wildly, blowing it until his eyes distended with his breath, until his jaws ached with the pressure; blowing, blowing the alarm. The *Spider!*

"The *Spider* wrecked a train!" he gasped.

And the police were off on their wild chase again, while the *Spider* raced forward to save the hundreds trapped in that blazing hell below the surface of the streets. The police would close in behind him, seeking to destroy him. And ahead there was fire and smoke, and panic and death! The *Spider* raced on!

Aboard the train as it lurched out of the station, Jacob Jones was very pleased with himself. He did not even mind very much having had his derby hat knocked off and dented. He smoothed it again and blinked through his glasses out the door's pane. It was very unlike him, Jacob Jones knew, to have made that wild dash for the train. He always preferred to wait for the next one, or ride the local.

But today, he was suddenly tired of being the old mild Jacob Jones. To begin with, he had lost his temper with Mrs. Jones this morning, something he had never done before; and he had even dared to snap back at a fellow clerk. The reaction of Mrs. Jones and the clerk was alike pleasant to Jacob Jones, and so it had prodded him into a new belligerence.

He blinked out of the window and thought about getting home. He built a little day-dream about getting home. He saw himself entering with a solid tread, a half hour earlier than usual because he had ridden the express and bawling out Mrs. Jones because dinner was not ready. She would be meek and contrite. . . . Jacob Jones smiled. He knew damned well that she wouldn't be, but it didn't hurt to think about it, did it?

Then the train was sliding past the end of the platform. He had an amazed glimpse of a man throwing a bundle wrapped in paper toward the car. There was a tongue of flame behind the bundle. For an instant, it looked as if the bundle would smack into the glass, but the train moved, and the bundle broke between the two cars. There was an instant after the smash of breakage when nothing happened; and then there was a rolling puff of flame with explosive force! The heat struck right through the glass window.

It was strange that a mild little man like Jacob Jones should be the first to act. He turned around and there were three boys of 'teen age beside him.

"Get up through the car and open the doors," he ordered. "You know where the emergency handle is?"

The boy nodded and excitement was in his eyes. He turned and began to worm through the crowd, and Mr. Jones reached up and seized the cord that ran overhead from car to car. He jerked on that cord three times: emergency stop signal. Mr. Jones had looked up at that cord many times and wished that he had the courage to pull it. He had thought that some-time, if he got drunk . . . then Mr. Jones never got drunk. Now he had a perfectly legitimate reason for pulling the cord. As he yanked it, he heard another muffled explosion behind him.

The brakes took hold an instant after he had pulled the cord. He saw the kids up forward, smashing the

94

glass over the emergency handle. People were heaved off their feet by the sudden application of brakes. They tumbled in piles. Some went down on their knees; a man fell flat on the floor; a woman screamed and stepped on his back with her high heel shoe, so that the man roared and wrenched over, and the woman screamed again and fell.

Mr. Jones was flung across the rear platform, and both his hands were braced against the steel wall. Outside the window, the flames were a tower, and the heat was suddenly intense. He pushed back, settled his derby hat. He was quite proud of himself. And then, suddenly, he remembered the third rail! The current was still on in it! These people, plunging out the doors, would be wild with panic! They would be electrocuted by the score!

"Don't open that door!" Mr. Jones shouted. "Hey, boy, don't open that door!"

He started pushing his way forward through the train. They were fighting there now, as they tried to get up off the floor. There were flames outside the windows, outside all the windows. Up forward, there were more flames, flaring redly against the doors. This car had been between two of the gasoline bombs, and flame had dribbled down to the tracks beneath it. Oil on the operating mechanism had caught fire, and the rubber insulation of wires had caught fire. There was a stench of flaming oil, and gasoline, and the smoke was dense and strangling. Rubber insulation burned through, and there was a sudden dazzling flash of blue-white light from beneath the train, and the lights went out.

There was still illumination, plenty of flame there. The light was red and dancing and horrible. Mr. Jones struggled on. He shouted, "Don't open that door!"

The door was open, and one of the boys writhed out. His face was frightened, and there was a silly grin on his mouth. This was exciting, but it was also terrifying. He jumped down from the side of the car, and he stumbled. It was his head that struck the third rail. There was more blue-white fire, and after that another stranger odor of something burning, sweet and sickening. One of the boy's companions seized him by the legs to pull him away, and he gasped and fell across his friend's body. His legs slowly contorted, as he writhed with the contraction of the electric current.

"Don't open the door!" Mr. Jones begged. "Don't jump out the door. The third rail! The third rail!"

He tried to work his way forward. He was a small man. A flying fist drove his glasses back against his nose, and they broke. After that, he couldn't see very distinctly. His hat was knocked off long ago. There was a rip, and half his coat was gone. A woman screamed in his face, and beat at him with her fists, and then they were both hurled aside as a big man fought his way toward the door.

Mr. Jones scrambled in his wake. "Don't go out the door!" he pleaded. "Wait until they turn off the current!"

His voice was lost in the bedlam of sound, screams and groans and curses. The floor was hot now, and the windows were cracking under the heat. A woman fell across Mr. Jones' path and he stooped to help her. That was a mistake. The weight struck him from behind, and he went down, and then something terrible pounded down into the middle of his back. He was sort of suspended, his knees on the woman who had fallen; his head had struck something. And that intolerable weight on his back. It increased. There were two people stepping on his back now.

"Please!" Jacob Jones screamed. "Oh, please! I—" His voice broke off then in a soaring shriek.

The weight moved off his back, but it was too late, then. He kept on shrieking. He couldn't think now. He was all pain. He beat the floor with his hands, and the floor was hot, and flame licked up through a crack in it. The smoke was thick and black and strangling. Someone fell on top of him, and he didn't feel it, but the weight bore his head against the floor. It was worse not to be able to scream. He screamed, and sucked in smoke and heat. It hurt. It hurt. . . .

Suddenly, there was a man in the doorway of the car, a man with a gun in each hand. The guns crashed, but the shots went upward. The blast of it shocked silence into the car.

"Plenty of time," he called quietly. "Take it easy. Step out on this side ledge, and then run forward. The flames are thinner up that way. Run fast through the flame, and then keep moving. You'll be all right. Take it easy now. One at a time. Here, you two, take this woman with you. . . ."

The man's voice was cool and steady, and there was a thin edge of command in his tone that sane men would not disobey. A man tried to rush past him; a big man whose foot had ploughed into Jacob Jones' spine. A gun reached up and caught him under the ear, and the big man spilled on his hands and knees on the ledge, and was still.

"Plenty of time," that coolly commanding voice went on. "Plenty of time. Easy does it."

The people did not know this man, but they knew authority when they heard it. They became more quiet. They could hear screams up ahead, and cries behind them. But the cries from behind were calmer, and with order in their sound. Somehow, they knew that this man had been at the other car, and that there was order and peace, and that people were being saved. They began to pick up the wounded and the injured. They heard the man tell them to breath lightly, through their nostrils, to cover their nostrils with their arms, keep their heads down.

Flame spurted up between the car and the ledge and made a sheet before the man's face, but he did not even step back. He picked up the body of a man who was dead and laid it on the flames. The flames went out, and the man felt no pain, for he was gone. And now people could get out of the door.

Swiftly now, the car emptied and the people raced forward along the ledge, spurting through the gushing flame there. They cried out, but beyond that spot, there was a surcease of fire. The smoke was heavy, but that could be borne. They hurried on, carrying the injured with them. The car emptied—and the last of the people disappeared.

The *Spider* sprang into the flame-washed car, moved swiftly among the bodies that remained. Here and there he found a flicker of life, and carried them out to the ledge. The flames were dying. There was little fuel in a steel car, just the oil on the trucks and the rubber of the insulation. A straw seat had caught, but he put that out.

He came now to Mr. Jones and started to lift him, and Mr. Jones raised his head.

"Don't," he said. "My back is broken. It won't do any good."

There was a strange dearth of pain now. Instead, he felt numb all over. He was numb right up to his shoulders, but he could still move his head. His face moved in a faint smile.

"I shouldn't have opened the door," he mumbled. "People got killed."

The man knelt beside him and smiled. "You did

exactly right," he said. "If you hadn't stopped the train, it would have been wrecked and many more would have died. Why, you're a hero, sir!"

Jacob Jones' smile was shy. "Me?" he shook his head, feebly.

"A hero!" the man said. "I, the *Spider,* tell you that you are a hero! Remember that! I never lie! You're a hero!"

The man looked at the *Spider's* face incredulously, then he smiled again. "Yes," he said, feebly. "Yes, I guess I *was*—a hero."

His head dropped then, and the life went out of him.

The *Spider* carried his broken body to the ledge and there was a smile on his lips but his eyes were terrible. Damn the men who did these things to little helpless people, to small heroic people, to the great common people who made up the world! Damn the murderers who killed for greed!

The *Spider's* lips were a-grin. He began to walk forward along the ledge. It was a slow and ponderous walk. His shoulders rolled a little, and the bulge of his twin guns was heavy beneath them. Just beyond the pall of smoke, he met a policeman. The man was running, frantic. He started to speak to the *Spider,* and his flashlight washed over his face. He swore, and squeezed aside, and let the *Spider* pass.

He whispered, "My Lord! Oh, my Lord! I'd hate to get in that man's way!"

CHAPTER TWELVE

Cash for Corpses

The emergency exit from the subway opened under the grating in front of the Big Bank. That, too, was part of Perfect Crimes' plan. There would be a crush of injured, panicky people pouring up from below, and it would create a lot of confusion. It would be easy for the robbers to merge themselves with the crowd and disappear. The timing was perfect, too. The police and ambulance sirens began to scream at exactly 5:09 and the robbers, waiting in the lines before the tellers' windows in the bank, looked at each other, and caught the leader's nod.

He jumped out of line, and his machine gun, hidden under his coat, came out and fired a burst. It was not a wild burst, but one that was carefully calculated. It caught the two guards at the outer door and cut them in half. A woman happened to be in the way, and that was too bad for her.

One of the crooks was beside the guntower where a watchman stood all day long, on duty. He lifted his revolver and fired a careful shot that was lost in the first wild gush of machine-gun fire. There were seven other men and five of them stepped up to the tellers' windows, while the other two hurled the customers over against the wall, and faced them up with their guns. It all went like clockwork. No improvisation; everything moving according to plan.

The tellers were pinned helpless by those guns. One man made a move with his foot, and a gunner, expecting an alarm, shot him without a heart-beat's pause. The other tellers began to shove out the money. The leader and one other man were behind the cages in a moment and stripping the vault. The workers crouched in fear on the floor. There was no interference.

Within less than three minutes, they were moving toward the doors in a compact bunch. The machine gun fired a last warning burst, killing two or three of the customers, and then the killers were slipping out of the door. The timing was perfect here, too. People were pouring up out of the escape exit, and nobody had any time to look toward the killers. The street was full of the sound of fire and police apparatus, and the shots inside went virtually unnoticed. The clangor of the vault alarm, cutting loose suddenly, brought one policeman—to his death.

That was the situation when one more man climbed up out of the escape way of the subway. He was a black-smeared man; his clothing was scorched, and his shoulders were curiously hunched. And there was a burning fury in his eyes. He stepped clear of the subway hatch just as the men burned down a policeman.

And the man flung back his head and laughed. He sent the wild, cold sound of it slashing toward the gangsters. These were the greedy men, these were the robbers for whose profit those people had died

101

below the surface of the earth, for whom others would die, terribly, of burns. He flung out his laughter, and the criminals heard it—and they recognized it! They had heard its echoes before—and they had heard about it—and they knew what it portended.

They were face-to-face with the *Spider!*

The machine gunner pivoted, off-balance, terrified. He saw the battered man, crouched there on the street's curb with a gun in each fist. That was the last thing he saw. The bullet took him between the eyes. After that the *Spider* walked toward them. There were ten men in that robber band, and the *Spider* walked toward them with a flaming gun in each hand.

He did not dodge, nor alter his pace. It was as if he knew that death could not touch him now while he had this task to perform. His eyes were a pale blaze, and his lips spat out that taunting, fearful laughter!

Those ten men could have killed the *Spider*. They could have killed an ordinary man. They had already killed many of them. But that laughter was an echo of doom, and there was no fear at all and no doubt in the *Spider's* face. Death was not for him—but vengeance was. Their leader went down without using his machine gun. In the first swift sweep of the *Spider's* guns four more men went down. One of them was screaming. Half of their number dead, and the man had taken only two strides!

Superstition, terror, panic seized the remaining five in that heart-beat of time. Three shots were fired, and they seemed to speed true, but they made no impression at all on the *Spider*. He did not even waver, and the big guns at his hips kept blasting, blasting.

It takes so little while for a bullet to reach its mark. It is the sighting and the aiming that take time,

102

and the *Spider* had no need for that. These guns were extension of his flesh, fastened to his nerve ends.

He could point them as unerringly as a man looks at a light. Both guns had blasted at the leader; then each of them had rattled out four shots, kicking against his wrists, dropping on the new target. Ten shots, and nine of the bank robbers were on the ground.

The tenth man turned and began to run. He screamed as he ran. He screamed and twisted about to fire back a single wild shot at the *Spider!* The *Spider* was pivoted half toward him, and his left gun hung at his side. His right gun was pointed with a stiff arm, and his eye ran along the barrel.

The man screamed again and tried to throw himself aside, but the bullet had already sped. It caught him in the base of the skull, and the man's body kept running for two more steps, tipping, inclining, until the feet were pawing and slipping. His face and shoulder hit the pavement together, and his legs flung up and flopped over. He lay there, unmoving.

The *Spider* bent over one of the dead and scrawled in crimson upon his forehead his warning symbol— the seal of the *Spider!* And then, in the same awful red, he wrote upon the pavement beside his prey:

"I make criminals pay!"

The public wouldn't know what that meant, but the crooks of Perfect Crimes, Inc., would know! They would read that twist of their own motto and know that the *Spider* had doomed them!

Once more, the *Spider* laughed, and men told about his laughter afterward and shuddered. But when the police arrived, they found only the dead who had tried to rob the bank, and the grim warning of the *Spider*.

The *Spider* himself had vanished.

*   *   *

Stanley Kirkpatrick, the commissioner of New York City police, reached the scene only a short while after his first men. With a series of curt questions, he learned the whole picture as far as his men knew it—and they had learned a lot. They knew that the man who had rescued the people from the subway and the man who had killed the criminals answered the same description; and that the signature on the dead identified that man even if his uncanny marksmanship and courage had not.

And Kirkpatrick, feeling an upsurge of hope for the first time since this long series of murderous bank raids had begun, stood rigid and stern beside the bank and whispered, "Thank God for the *Spider!*"

He smiled then, with a twist of his stern lips beneath the points of his military mustache. He hunted the *Spider* because it was his duty to enforce the law without favor. The fact that the men the *Spider* killed were criminals could make no difference. Kirkpatrick felt that no man had the right to take the law into his own hands, as the *Spider* did, but sometimes, as now, he could not help but feel thankful that the *Spider* had struck.

Kirkpatrick turned crisply to the sergeant who was his personal aide. "Gallagher," he said curtly, "put out a general alarm for the *Spider,* giving the description of the man as he was seen here. Also notify doctors and hospitals to get in touch with us immediately if any man presents himself for burn treatment."

Gallagher had a big hearty face and now, as usual, he wore a grin. "Right, commissioner," he said, then laughed. "Aye golly, this *Spider* did himself a good job here!"

Before Gallagher could return, Mayor Mace dropped from a police car and came striding sharply across

104

the street toward Kirkpatrick's side. His heavy jowled face was grayish at sight of the dead, but his voice was bullying and harsh.

"You've got to put a stop to this business, commissioner!" he said, violently. "Ten men dead here. Six more men shot in the subway, I hear, and from all accounts the *Spider* set the train on fire. Lord knows why!"

He stared belligerently up into Kirkpatrick's saturnine face, and the commissioner's clear blue eyes flicked him impersonally. Kirkpatrick was a fixture as police commissioner. He had lived through many administrations and his popularity with the force, and with the public, made it mandatory upon the changing governments to retain him. But they resented it, these politicians. They resented also that they never gained a concession from the police while Kirkpatrick was in power.

"You have your reports a little twisted, Mr. Mayor," Kirkpatrick said shortly. "The subway wreck was planned to create a disturbance so that criminals could rob this bank. The *Spider* completely smashed the gang, and prevented a heavier death-toll in the subway fire. There would have been a wreck also if he had not intervened. This is one time when we owe him a big vote of thanks."

Mayor Mace's eyes glinted shrewdly, "So you defend a criminal! Why didn't he notify the police? No man has the right to take the law into his own hands."

Kirkpatrick smiled thinly. "I agree with you. I can only tell you that the *Spider* invariably notifies the police of such impending crimes, when he learns about them, and if there is time. I can only assume that there was not time."

Sergeant Gallagher came back and saluted. "General alarm for the *Spider* is on the air, sir,'' he said. ''Headquarters is notifying hospitals and doctors to watch out for him, if he shows up for treatment of his burns.'' Gallagher's Irish eyes were bland as they swept past the mayor, but Gallagher was a staunch henchman of Kirkpatrick, and he knew the full situation. He laid it on, thick. ''Also, Mr. Commissioner, according to your orders, the police have thrown a cordon around the district and every man who bears any trace of having been through the fire will be carefully examined for traces of disguise before being released.''

Kirkpatrick's smile moved his mustache. ''Very good, Gallagher,'' he said quietly. He had not been wrong in his choice of an aide since his former assistant had been killed.

Mayor Mace looked disappointed. He said shortly, ''I will expect results.''

Kirkpatrick said, ''Don't be too sanguine. It's very rarely that the police even catch sight of the *Spider*. The man has a knack of vanishing into thin air, and—''

He caught his breath. Walking casually toward him along the street, resplendent in black broadcloth, gray gloves, swinging an ivory headed cane was— *Richard Wentworth!*

Kirkpatrick's jaw set solidly. Wentworth was his personal friend, but unfortunately for their amicable relations, Wentworth had often fallen under suspicion as the *Spider!* It was like his insouciance to appear here—after the *Spider* had killed!

Wentworth checked beside them. He bowed suavely to Mayor Mace, lifting his hat with his left hand. The mayor was immediately friendly. Richard Wentworth was a man of great wealth and wide influence. But

106

when the mayor thrust out his right hand to shake hands, Wentworth apparently did not see it. He had turned toward Kirkpatrick.

Mayor Mace flushed and said, quickly, "Lucky you weren't here a little earlier, Mr. Wentworth. This is a terrible affair."

Wentworth glanced curiously at the *Spider* message on the pavement which a police photographer was recording. "I make it a rule," he said, "always to be somewhere else when the *Spider* is operating."

Grim amusement crept into Kirkpatrick's eyes. "In police parlance," he said flatly, "we call that an alibi."

Mayor Mace forced a quick laugh, glowered at Kirkpatrick. "You will have your little joke," he said. "Drop by my office any time, Mr. Wentworth."

"Delighted," Wentworth murmured, bowing and lifting his hat as the mayor stumped off. He confronted Kirkpatrick then, and his face was deadly serious. "I prefer meeting you here to in your office, Kirk," he said quietly. "I have been warned to avoid contact with the police. I have been notified by someone calling himself 'The Judge' that he holds Nita van Sloan, Ronald Jackson and Ram Singh as prisoners! Would you care to see the message?"

He produced an envelope, held by diagonal corners between finger tips. He used a pencil to slip out the letter. Kirkpatrick used the same care in opening it.

It began without salutation:

"The Nazis are excellent initiators of criminal practices. While I dislike to copy others, I feel called upon to emulate this particular device. I refer to hostages, held for the good conduct of others. The 'others' in this case is yourself; you will keep away from the police, and you will find it convenient to

107

keep hands off of my chosen field of endeavor, or I shall be obliged to copy a good old Nazi custom of reprisal executions. I might mention that the hostages I hold are Nita van Sloan, Ronald Jackson and a curious individual known as Ram Singh.''

The signature was ''The Judge'' and the name was followed by a crude drawing of a gallows, an upright, a cross-arm and a dangling noose.

There were cold fires in Richard Wentworth's eyes, ''I thought you might tell me about The Judge and this chosen field of endeavor from which I am to keep my hands!''

Kirkpatrick said, ''As a matter of fact, Dick, I was under the impression that *The Judge* and *The Spider* were one and the same man.'' His eyes narrowed. ''I find nothing in this letter that would contradict that idea!''

There was challenge between the two men. Kirkpatrick made no secret of his frequent suspicions that Wentworth and the *Spider* were the same man; so long as they remained only suspicions, and he had no proof, he delighted in Wentworth's friendship, and it was a warm and close association. But the events of the day, and the goading of the mayor, had him on edge.

Wentworth frowned swiftly, but his voice did not change. ''Then The Judge defends humanity?''

Kirkpatrick said harshly, ''He robs criminals and then hangs them!''

Wentworth said, ''Thank you, Kirk. My report to you was, of course, unofficial. I think it best that the police keep hands off this case.'' He lifted his hat, turned away.

Kirkpatrick said, shortly, ''Just a minute, Dick. Would you mind taking off your gloves?''

Wentworth turned back and lifted his eyebrows in

108

polite inquiry. "If there is some purpose in the procedure—"

"There is," Kirkpatrick said shortly. "I notice that you lifted your hat with your left hand, and you have not shaken hands either with the mayor or myself—and the *Spider* suffered a rather severe burn to his right hand in the subway fire!"

Wentworth touched his right hand with his left, almost protectively. He allowed his face to show a slight alarm.

"Really, Kirk," he said shortly. "I find your repeated suspicions rather tiresome at times!"

Kirkpatrick took a step toward him. "I can arrest you and take you to headquarters," he said.

"You can," Wentworth admitted, "and I find the idea objectionable, especially in view of The Judge's threat."

The two men looked at each other steadily, but Kirkpatrick's jaw grew dogged. "Take off your right glove."

"You wouldn't care to accept my word that the hand is uninjured?"

Kirkpatrick's eyes widened. Wentworth's word was as inviolable as cosmic law, but slowly Kirkpatrick shook his head. "It is enough for me," he said, flatly, "but it is not enough for police procedure. Kindly remove your glove."

Wentworth said angrily, "All right!"

He stripped off the glove and exposed his hand, both sides of it. Kirkpatrick flushed and apologized. "I'm sorry, Dick," he said. "And frankly, I was just guessing. You were protecting your right hand, apparently, and the *Spider* was in a fire. . . . Pardon me, Dick."

Wentworth shrugged, "Oh, you have your duty, Kirk. I'll bid you good evening."

He lifted his hat with his left hand and stalked away, swinging glove and cane in his right. It had been necessary to arrange this bit of ''proof'' that he wasn't the *Spider* because he needed to be free of police surveillance. He had deliberately favored the right hand so that Kirkpatrick would demand to inspect it. He had deliberately maneuvered affairs so that Kirkpatrick would be ashamed—and would not ask to see the *left* hand!

It was the left hand which was severely burned!

Stanley Kirkpatrick was deeply embarrassed. He valued Wentworth's friendship. He knew that it was inconsistent that he should be fond of the man, and yet suspect him, but that was the way the matter stood. He was still chagrined when he reached his home. He knew that Lona, his wife, was out, but he wanted a quiet hour before attacking the accumulating work at the office.

He let himself in with his key and went toward his library and den with his head down. He hung up coat and hat absently in the hallway, flicked on the light in his office—and then swore and started to grab for his gun. It was futile, as he instantly recognized.

Seated behind his desk, a gun leveled in his left hand, was a man who smiled at him, mockingly.

''I thought this was an appropriate place for an interview, Kirkpatrick'' the man said. ''Sit down, won't you?''

The man was—the *Spider!*

CHAPTER THIRTEEN

The Right to Die!

Stanley Kirkpatrick was rigid with anger and surprise at discovering the *Spider* in his own home. His mind flicked back to the meeting with Richard Wentworth and his embarrassment at accusing his friend deepened. Obviously, his many doubts were unjustified; Wentworth had just spoken to him, there was no reason why, if Wentworth and the *Spider* were one, the *Spider* should now be awaiting him in his home! He could not guess that this was another reason why Wentworth had spoken to him on the street!

Kirkpatrick's voice was sharp. "I know you will not kill me," he said. "Why should I not draw my gun on you?"

The *Spider's* voice, a flat whisper, reached him clearly. "I hope you will not put the issue to trial, Kirkpatrick. This is a lighter gun than I customarily use. I am quite confident of being able to disable you with it without serious consequences to either of us. But stay your ardor for awhile. I merely wish to talk. You might, presently, catch me off guard!"

Kirkpatrick was forced to smile. He dropped into a chair, but he sat there alertly, and he was intensely conscious of the gun tucked into his trouser band where he always carried it. His eyes rested curiously on the face that he knew was disguised, the lipless gash of the mouth, and the predatory beak that was the nose. It made the eyes seem smaller than normal; they were slitted and shadowed under the black brim of the hat. The ears were covered by lank black hair. It was an excellent disguise.

"I have come to lay certain information before you for action," the *Spider* said quietly. "I tried to lead the police into the World Brotherhood Building, and they missed the cue. That building is headquarters for a hidden empire of crime!"

Briefly then, he summarized the things that he had seen there, the secret city with its Easy Street; the multiple barriers that must be passed either to enter or depart. "Unfortunately," he concluded, "every person who leaves or enters that place goes under anesthetic at some point in his passage. Naturally, he cannot be sure how he has been shifted around, or what route he has traversed while unconscious. It is a subtle means of guarding the hideout."

Kirkpatrick said, incredulously, "I have never known you to lie, *Spider,* but this sounds fantastic. Donaldson Gust, who built the building, is a splendid chap." While he spoke, Kirkpatrick was considering what means he could use to entrap the *Spider*. Lona would be returning home soon. If he could signal her—the *Spider* had been clever in taking the seat at the desk. There was a secret button there that connected with the police. . . .

The *Spider* said dryly, "I don't know what it is about me, but you police seem to concentrate your best efforts on catching me, rather than employing the information I give you to catch criminals!"

Kirkpatrick flushed. "I know everything you have said," he answered stiffly.

"Good," the *Spider* was still ironic. "This organization, calling itself Perfect Crimes, Inc., is the reason that your usual methods of detection have failed to solve recent bank robberies. They deliberately vary techniques so that there will be no clue. I think that they undoubtedly plan a gradual expansion of their organization until they encompass all efficient criminals. That is where The Judge comes in."

Kirkpatrick's head jerked up at that. Wentworth had asked questions about The Judge; the *Spider* apparently had solved the mystery of the man who used the gallows signature.

"It is fairly obvious," the *Spider's* whisper ran on. "The two men he killed were a fence and a man suspected of one of the bank robberies. A fence, any fence of stolen jewels or other property, would be a rival to the shops in Easy Street. The bank robber was not actually guilty, but the Underworld thought that he was. So The Judge is merely a name for whatever executioner the Crime Empire sends out to eliminate competition. It is an added incentive to force the Underworld into the Empire!"

Kirkpatrick came slowly to his feet. "By Jove!" he said sharply, "I am beginning to believe you're right!" He took a step forward, and the *Spider* did not move, but his lips were smiling faintly. "Such a criminal organization would be an incredible menace! Why, the whole structure of the city is threatened, its entire government! There is no reason to think this bunch of crooks will limit itself to New York City."

"Now take three steps backward and sit down again!" The *Spider* ordered.

Kirkpatrick stood rigidly, and did not seem to hear him. "Wentworth's three closest friends are prisoners of The Judge. Do you think they are in the World Brotherhood Building?"

The *Spider* was abruptly on his feet. He went around the desk in a movement so swift, it seemed merely a shifting of shadows. He stood beside the door, and now he was behind Kirkpatrick. At that moment, a woman stepped into the office. It was Lona Kirkpatrick, whose arrival the commissioner had tried, and failed, to cover.

"I'm just leaving," the *Spider* said softly. "Come right in, Mrs. Kirkpatrick, and be seated!" The *Spider* bowed to the police commissioner's wife.

Lona Kirkpatrick whirled, a movement as light as a dancer's. Her pallid face was startled, but not frightened. When her eyes touched those of the *Spider*, she smiled and then, deliberately, winked! Lona was not the rigid law supporter that her husband was, and she had reason enough to like the *Spider*.*

Lona began to talk, "You're as good as trapped, *Spider*. There are police in the building and the doors are sealed. They even tried to keep me from coming in, and they warned me I couldn't get out again, not even with my husband! It seems that Sergeant Gallagher had a report you entered here, and he is taking no chances!"

Kirkpatrick uttered a triumphant exclamation, whirled about with his gun in his hand—and the door clapped shut, and locked! Beyond it, he heard the mocking laughter of the *Spider!*

"Many thanks, Mrs. Kirkpatrick, for the warning!" he said.

---

*NOTE: Lona Kirkpatrick said she owed not only her life, but her happiness and self-respect to the *Spider*. Their adventure together was described in the novel called *Satan's Seven Swordsmen*.

Lona clapped her hand to her mouth. "Good heav ens!" she gasped. "I was trying to frighten him, and—"

Kirkpatrick put his arm about her shoulders. "You did well, my dear," he said. "After all, you were taken by surprise."

Lona pressed her forehead against his shoulder. She was smiling, but there were tears in her eyes. She did not like to trick this bluff and straightforward husband of hers, but she was protecting him against himself. If he ever succeeded in capturing the *Spider*, and it should prove to be Richard Wentworth— Kirkpatrick would never forgive himself!

There was the distant sound of a bell ringing, and then the beat of fists on the door. The police were at the entrance of the apartment! Kirkpatrick shouted:

"Break the door in, sergeant!"

There was a muffled answer, and presently the crash of a broken door, then the heavy pound of footsteps. There was some more muffled shouting, but it was sometime before the footsteps came to the door of the office. Then the key was turned and the door flung wide.

"Sorry, commissioner," the man said. "Couldn't locate you right away."

Kirkpatrick nodded shortly. "Come with me," he said. "I'm going to take charge of the search of this building for the *Spider!*"

The police officer saluted and fell in behind Kirkpatrick as he stalked down the hallway. Lona Kirkpatrick looked down at those clumping feet. The shoes were obviously too big for the man who wore them. Lona caught her breath, then covered her smiling lips with her hand.

A policeman, she knew, always took good pains to have his shoes fitted carefully. He couldn't afford to have sore feet! She called out.

"Stanley, you be careful, the *Spider* is dangerous!" She ran after them, touched the man in police uniform on the arm. "You be sure the *Spider* doesn't hurt him, won't you, officer?"

Kirkpatrick said indignantly, "I'll look after myself, Lona."

The police officer saluted Lona. "You may rely on me, ma'am," he said stolidly.

Five minutes later, Lona, peering from her window, saw the police officer pace with businesslike efficiency off into the darkness—and she knew that the *Spider* had made good his escape!

As soon as he was out of sight of the building, the *Spider* raced toward where he had parked his car. His night's work had only begun! He knew that Kirkpatrick, failing to find him, would begin to think over the *Spider's* information and would act on it.

Kirkpatrick's first step would be to place a secret police watch on the World Brotherhood Building. Before that time, the *Spider* intended to be within its walls! He had small doubt that Nita van Sloan and Jackson and Ram Singh were imprisoned there. Now that all his information was in the hands of the police, the *Spider* now had the right to risk his life for his friends!

CHAPTER FOURTEEN

Betrayal

Nita van Sloan groped back to consciousness with a burden on her heart, and that burden was despair. She needed no knowledge of her surroundings to realize that she and Jackson and Ram Singh had been captured in their foray to rescue Richard Wentworth. She hoped that they had been in time to permit him to strike a blow against the criminals. He had said something about a subway wreck. That was her only possible consolation.

Nita opened her eyes cautiously, but her first secret glance revealed no reason for subterfuge. She apparently was in a windowless, doorless room. It was furnished in conventional fashion. She was slumped in an overstuffed chair, and Jackson was stretched upon a couch with a stained bandage about his naked torso. His shirt and coat were tossed beside him. Ram Singh had been tumbled carelessly on the floor. The room was unremarkable in every way. The prints and mirrors on the wall might have come from any furnished apartment—except for the absence of doors and windows.

Nita knew about Argus glass, one face of which gives the aspect of a mirror, the other of which affords clear vision, as if through a window. But it did not occur to her as she pushed herself heavily to her feet and stumbled across to look at herself in a mirror that another woman was looking at her through that mirror. The girl was the office attendant, May Connel, and the man beside her was Sam Martin, who was the "front" in the office of *"Self-Help to Greatness."*

Martin looked uncomfortable and angry. May was disgusted. You'd think that in a cubby-hole like this, any guy that was worth a lick would make a pass at a good-looker like herself, but he had only sworn at her archness in a low, vicious monotone. May didn't know, as Sam Martin did, that their every movement and word was under observation.

So May Connel was pleased when the girl inside the room finally woke up. May shrank back a little as the girl stumbled over and peered into the mirror. It was funny, as if those deep violet eyes were reaching right through the glass and touching her.

May looked at Nita van Sloan's face critically. She had class all right; and even after being knocked over and hauled to this place, her face had freshness and life. Not even a hangover! May's eyes narrowed. It must be that hair-do made Nita look so innocent. No babe who could use a rod like her could be as sweet and melting as she looked now.

"My dear Miss van Sloan!" the voice was oily, smooth—but forceful. It dropped down from the ceiling somewhere. May Connel almost squeaked, and clapped a hand over her mouth. The girl outside didn't look around her at all. She just said, quietly, "Well?"

"Behind the mirror on your right," the voice continued, "you will find a bathroom. The cabinet is equipped with restoratives. I suggest that you revive your two confreres. They received a somewhat heavier dosage than yourself!"

Nita's face was perfectly placid as she followed the suggestion of the voice which, from its sound, came over a speaker-system. It was also apparent that she was under full observation. Inevitably, there was a secret exit from this room, but if she had no way of telling when she was being watched, there was no opportunity to search for it. Her best chance she knew, without need for long thought, was to induce someone to enter the room from outside.

Under her ministrations, Ram Singh exploded out of unconsciousness, and leaped to his feet. He stared about fiercely for enemies and then remembered how he had been overcome. He folded his arms and rumbled in his beard.

"They dared not face our valor, *missie sahib!* We are the conquerors!"

Nita spared him a smile as she bent over the wounded Jackson. One thing she could count on always from Ram Singh and that was his undimmed courage and loyalty. Even under the stimulation of drugs, Jackson came back loggily. It was apparent that his wound had taken a heavy toll on his vitality. Ram Singh jeered at him.

"Wah! A scratch—and you allow them to imprison us!"

Jackson scowled, said weakly, "So the clay pigeon is on his feet for once!"

"Silence, both of you," Nita said shortly. "We are under observation, seen and heard."

Ram Singh's hand crept to his sash, but there was no familiar knife there. His dark eyes glared about, at

119

the ceiling, at the unresponsive walls. He was primarily a fighter, but they did him injustice who believed that Ram Singh was not capable of guile. More fights are won by shrewdness and trickery than by front-to-front warring. The Sikh came of hills warriors.

Behind her mirror, May Connel looked at the big Sikh with widened admiring eyes, turned her gaze toward the supine Jackson. Nita stood between the two men and she was looking—toward the mirror! Sam Martin sucked in a breath. He would swear they had made no sound, and yet the woman was looking this way. His strained attention was broken as the oily voice dripped again from the speaker system.

"I am prepared to offer life to one of you," the man said. "One of you can accept orders, a chance to win honor and wealth, a chance to fight your way to freedom. The other two—must await my pleasure. I am indifferent as to which of you accepts this offer."

Ram Singh growled in his throat. He made no movement, but somehow his great body seemed crouched to spring. His eyes rolled wildly about the room, seeking the origin of that voice.

Nita smiled faintly and made no response; Jackson closed his eyes.

There was laughter as smooth and fat as the voice. "Well, well, so you choose to die together? It is very noble of you and very foolish. You won't have a chance, you know. I'll merely touch a button here under my hand and gas will flood your room. This time it will be no harmless anesthetic, but hydrocyanic gas. They say men survive about two minutes after they get their first whiff."

Ram Singh's hand crept up to his throat and he

loosened his collar. He stretched his neck. It looked as if he were frightened.

Nita said, shortly, "We don't deal with voices. Send us some one we can talk to, and one of us may make a deal, provided the others are safe for the time."

The voice sounded amused now. "I make the proposals, not you," he said. "This is the last opportunity, will one of you live to fight and acquire honor and wealth—or will you strangle like trapped rats on gas? I will give you three seconds. *One—two—*"

Ram Singh uttered a strangled cry! "Wait!" he said. "Wait, not gas!"

Nita whirled toward him incredulously. His arms were no longer folded. He crouched, but it was like an animal at bay, not fiercely ready to attack. His eyes rolled wildly.

"Not gas!" he cried again and his voice was almost a whine!

"Ram Singh!" Nita's voice cracked like a whip.

The Sikh winced, then snarled back at her! "What is my life to thee, woman-thing!" he rasped. "You would have me strangle here! For what? For nothing except a foolish idea! I will go! I will go, man-I-cannot-see!"

Jackson pushed up on an elbow. "Over my body, you'll go!" he snapped. "By the heavens, I'll—" His head rolled. He said, "Lord, Gas again! Damn it, they—"

Ram Singh screamed, and the sound of his terror was awful. Behind the mirror, May Connel's lips curled. "He made a big noise," she said, conversationally, "but so does a bag full of hot air when you break it."

Sam Martin smiled, with a thin twist of his lips. "I feel better now," he said. "I've got to handle that

121

lug. If he can be scared, that makes it easy. What a sucker!''

May cut her eyes toward Martin. "He's going to get bumped off, isn't he?" she asked.

Martin chuckled. "And how!" He looked at her appraisingly but not with interest. "You're going to finger this job, you know. The Brain says all of us have to take 'refresher courses' every now and then to keep our hand in. This is yours and mine, baby."

May spat like a cat. Sam Martin laughed shortly. It made him feel better to have her hate the job, too. He'd taken this as a reasonably safe proposition with good pay . . . to find it was something much tougher. But the pay was worth it.

He sucked at his teeth and continued to watch through the mirror while the entire bathroom moved downward and revealed an elevator cage above it. Two men in gas masks walked into the room, picked up Ram Singh and struggled back to the elevator with him. Then the bathroom rose again to its normal position. Sam Martin chuckled and reached out for May.

She spat at him again. "And I hired out for a nice soft spot!"

There were six of them in the car when finally it pulled away from the hideout, and it was dark night. Ram Singh sat in the back between two men. Martin was wedged in the front with two others, but he was in charge. May had gone on ahead. She had already made the pickup. Sam Martin pushed distastefully at the length of knotted rope at his feet. In the back, Ram Singh sat with folded arms and glared ahead of him. He had not yet been given back his knives.

Martin twisted around and glared at him. He held up a ball of glass. "Remember, mug," he said

122

shortly. "One false move, and I chuck this in your face. Gas. You'll choke!"

Ram Singh's eyes rolled frantically. He made no other reply. Martin chuckled. It was fun pushing around this big muscle lug. Easy, too, since he'd found his weak spot. His eyes narrowed. The plans were as faultless as all the jobs of Perfect Crimes, Inc. May was corraling a moderately successful crook who had pushed over a twenty-thousand-dollar safe two nights before. His partner had been knocked over by a cop, but the crook, Jack Smithers, had made his get-away. So they were going to hang Smithers, more or less, and leave a note from The Judge. . . . Then, just as they were pulling out, the cops would be tipped off and they'd shoot Ram Singh. It would put the heat on Ram Singh's boss, which the Brain seemed to think was a good idea. The cops would figure Ram Singh was hooked up with The Judge.

The car pulled up at the curb, and the driver said, "There goes May in with the lug now."

"She's going to leave the door on latch," Martin said easily. "Remember, we want this Smithers alive, first. We got to find his roll."

Ram Singh growled, "Is that the man I fight?"

Martin chuckled. "Sure," he said. "That's the guy you fight."

The men trooped out of the car, and there were two guns at Ram Singh's back as they entered the hall of the apartment building. They stayed there while they moved up the stairs. Martin rehearsed it carefully. The timing had to be just right. The Brain wanted the cops to arrive before Smithers strangled to death, so he could testify against Ram Singh.

At the entrance to the apartment, Martin stepped aside. "Okay, mug," he said contemptuously to Ram Singh. "You go inside and take this bird apart but

123

don't kill him. We're right behind you, with guns. And I've got this nice little globe of gas.''

Ram Singh looked at him quietly, and Sam Martin was shaken by a sudden doubt. He held the glass ball prominently displayed.

"Get in there and get in fast," he snapped. "That guy has a gun!"

The door was wrenched open and Ram Singh went through in a single fierce bound. The crooks with their guns crowded in behind him.

CHAPTER FIFTEEN

The Traitor

May Connel knew, within limits, what was going to happen, but she couldn't help a small scream when Ram Singh bounded into the apartment! Jack Smithers crouched and whirled, clawing at his gun. What he saw fairly paralyzed him. The Sikh was enormous and there was an almost animal ferocity in his eyes. His big hands were reaching forward. Jack Smithers took a stumbling step backward, tried to get up his gun. It was plucked from his hand. The impact of a fist against his jaw knocked him half across the room and slammed him into a chair.

May saw one of the crooks bring a blackjack down on Ram Singh's gun wrist. The weapon thudded to the floor, and two of the men shouldered the Sikh back against the wall. Martin stood ready with the globe of gas, but Ram Singh spoke calmly.

"You are strange fellow warriors for a Sikh," he said. "Do you trust even yourselves?"

One of the men drew back a gun to slap at Ram Singh's face but the fierce eyes of the man struck him like a blow. He cursed and jumped back, weapon ready in his fist.

"Bring that guy around," Martin ordered shortly, "and find out where the loot is."

"In the closet," May Connel spoke then for the first time. "He's got it all packed for a get-away. Suitcase handy and everything."

She sounded flip and cheerful. Her face was very white. She kept watching the Sikh. There was something about the man that worried her. He was really a swell guy when you came right down to it. Who wouldn't be afraid of getting a load of gas in the face! Even a fighting man didn't have a chance against that. And they weren't going to give him a chance, anyway. They were going to shoot him.

May Connel swung toward the door. "I want to get out of this," she said shortly.

Martin put the flat of his hand in her face and pushed her back. "You're staying, babe," he said. "Got the dough? Okay. Here's the rope. Slip it over the top of that closet door. This has got to be timed just right." He moved toward the telephone, looking at his watch, and watched three of them put the rope around Smithers' neck, stand him against the door, and prepare to haul him up. He looked at the man who held a gun on Ram Singh and nodded. The man lifted his gun and pulled the trigger all in one smooth movement.

Ram Singh was already in motion. This was the moment he had waited for. Three of the men were busy with the crook, Smithers, and Martin didn't have the gas globe in his hand. Ram Singh came out from the wall—but an instant too late. The bullet took him. He felt its shock, and he bent forward slightly against the impact. Then his hands reached the man with the gun. He took the man's gun wrist,

126

and put his other hand against the man's face and jerked. The man screamed but the sound of it didn't last long. His neck snapped under Ram Singh's hand.

Ram Singh had the gun in his left hand, and Martin was groping for the gas globe when the Sikh fired. The bullet went through his hand and the globe smashed against Martin's jaw. He yelled, tried to get away from the stuff, but it was greasy and thick and clung like oil. It curled around his face and he hit the floor screaming. But Ram Singh scarcely noticed him. He went straight at the other men.

One of them had a gun and attempted to use it. It had been so swift, and he expected one shot, had expected even a scream and the fall of a body. It was only when the second shot came, that he started to turn. He started and Ram Singh reached him. Ram Singh was saving bullets. He lifted a knee and set it in the small of the man's back, hooked his right elbow under the man's chin and wrenched. He straightened his leg and hurled the corpse against the other three men as they whirled from their gallows work and charged toward him!

Two went down under that assault. Over their tangle, the Sikh went in a single leap. He was singing softly now, a rumble in his beard, and it was a deep, menacing sound like oncoming thunder. He used his weight as a battering ram against the one man who was on his feet, and reinforced it by a chopping uppercut that almost wrenched the man's head from his neck. The crook went backward in a clean arch, whose end was the window. The glass smashed, and the crook was gone.

Impassively, Ram Singh used his feet on the two men who were struggling to arise. His heel caught one in the jaw, the other in the throat. They scrabbled, helpless, on the floor and the Sikh reached the door in a long stride. May Connel had been clawing at it; now she shrank back, staring at the Sikh's face, screaming thinly. There was blood on the Sikh's beard. It was his own.

"Cut down the man they hanged," he ordered thickly.

May Connel started to run, anywhere, away from him, and Ram Singh's big hand cracked against her cheek. It was almost gentle, for the Sikh, but it sent her reeling against the wall. It stopped her screams.

"Cut him down," he said thickly, "I don't murder unconscious men, and I don't help to do it."

May Connel staggered across the room and got the rope loosened, so that the man slumped to the floor. She turned and stared then at the grim, bearded warrior against the door. He laughed at her—and when he laughed, there was blood on his lips.

"Come!" he ordered hoarsely. "Come, you will drive for me. Martin has the keys. Get them."

May Connel obeyed in a daze and found herself walking swiftly ahead of the Sikh down the hall, down the steps. She heard the Sikh laughing softly, and rumbling a song. It was nothing like his usual deep bellow. There was a pain in his chest. That treacherous ape with the gun had skimmed his lung with a bullet. It might be bad.

May Connel was finally behind the wheel, speeding across the city in the gang car, and the big Sikh was beside her, hunched a little forward, a hand grinding into his side. May didn't know where she was driving, but Ram Singh knew. He was headed toward the home of Kirkpatrick, *sahib!* The *sahib*, Ram Singh's *sahib*, was fighting somewhere, as always when a battle was on. He could not wait to find him. His wound would not wait.

128

As they drove, May Connel lost some of her fear and began to cast speculative glances toward the huge man beside her. "I thought you were a yellow belly like the rest," she said wonderingly. "You never were scared. That was a trick."

Ram Singh grunted, "Drive faster."

The street was reeling before his eyes. By Kali, he would not fail now! He turned his glazing eyes toward the girl.

"We are going to the home of the Kirkpatrick *sahib,* of the police *wallahs,*" Ram Singh said, more thickly. "You are going to tell him where those two are held prisoners, and how to get them out. It is not in the big building. I know that. If you do not—" He set a hand on her neck. He reached up his other hand, and there was blood on it, and he put it on her shoulder. He exerted a little strain. "If you do not," he said again, "I shall begin with your white right arm, and I shall tear it off."

May Connel smothered a small shriek. "You're hurting me!" she cried.

Ram Singh chuckled. He left his right hand on the back of her neck, and looked ahead of him. He couldn't see the street at all now. It was a blur of movements and lights.

"Faster!" he mumbled.

After that, he did not speak again. When he reached the doorway of Kirkpatrick's apartment, he was unconscious. May Connel sat shuddering under the grip of his hand. It was not for some time that she realized he was no longer conscious. Then she leaped out of the car and ran frantically along the street. Ram Singh sat unmoving, head staggering forward. He had made his great play. He had allowed the *missie sahib* and Jackson to think him a traitor in order to

129

gain an opportunity to fight his way clear and to bring help for them. He had made his great play—and he had failed.

The cold crept into the stationary car. Ram Singh made no movement except for the convulsive heave of his lungs, and his breath was a moan. There was blood on his mouth again.

CHAPTER SIXTEEN

The Red Pin

There was an ugly twist to the red lips of the man whom Perfect Crimes, Inc., knew only as a voice and a grim executioner; the man they called the Brain. He was seated beside a sand-covered pit that was about six feet in diameter, an equal distance deep and railed in steel wire. He was leaning atop that wire, and in the pit were two dogs. They were pit-bred fighters, and they were snarling, growling, tearing at each other with their teeth, circling for an opening, springing in, slashing, intent on the kill.

The man's eyes glittered as he watched them, but it was a surface emotion. He was deeply involved in plans. Presently, he left the pit rail and walked across to where he had laid out a huge chess-like board. There were pins on it, indicating activities. A red pin had been twinned by a black one—that was where the *Spider* had checkmated his robbery of the Big Bank and dealt out death. The Brain was awaiting another report.

He sauntered to the pit, and the dogs were separated, glaring at each other, but both intimidated.

He went back to his chessboard and one of the dogs began to howl. On his desk there were no written reports, but he picked up a telephone like arrangement and let come to him again the report which had been recorded on a spool of wire:

"Big Bank a washout. Total casualties in subway and in bank. None escaped. Spider responsible."

Decidedly, this *Spider* was a worthy foe! But he would drop a wedge between him and the police, that would help. When Ram Singh was arrested . . . there was a whir of the phone, and he received a report on the hanging of Jack Smithers. As he listened, his eyes grew hard as agates and his smile grew vicious.

"You're sure the Sikh is in the auto in front of the apartment?" he asked. "Very well. Tip him to the police and capture that girl, May Connel. When you have her, report back."

He plucked his lower lip between a thumb and forefinger, looking indirectly at his chessboard. He leaned over it. There were only red and black squares and pins of different colors, but to him it was a map of all his plans. He knew what each pin represented and each square. The vicious saint-like face grew merrier. He picked up a red pin and thrust it viciously into the square that represented Stanley Kirkpatrick, commissioner of police.

He scooped up his phone and manipulated the radio device, dialed happily. When he spoke, it was with the snap of machine-gun bullets.

"The police will set a secret watch over the building," he said shortly. "Start using alternate exits and entrances. Let the word go out. Plant a fragmentation and a flame bomb in the Donaldson Gust office, wired to be set off by 7. Because the *Spider* will call on him, fool! Attend to it personally, and keep it quiet. Tonight at midnight, we attack. Plan Seventeen."

The man at the other end of the radio did not speak for a moment. "I just want to verify that. It's plan *seventeen,* plan *one-seven."*

The Brain laughed, almost silently. "That's right! We're taking over!"

He replaced the phone, and smiled at his chessboard. It was a very beautiful plan. It would begin with the murder of a policeman, a blatant bank robbery and a riot. It would end with a clean sweep of every major bank in the city, and the murder of the police commissioner—preferably by The Judge, though that did not matter too much. Tomorrow, he who ruled the Secret City of Crime would also rule the world's greatest, richest city!

The Brain slammed his clenched delicate fist down on the desk. It didn't make much sound, and it hurt. He laughed, looked lovingly at his aching hand.

There was just one uncertainty in his scheme, and that was the *Spider.* The man never made orthodox moves. He could be certain about the call on Donaldson Gust. If that failed, he would have to allow the *Spider* to find a clue to the place where Nita van Sloan and Jackson were hidden, and use the girl, May Connel. If it were timed just right, he could arrange matters so that the world thought it was the *Spider* who hanged Kirkpatrick and signed the crime *"The Judge."*

Not that the *Spider* would care! He and all his colleagues would be dead!

The man got to his feet and paced meditatively toward the dog pit, hands clasped behind him. He looked like a priest at his offices; he smiled now and then, happily, viciously. There were so many beautiful ways to kill a man like the *Spider*. It was really a shame the man had only one life!

For all his violent haste, the *Spider* ultimately strolled very casually toward the World Brotherhood Building. The huge statue at its peak was washed with floodlights that changed color slowly. Formerly, they had all been brilliant white, but the dim-out had changed that. Blue and dull red and gold illuminated the formally draped robes, the gaunt cavern of the face and eyes, the outstretched hands.

Wentworth went in seeming idleness into the lecture hall on the first floor. He was not conspicuously ill-dressed, but there was nothing dapper about his appearance. His face had been altered, and his carriage was sloppy. He let his eyes quest over the persons in the lecture hall, but there was no face he recognized. Two men pushed past him, entering the hall and Wentworth smiled faintly. They were police officers in plain clothes. He had been only minutes ahead of Kirkpatrick!

The man on the lecture platform was saying ". . . free copies of lectures delivered here may be obtained in any language at the offices of Donaldson Gust on the nineteenth floor; Donaldson Gust who has made all this great work possible with his philanthropies. . . ."

Wentworth frowned and moved toward the elevators. He could not suspect Donaldson Gust of any part in the criminal proceedings here; he was an almost saintly man, though Broadway whispered about him. But Broadway whispered about everybody. But it was a very *obvious* move for the *Spider* to call on Gust.

He rode up in the elevator and walked quietly toward the offices of Donaldson Gust. The place was brightly lighted and there were a dozen or more clerks, all with intent and serious faces, who presided over selections of printed matter. There were signs indicating that many languages were spoken here by the various clerks.

Wentworth stepped up to a clerk whose sign stated: *Ici on parle francais.*

"I've just come in from Paris," he said in French, "and I have some information to lay before Mr. Gust personally."

The clerk nodded, scooped up a phone and spoke into it, and presently rose and led the way through aisles among the desks to a remote corner of the big office where there was a door without any label on it at all. She knocked and then opened the door.

The man behind the desk rose nimbly. He was not a large man. He had a very red mouth, and his face was saintly. He gestured Wentworth forward with both hands, placed a comfortable chair beside his big desk.

"Sit here!" he cried. "Sit here and tell me all about it! Ah, I am glad to see some one from my poor suffering France!"

The clerk was gone, but Wentworth did not immediately move forward. He had expected his entrance here would precipitate trouble; perhaps it was too early to expect action from the criminal gang.

Wentworth spoke abruptly, in Norwegian. "Herr Gust," he said. "I have reason to think your office is under observation. Couldn't we talk together somewhere else, more public?"

The man frowned, came forward around the desk— and there was, beneath it, a sudden metallic click. Wentworth heard it, and cried out a warning. He dove forward across the room. His shoulder caught the man in the stomach, and catapulted him into a heavy chair, overturned the chair atop both of them.

It was while the chair was still wheeling over, legs high in the air, that the explosion came. It was shattering and terrible. The glass partitions were blasted out. The metal frame and base was torn with a dozen jagged fragments. Immediately thereafter, a violent fire broke out. The outer office blazed in four different places from the spewing of liquid flame. The cubicle of Donaldson Gust was an inferno!

Two of the clerks ran across the office, and they had machine guns in their hands! They sprayed the flaming pocket in the corner with deadly lead. When their drums were almost empty, they whirled about. There were only two clerks left in the main room. They killed those and, hiding the machine guns under their coats, ran out of the place.

They ran up two flights of stairs to the twenty-first floor and ducked into an office. There was a man there, and he was holding open the door of a closet.

"What luck?" he asked.

The machine gunners laughed. "Hell, a guy would have to have nine lives to get out of that. It was a mass of flames and we gave them a hundred bullets between us."

The man grunted and closed the closet door behind them. He reached up and squeezed together the top and bottom pins of the upper hinge. He picked up his phone and spun the dial at two and then *three*. He waited until the phone buzzed three times, then he picked up his hat and coat and left the office, locking the door carefully behind him. He was frowning. Seemed as if the *Spider* ought to be dead, but you never could tell. The guy seemed to have more lives than any cat. He had reported, *"Probable success, unconfirmed."*

He straightened up from locking the door, and very conscious of the hidden gunman in his cubicle—there was one on every floor—walked staidly toward the elevator. The organization certainly went to extreme lengths to see that everything was well protected.

He got in the elevator that stopped in answer to his signal—and the cage instead of going down, moved upward! He turned, startled, toward the operator—and looked into the muzzle of an automatic pistol. He looked quickly at the other occupant of the elevator, and saw that it was the operator, equally immobilized by the gun!

"Gentlemen," spoke the third man in the car, "when you use fire and bombs and guns to trap a man, you should first make sure there aren't any steel files in the office! They offer excellent protection from all three—especially when there is a window beside it."

And the man laughed. The sound of it was flat, mocking—*the laughter of the Spider!*

The prisoners shivered, and one of them remembered his message: *"Probably success, unconfirmed!"* He'd never get a chance to send a message: *"Spider alive!"*

"Gentlemen!" said the *Spider* again, "it's a lovely night, had you noticed? Let's go up to the observation tower and have a nice, cozy chat."

CHAPTER SEVENTEEN

Night of Doom

Wentworth knew that he could hope for only a few minutes of safety, even in the observation tower of this tall building. The movement of the elevator, contrary to signal, would be spotted at once. It was possible that the hidden gunmen were placed even in the tower, and he had no means of spotting their whereabouts. But the slow cold anger of the *Spider* was flaming within him now. His escape from that inferno had not been as easy as he had made it seem. The first burst of machine-gun bullets had smashed into the man he was trying to save, as he dragged him away from the already blazing chair that had broken the first force of the blast. He had barely made the protection of the filing cabinet himself and there had been uncomfortable moments before he had managed to get out upon the window ledge, cross to another office in time to follow the escaping murderers.

It was when the *Spider* stopped the elevator at the tower floor that panic fear got the better of his two prisoners and they made a concerted attack upon him! The operator leaped for his back, and the other man whipped out a gun!

The *Spider* moved with the speed of a sword-thrust. He slid aside from the man's leap and hooked his right into the man's solar plexus. The double violence of that blow doubled him over like rag doll, and he was like that when his companion started shooting. In the close confines of the steel-sided elevator, the noise was incredible.

It beat with the violence of blows upon the *Spider's* ears; it completed the panic of the man who was wielding the gun. His first bullets slammed into the body of the elevator operator. Two others missed and caromed, screaming, off the steel walls. It was like being inside a boiler when the sledge hammers started to swing outside.

Wentworth dropped to one knee and his gun jerked once in his fist. He was in deadly peril, but he still shot coolly, aiming at the killer's gun-wrist. But the man was crazy with his fear, with the sound of his own attack. He dodged wildly—the wrong way! The bullet took him full in the heart.

In the sudden silence that followed the last shot, the man's fall was a crashing explosion. Wentworth reeled to his feet, almost stunned by the concussion. His ears rang with it. He could hear nothing but the ringing. The air was thick with the acrid sting of gun-powder. He coughed, but he did not open the door. If there were gun-guards anywhere on the two or three floors around here, they would be concentrated on the elevator door now. He dared not open it!

Almost violently, the *Spider* wrenched the gunman over on his back and went through his pockets. He found a penciled notation: *"Plan 17, midnight! Your job, 21-b, address 4961 West Sixty-First street. Kill them."*

Wentworth's hand groped for the control stick of the elevator and sent it upward to the top of the shaft. He reached up and with hands that still shook a little from the tremendous shock of the shouting, forced open the trap in the elevator's top. He climbed out, reached to the overhead mechanism and muscled up into the machinery house. He was just in time. The elevator suddenly lurched and started downward. There were external controls, then!

The *Spider* smiled thinly, and crossed the machinery house to a door that opened on the wind-swept roof. His mind was racing as he darted across to the balustrade and threw himself over to the ledge outside. There was half a gale blowing here. Above him the chill stainless steel statue was bathed in blue and crimson. Wentworth spun out a length of silken rope and began to loop it through a paling of the balustrade. He was fifty-six stories above the street, but he was not thinking of that, nor of the perilous climb he must presently make. He was thinking of the note he had found in the man's pocket.

Incredible that a man in this rigidly disciplined organization should make a penciled note of his job! What was this *"plan 17"* which the man had followed by an exclamation point? It must be something big to move the man to use that punctuation in a note for himself. Midnight—Wentworth took an instant to glance at the luminous dial of his watch. It was just after ten o'clock. Before midnight, many things might happen!

Up to now, Wentworth had not dared to let himself think of the rest of that message. Was it possible that it referred to Nita's hiding place and that she was not in the Secret City? *"Kill them,"* the message had ended—Wentworth had his silken Web ready and he took quick turns about thigh and arm, and slid over the edge of the balustrade.

The wind caught him and whirled him away from the face of the building. The lower he slid along the silken rope, the farther out he would swing. Nevertheless, he pushed on, swiftly. That notation was very pat. It wouldn't be possible, would it, that the head of this fantastic organization had deliberately *planted* that message on his own man?

Wentworth had descended three stories now, and he was at the tend of his silken rope. The wind buffeted him a good six feet away from the face of the building, but now and then it relented and he swayed closer. He would have to bide his time. The *Spider's* face was very grim. He knew his own reputation for miraculous escapes, and criminals were well aware of it also. If he had survived the bomb-attack, it was logical that he should follow those two killers. They would escape by some secret way, but this man would be left behind. Yes, if the *Spider* escaped, it was logical that the Brain should expect him to take this man prisoner or kill him.

The *Spider* was suddenly sure that the note had been planted deliberately. Either Nita actually was a prisoner at this address; or else there was a trap set there for the *Spider*. Either way, he had no choice except to follow through on it.

The wind pushed him constantly, and from above the *Spider* heard voices call out cautiously. The men were closing in upon the observation tower! Swiftly, Wentworth knotted the dangling end of the silken rope about a gun, and tossed it through the nearest window. It sagged down over broken glass, but the gun caught in the radiator placed, as usual, just below the window.

Cautiously, the *Spider* drew himself in. He got a

foot on the sill, managed to pull himself in, and cautiously, to snake the silken line down from where it was looped about the balustrade. Perhaps they had heard, perhaps seen the line. It was a chance he had to take. Swiftly, he raced across the office he had entered.

From another window, where the wind would be helpful instead of a hindrance, he once more rigged his silken line. It was his only chance, for the halls were guarded by hidden gunmen, and the police would be swarming over the building to investigate the fire and explosion in Gust's office. Slowly, step by step, he made his way in three-story drops down the side of the building. It took time, *time*.

When finally, somewhat drained physically by the struggle, Wentworth reached his car it was almost eleven o'clock. He drove swiftly to a spot from which he could phone Commissioner Kirkpatrick and warn him that the criminals were springing something big at midnight. That was all he could say; he didn't know the details. As he raced through the streets, he flicked on his radio and caught a news broadcast.

He cursed harshly then at the glib voice of the announcer, narrating the adventures of Ram Singh, who was accused by one Jack Smithers, twice convicted felon, of attempting to hang him! The announcer said police were quite certain that Ram Singh was *The Judge*.

A note had been found, with that signature, about Smithers' neck. Only the police had arrived in time to revive him. Apparently, the rope had been carelessly tied and had come loose from the door knob. And Ram Singh was in the hospital, critically wounded. Smithers, and the police, were totally unable to account for the five dead men found in Smithers' apartment and the sixth, who had been thrown out the window.

A girl had been seen leaving the place with Ram Singh by two people who lived nearby; Ram Singh, curiously, had been found, wounded, in a car parked in front of the police commissioner's apartment house! He had not yet regained consciousness.

The *Spider* did not alter his plans by a hair's-breadth. He phoned Kirkpatrick, giving the commissioner no opportunity to interrupt his talk, and then raced on toward the West Sixty-First street address.

He heard the police sirens rip out behind him as they raced to the phone from which he had called. That was normal procedure, but they had no way of identifying him. He was not in the *Spider* disguise— but he would be! There was no longer any doubt in his mind that this was a trap. His mind cast back to the woman who had been seen escaping with Ram Singh. Could that possibly have been Nita? But who else would have been with Ram Singh?

Nevertheless, Wentworth pressed grimly on. He was going to take the bait of this trap, and let the jaws snap at him! The *Spider* was tough. He had broken the steel jaws of traps before this! It took him perhaps five minutes after he had stopped the car to don the *Spider* disguise. It took him three minutes, clinging to the shadows, to reach the rear of the small apartment building whose address he had so conveniently found.

The *Spider* smiled thinly as he made his way up the slender black skeleton of the fire-escape. Room after room, which he passed, was vacant and unfurnished—in itself a curious thing in war crowded New York. But the *Spider* kept straight on to the roof.

When he found a lighted apartment, he rigged his silken rope swiftly and let himself downward. There were three men in the room. They sat, in their shirt-sleeves, playing cards. Their guns swung from shoulder holsters. The *Spider* pushed away from the building wall with a sharp thrust of his legs—and sailed, feet-first, at the window! The smash of glass made an explosive sound in the room. One man pitched over backward in his chair. One dived for the floor. The third, crouched out of his seat, and clawed for his gun.

The *Spider* laughed as his feet struck the floor, and the chill sound brought a curse of terror from one of the men. Before the gunman could fire, the *Spider* had crashed his left against the man's jaw. He was straightened out, sent crashing over the table. Coins rang on the floor; liquor glasses crashed; an ashtray rolled lop-sidedly across the floor.

Two guns blasted up at the *Spider* and he caught one bullet on the bottom of a snatched-up chair; his own automatic poured instant hot death into the face of a second assassin. He kicked the table, then, and it lifted and smashed, top-down, upon the one gunman who remained in the fight. The man's gun-hand flung outward in pain, and the *Spider* kicked the gun from his fist. He put a foot on the table, weighting it, pressing it down.

"Where are they?" he asked, in a chill whisper. His gun looked over the table's edge and into the man's face at a distance of six inches. The man could see the tense finger on the trigger, could smell the reek of gunpowder.

The man groaned. "I don't know! I swear I don't know!"

The *Spider* pulled the trigger. The bullet missed the man's head by inches, but the blast was deafening. He jerked convulsively. His teeth chattered in fear.

"*I don't know!*" he whimpered.

The *Spider* hit him above the ear with the pistol barrel and put him out. He found a slip of paper in his pocket, giving this address. "*Guard duty*," it stated. The man was probably telling the truth, then. Abruptly, Wentworth straightened. He heard someone calling out, and the voice was clear and high: the sound was the three-toned signal that he used to call his companions!

It came again, and Wentworth leaped into the bathroom. It came, apparently, from the other side of the wall. With narrowed eyes, he jerked open the medicine cabinet. It was empty of everything, but the second glass shelf was smeared with fingerprints. He jerked at the shelf, and the whole cabinet swung toward him. He was looking through a sheet of mirror-glass into a room where Nita van Sloan stood at rigid attention, listening!

Wentworth struck the glass with his gun barrel, and it shivered into fragments under the blow. Jackson was propped up on the couch, obviously wounded, and there was a third person in the room—the reception clerk from the offices of Self-Help to Greatness!

Nita looked at him without words and, slowly, smiled. Jackson's grin was wide. The girl, May Connel, stood stiffly against the wall and shivered. The *Spider's* gun sought her out.

"What is the exit of this room?" he demanded, for the hole in the wall was too small for even a child to climb through.

The girl lifted her fists to her cheeks. "The bathroom is an elevator," she whispered. "You can't work it from in here. Only from upstairs."

Wentworth spoke in French to Nita. "This is too easy," he said. "There's a trap of some description. And elevators are favorites with this gang."

"The girl is really terrified," Nita said. "Not of us, but of the men who put her here. She says she's one of the gang, but is scheduled to be killed."

"I'll risk the elevator," Wentworth said quietly. He looked toward the girl. "Come here, May," he directed. "I'm going to ask you a question to which I know the right answer. By your answer I'll know whether I can trust you. *What is plan seventeen?*"

The girl grew even paler, so that the rouge stood out on her cheeks. She twisted her hands together. "I don't know much," she whispered. "I overheard something once. Seventeen is the big knockover. It's a big cleanup. I heard Sam Martin say it meant they'd take over the city. The only thing I really know about it is that one part of it means—" She sucked in a breath and it quivered. "It means they kill the commissioner of police. You know, Kirkpatrick."

Wentworth uttered a muffled cry, glanced at his watch. It lacked three minutes of midnight! He had to get them out of here fast; a phone call to Kirkpatrick . . . It would bring the police here at once, but he would have to risk that. He could not endanger Kirkpatrick's life through thoughts of personal danger. He sprang to the door of the bathroom—and found himself looking into the muzzles of four machine guns. The four men all held guns to their shoulders like rifles, and it was plain they knew how to use them.

"This is it, *Spider*," one of them said flatly. "*Drop the gun—or take it!*"

CHAPTER EIGHTEEN

Plan Seventeen

It started with the murder of a policeman walking his beat on an East Side street. He'd just stepped out of the side door of Mike's Bar where he had been warming his cold-stiffened body. A man stepped out of the darkness and said, "Hello, Flynn."

Patrolman Flynn had been trained in a hard school. This beat was like that. Men who moved up toward you unexpectedly were apt to pack trouble. He'd learned that lesson, at cost, three years before, when he had been laid up at home for three months with Mollie alternately loving him and quarreling with him because he wouldn't leave the force.

So when the man spoke to him like that, Flynn shoved his hand in his right-hand overcoat pocket and through the slit to his gun. He didn't have time to do more than that. The man who had spoken carried a double-barreled shot gun, sawed off about six inches from the stock. He shoved the small cannon-like weapon up against Flynn's belly and pulled both triggers.

The charge tore Flynn apart. It picked him up and

147

blew him backward against the door of Mike's Bar and the door went open and he sprawled backward in the dim light from inside. His arms were flung wide now, and his head was wrenched backward, but there was no life in him. The hole in the middle of him took care of that. His hair was fair, and there was a careless lock down across his forehead.

There's nothing that gets the cops so sore as the death of a policeman, especially a wanton murder like this. It brings the homicide squad on the run and starts a wholesale roundup that will take the services of a big lot of police. It brings out high officials, and because Commissioner Kirkpatrick loved his men, it would always bring him to the scene.

Patrolman Flynn was a pawn on the Brain's chessboard of crime.

Across the city, the Knight of the Brain's attack, swung into action. It was a small bank robbery and it had been planned with deliberate holes. The planners, for instance, had neglected to mention that the place—an all night loan office was equipped with tear-gas jets, and that the guard who operated it was stationed in what looked like an elevator, but was really a fort-like room. Consequently, the ten crooks who were involved in the bank robbery ran into heavy trouble.

They were vicious and heavily armed and they fought like cornered rats. They slaughtered three tellers and four customers of the bank. They tossed a grenade at the door of the elevator and blew it in. By the time they ran toward their get-away cars, their eyes were streaming from the tear gas. A radio car slammed into them, and a truck was wrenched about to block the street. They forted up in a closed store, smashing their ways through the windows, and the cops turned in a call for reserves.

All very nicely planned, and it called out another big block of the police who were on duty, drained off some of those who were held against emergency at headquarters. This was at quarter past twelve.

The other trouble had started a little before twelve, because it took time to get a mob organized. It wasn't hard to do, if you would pour out enough free liquor and go to the places where men would sell their souls for an extra drink—down in the districts that bordered on the slums, where the men out of work, and the men who never would work again, were sleeping nights in barrooms and in sheltered doorways with newspapers for a blanket. Not a very courageous mob, perhaps, but liquor would blind them and dull them, and they would follow the lead of the few killers who were assigned to the job.

It was about half-past twelve when they all trooped out into the street and moved resentfully toward the wealthier districts that bordered on their sullen streets. The mob picked up others as it moved along, and there were shouts like, "Kill the rich! Pull 'em out of bed!" There were yells of, "They got food! They got liquor! Come on, pull 'em out! String 'em up!"

It was madness, liquor madness, but it's the sort of yell that will pull a crowd any time, catering as it does to envy and greed. A few determined leaders, a motley mob of drunks, and skulkers who thought to take advantage of the impending riot to loot and steal. They slammed into the exclusive Gramercy Square district and streamed into the lobby of an expensive hotel before the doorman half-realized what it was all about.

There was a detective, but one of the crooks put him to sleep with a blackjack. Some of the mob went into the barroom, and others began to rampage through

149

the halls. There were screams, and the calls went through to the police.

The crooks waited until the mob was pretty well scattered at its wrecking, and then carefully killed three innocent bystanders.

The squad cars rolled, and police reserves poured into the district. The cops were run crazy with a dozen minor outbreaks like that, all over the city, including some that were dead serious. And, behind that smoke screen, the real work of Plan Seventeen stealthily gathered headway. Certain men were quietly strangled in their beds; and certain others were carried, unconscious, away from their homes to the banks whose vaults they could open.

Every bank in the city was quietly invested by squads of well-dressed men who, in every case, knew the name of the watchman and the names of the bank officers; who, where they did not have the bank officers as their prisoners, were disguised to resemble them. In each bank, after the watchman was killed, one of the men took over the clock and made the rounds—and didn't skip one punch, or punch one off-schedule. Such was the perfection of Perfect Crimes, Inc.

And all this started with the murder of Patrolman Flynn just three minutes after the men with machine guns challenged the *Spider*, pinned him in a narrow doorway from which there was no retreat, with carefully aimed machine guns that did not even need to be aimed. There was only one thing wrong with this phase of the Brain's plans. He himself had named it: the unorthodox behavior of the man called the *Spider*.

This was a spot for a man to surrender or die—and the *Spider* looked his assassins in the face . . . and laughed!

He did several things with the lightning-like rapid-

150

ity of a stage magician. He had expected to walk into a trap and he had made his small preparations. He flipped off his hat and sailed it out into the room. He fired one shot, which caught his hat in mid-air. Then he hurled himself sideways behind the protection of the wall, pushed off from the wall—and fell neatly into the bath-tub!

A hell of gunfire burst loose. Impossible to tell which had happened first, the *Spider's* dodge, or the ripping deluge of lead. The bullets tore the edges of the door to bits; chewed through the thin partition of plaster and lath, smashed the back wall of the bath—and played a devil's tattoo on the bathtub. It sounded like the ringing of a cracked bell, but it was a double tub; one whose metal rim arched over to the floor. It might be cast iron, or it might be steel, but one thing was certain: bullets that had clawed through the wall would not be able to pierce two thicknesses of the metal!

The *Spider* drew himself wholly into the tub, lay with his legs doubled under him, his guns ready in his hands, and waited.

When his bullet smashed through his hat, it hadn't made much sound. There had been a minor explosion. The hat had leaped, and then settled to the floor. Afterward, vapor poured out of it. Black vapor, and gray vapor, mushrooming and spreading with oily thickness, and gaseous speed. In a space of heart-beats after it started, the room was choking thick with black chemical smoke, and the tear gas it contained was beginning to work on the killers!

"Into the bathroom," one man ordered in a choked voice. "Go in, shooting!"

But they couldn't see. They stumbled and collided with each other as they worked toward the door of the bathroom where the *Spider,* fairly comfortable in his tub of armor, waited with his guns. They reached the bathroom door, eventually, and three of them died there.

The fourth turned from the maw of death and, screaming, fled through the murk. He left the door open, which set up a dissipating draft on the vapor. The *Spider* did not wait. He moistened a chemically impregnated cloth and, pressing it over his face, he walked through the death-strewn room and raced for the upward steps.

He found a phone there, and put through his phone call. He had been delayed a few minutes, and there was more time lost while the call went through—and he was too late.

"Commissioner Kirkpatrick just went out. A murder," the man reported. "Any message?"

"Get this on the air, and get it there fast!" the *Spider* snapped. "Warn Kirkpatrick there's going to be an attempt to kill him tonight! This murder may be a part of the plot to put him on the spot! Make it fast!"

The cop on the wire was startled into an oath. "Who is this?" he demanded.

The answer was a laugh, but a laugh he could recognize—the laughter of the *Spider!* The cop had already pressed a button which would signal the operators to trace the call. Routine procedure on this sort of thing. He jumped from his desk and grabbed another telephone.

"*Spider* just called in on my line," he shouted. "Get after him!"

It was only afterward that he thought about the warning to Commissioner Kirkpatrick. He was a little worried about that. Crazy to think anybody would try to kill the commissioner, but maybe he'd better do something about it. He couldn't put it on the radio.

Every cop who heard it would go straight up in the air. He could send out a request for the commissioner to call him at headquarters, then he could tell him. He made his decision and put it into action, but he was still a little worried. After all, the *Spider* might be right!

Wentworth took ten minutes to work out the secret of the elevator that gave access to the prison room in which Nita and Jackson and the gang girl were locked.

It was quarter past twelve when they ran out of the building, and the raid on the loan office was under way then. They caught the police alarm for it as they raced across the city.

May Connel was twisting her hands. She said, desperately, "Don't kill me! I can save that man, Ram Singh, from burning! I know he was framed! Just protect me, and let me tell my story to Commissioner Kirkpatrick! I'm afraid of anybody else on the force!"

Nita was behind the wheel. Jackson and the girl were in the rear and Wentworth twisted about on the front seat to study the girl. He was doubly suspicious of any mention of Kirkpatrick, now. He could not fathom why this girl should have been placed in with Nita when he was known to be on the way to smash into the trap.

Jackson swore harshly, "That yellow punk!" he said. "He walked out on us, afraid of gas!"

May Connel turned on him furiously. "You're a fool!" she said. "He got out of there so he could tell Kirkpatrick where you were! He killed six men and got wounded himself getting away! He's worth ten of you! And he did it for you. He did it for you!" May Connel was suddenly crying. "I never saw a man do a thing like that for anybody else. He wasn't out for

153

number one. He was doing it for you—and you call him yellow!''

Nita laughed in sudden relief. ''I couldn't understand it,'' she said. ''It was a clever act. He looked frightened, and—'' She twisted her head about. ''I don't know whether it means anything, Dick, but the man who spoke to us could hear *and see* everything that went on in our dungeon.''

''That argus-window,'' the *Spider* suggested.

''*I* was there!'' May Connel said. ''I was behind that window, and the Brain wasn't there.''

They were racing downtown now, streaking to make contact with Commissioner Kirkpatrick. Grimly, the *Spider* flicked on the two-way radio of his car. It was damned risky business, with the town alive with the police prowl cars, but he had to risk it. He had to get through to Kirkpatrick. He realized that the police would hesitate to put that warning of his on the air. They couldn't use code for a thing like that.

He lifted the microphone to his lips and he was staring straight ahead. The statue that topped the World Brotherhood Building was very clear against the sky, bathed in its light of crimson and blue.

''*Spider* calling Kirkpatrick,'' he said steadily into the phone. ''*Spider* calling Kirkpatrick. All police cars please copy and repeat. *Spider* calling Kirkpatrick. Come in, Kirkpatrick.''

He closed the switch to listen, and there was no answer. He repeated his call, and this time when he closed his switch he heard a police alarm go out for him. They hadn't spotted him very closely yet, and were directing all patrol cars who heard him to close in.

Wentworth swore and opened his switch again. ''*Spider* called Kirkpatrick,'' he said. ''Cars please repeat. This is life and death. Repeating. This is life and death.''

154

He closed his switch, and a voice spoke out of the receiver. It was something like Kirkpatrick, but Wentworth knew that it was not. He had imitated too many voices not to recognize a fake when he heard it.

"Kirkpatrick here. What is it, *Spider?*"

The *Spider* spoke his message into the microphone, "Kirkpatrick, your life is in danger! The criminals known as Perfect Crimes, Inc., are looting banks wholesale tonight under cover of a round of other crimes. Disregard all except bank robberies, Kirkpatrick and smash into the banks! And, Kirkpatrick, protect yourself! Your life is in danger! They are planning to assassinate you and take over the city! I have full details of their plans, by confession of a member of the gang. I'm on my way to see you, Kirkpatrick! Protect yourself!"

Wentworth turned to Nita and his eyes were glowing coldly. "Slow down and let me out on this side street," he ordered. "Get Jackson to my home and take this girl with you. Ram Singh's life depends on her."

Nita's face was white. She recognized that cold, singing urgency in Wentworth's voice.

"Oh, Dick, what are you going to do?" she cried.

The *Spider* laughed, and the sound of it was bitter and edged. "I'm going to drive the Brain crazy," he said and laughed again. "Failing in that, I'm going to dash his brains out!"

He dropped out of the car as it bucked to a stop— and the shadows swallowed him.

The *Spider* had vanished!

CHAPTER NINETEEN

The Tangled Web

The Brain sat over his chessboard and smiled at the pattern that was growing among the pieces. Move after move had been successful, and only one had failed. He still could not put a red pin permanently in the square which represented the *Spider*.

The man smiled and spat out a vicious curse. One of the caged dogs whimpered, and the man looked up suddenly at the beast. It cringed and lay flat on the floor. The painting on the wall was illuminated by green light. He picked up a phone and said, *"Report."*

"Failure," a voice rasped in his ear. *"They were waiting for us! That damned Spider!"*

The voice clicked off. The Brain got to his feet very slowly. His lips writhed, and it was not a smile now. While he stood there, the light flicked on the painting again. He scooped up the phone, and once more a voice wailed in his ear:

"Failure! That damned Spider! You said you would kill him—"

The man shook his head and his eyes were shrewd. That was a little too much. None of his men would dare to utter a reproach to him. His messages were being crossed up, somehow. Someone had learned what wave-band to use.

The Brain looked about his room slowly. He opened a drawer in his desk and closed certain switches there. The light on the picture went out. If it burned again, it would mean that someone was trying to force an entrance to his stronghold! He took out of another drawer a vicious-snouted automatic. It had a curled clip extending from the butt. It would fire thirty-two cartridges without reloading, and with force enough to pierce thin armor.

He moved backward across the room then, and sat down in a chair. When he did so, screens of bullet-proof glass slid up from sockets in the floor, and a lid dropped into place on top of it. But he had a port in each face of the screen, and the chair in which he sat was a swivel. It also could drop through the floor if he touched a button in the left arm. He put his hand on the button.

He realized then that he had failed to shut off the radio that was tuned to police signals. He heard the warning of the *Spider* repeated by the police broadcaster, and this time Kirkpatrick's car came in briefly to acknowledge the report.

Suddenly, the Brain heard laughter—and it came from the radio. It was the laughter of the *Spider!*

"Poor Brain!" the voice whispered. "Poor befuddled Brain! Poor crazy, madman's Brain! Poor, poor Brain!"

The man behind his bullet-proof screen went stiff with anger. His face lost its mask of saintly gentleness. The laughter was repeated, and those same mocking, goading words. The man lifted the gun to the porthole—but didn't fire on the inoffensive machine that repeated those taunts. He realized suddenly that it was a recording he was hearing. The *Spider* had set it going with intention to madden him, to confuse him—and *to distract him!*

With sudden sureness, the Brain knew that the *Spider* had located his hideout and was on the way to challenge him! For a wild instant, panic touched him. He licked his dry lips.

Suddenly, different words were coming out of the radio!

"This is the *Spider* calling the police," it stated gravely. "I am on my way to the World Brotherhood Building where I will open all the Secret City to you. I have the operating mechanism of the secret doors under my hands and will open them all. All criminals take notice of this message. Cease your operations under Plan Seventeen if you wish to live through the night. I have its details under my hands and am relaying it to the police. That is all."

It cut off and once more there was laughter and those taunting, mocking words: *"Poor, poor Brain."*

The man in the bullet-proof cage swore horribly. But he listened; he listened with strained attention to find out what the *Spider* would say next.

"The whole system is really very simple," the *Spider* said, presently. "Constantly tuned continuously operating radio circuits keep the whole organization tied together. It's fine so long as no one grows suspicious and investigates the ultra shortwave band. Then the whole thing is an open book. But the Brain couldn't know about that. Poor poor Brain, failing under the strain of trying to think."

Abruptly, the Brain laughed. The sound of it racketed back from the close, thick glass walls about him. The *Spider* was working a neat trick, but it wouldn't succeed—not against the Brain. The man had merely recognized that answer, simulating Kirkpatrick, as false, and was using that wave band to torment him. He didn't really know anything at all. And he couldn't use the ultra shortwave radio to trace him, because he had shut them all off.

It was true that a small germ of worry remained in the Brain's mind. Had he shut those radios off soon enough? He had spoken only twice, at intervals of a few seconds. He had spoken one word: *Report*. Surely that wasn't enough to give the *Spider* triangulation on his hideout?

The Brain shrugged in bravado, touched a button that would drop the bullet-screens back into their floor-sockets. As he did so, one of the dogs twisted its head about toward the window—and *whined!* With a convulsive fling, the Brain was back in the chair, the screens up. He waited.

He touched a button in the chair arm—and sudden blue-white electric flame danced around the window at which the dog had whined! There was a grim smile on the Brain's lips. By compressing that button, he had touched off his first circle of defense. The entire stainless steel wall of his hideout was now charged with a death-dealing voltage of electricity!

He had more tricks in reserve if the *Spider* managed to survive that one!

Outside in the night, nearly seventy stories above the pavements of New York, the *Spider* dangled at the end of his silken web! He had climbed to the observation tower platform of the World Brotherhood Building, about the foot of the giant statue that crested the building, the giant statue with its outstretched arms!

There apparently was no entrance to the statue at all, but the *Spider* had painfully fought his way up the draped folds of the garment, while the gale whipped and tugged at him, until he could throw the weighted end of a line over one of those outstretched arms. After that, it was easier—easier until he heard the whine of a dog, and suddenly the whole blue-washed statute of stainless steel was alive with electricity!

He was glad then for the wind that kept pushing him out into space, but which equally, was likely to whirl him against the stainless steel, a touch of which meant death! He could see the glistening square of argus glass, fitted into a shadowed fold of the garments of the statue, and he knew that it was a window. But a window that was well-guarded by electricity!

The wind shrieked and flapped the *Spider's* cape out from his shoulders. It whirled him—and then there was a sudden cessation of wind. He was whirling straight toward the death-charged steel! With a frantic whip of his legs and body, the *Spider* wrenched himself aside. There was just time to brace himself, and then he did the only thing that he could do:

He catapulted himself bodily through the argus-glass window!

He went from darkness into dazzling light in a space of a split-second. He released his hold upon the silken web, struck on his feet, bounded into a somersault and brought up sharply behind a chair. His light-blinded eyes could just make out the man he sought seated in a chair across the room—a curiously pivoted chair, set upon a chromium rod. And the man had a gun in his hand, which he raised and was aiming carefully.

When the gun crashed, its sound was curiously muffled—and a bullet tore through his shielding chair with the whine of high velocity. But the face of the man in the chair across the room was convulsed. The

160

Spider laughed in sudden triumph! The man had failed to take into account the concussion that would occur in that tightly enclosed area.

At the same instant, there was an explosion behind him! Wentworth whipped about, flung flat to the floor. A masked machine gun, operated apparently by the man in the bullet-proof cell, was blasting away from a port in the wall. Its bullets fanned across an area of ten feet before it was silent. That near-escape made the *Spider* more cautious. It was apparent that the place was well trapped! But the *Spider* had a cure for that—if he could reach the lamp on the nearby desk!

The *Spider* stepped calmly out from behind the chair, and his gun was in his holster.

"We seem to be at an impasse," he said quietly, "but you're completely finished. You might as well surrender and take your medicine. The police are on the way here, summoned by radio, and as I told them, all the keys to the secret Doors can be operated from this room. In a short while, I can unravel the secret."

"If you live!" the Brain said.

He had the gun leveled again through the porthole, and his face was tightened in anticipation of pain. The *Spider* looked at him curiously. He didn't think the man would fire unless he were forced. He would prefer to give Wentworth opportunity to step into one of the prepared traps that must pitfall this room. Meantime, he must distract the man's attention for a while, for a little while—until he could reach that lamp.

"You haven't made many mistakes," the *Spider* said shortly. "But you made a few. I realize now that you intended me to go to Kirkpatrick with the girl May Connel. That's why you planted her in the dungeon. You had some scheme for murdering Kirkpatrick when I went to him—but my warning, and my setting the police on my own trail will dispose of that. They'll be on the lookout for the *Spider* everywhere. If you have a man masquerading as me—" the Brain's rising rage told him he had guessed right "—that man is doomed."

He was only ten feet from the desk now. He could reach it in a quick leap—but a bullet would be swifter.

"Your radio was very clever, too," the *Spider* continued, "but the television you used to spy on your dungeon had to be left behind. And it was possible to determine its wave length, as also with your listening devices."

The Brain spoke viciously, "I'll kill the fools who failed to destroy them, according to orders."

The *Spider* laughed, and the sound was flat, deadly. "I saved you the trouble!" He was very close to the desk now. "The other mistake you made—aside from enabling me to triangulate your hideout which was already, if it must be confessed, suspect because of its composition of stainless steel—and because it fits in so well with your personality.

"You have a macabre sense of humor, my madman, which turns a World Brotherhood Building into a Secret City of Crime; and the figure of the greatest and best man this world has ever known into the headquarters for a murderous fiend! You see, no matter how clever a man is, *he can't change the pattern of his character*. This is the only place where a man like you would make his headquarters.

"And the final thing was this, your fake philanthropist. The man you put in your office to meet me, to pose as you, and to die—so that if I escaped I could not suspect you: the man who played the benevolent

162

philanthropist, from Norway. Your fake Donaldson Gust couldn't speak Norwegian!''

As the *Spider* hurled that fact at him and laughed, he seized the lamp on the desk and wrenched its wires violently against the edge of the desk. They snapped, short-circuited—and the room went dark. And, at the same time, the *Spider* knew that he had short-circuited the man's electrical control of his traps!

The *Spider* flung himself aside, flat on the floor, but there was no shot from the glass trap in which Donaldson Gust, the real Donaldson Gust, had encased himself. The *Spider* moved toward it softly. He heard the man pant out a curse and knew that he was working on some safety device that refused to operate.

''I'm coming for you, madman!'' the *Spider* whispered. ''I'll take that glass cage apart with my hands and, afterward, I'll take *you* apart!''

There was a heavy thud—and after that silence. In the darkness, there was the sound of close breathing. The man had opened his own cage! He was in the darkness now, somewhere, probably behind a double thickness of the glass, searching for a target with his automatic that was like a small machine gun!

The *Spider's* outflung hand touched a dog cage, and the animal snarled viciously, struck at the hand, but bit only the wire of its cage. The gun of the Brain crashed! Its orange red tongue of fire leaped out, and the Spider saw that he had guessed correctly. The man was behind the bullet-proof screen. The *Spider* did not shoot. He smiled thinly in the darkness, and moved behind the dog cages. His sensitive hands, silent and seeing, found the fastenings of the animals' cages and opened them.

It took courage—or knowledge—to dare to open those dog cages. Every one of the animals was scarred with fang and whip wounds. They were vicious, and they were killers. But the *Spider* only kept behind the cages when he opened them, held a gun ready in his fist.

There was faint light from the window, where blue floodlights still washed the gargantuan statue. Apparently, they were of a different circuit from the mechanisms inside the room. Of course. They would be operated from the building below! But, dim as that light was, it would give Wentworth a target, should the dogs turn on him. It would reflect on their eyes!

But Wentworth was quite sure they would not attack him. He knew their master, and he knew that these dogs would have ample reason to hate that master! He thought he knew what prey they would choose in the darkness! Silently, the animals quitted their cages. The claws of one of them made a faint rasping on the floor. The *Spider* laughed.

"I have loosed your own dogs on you, Gust!" he said softly.

A soft cry of fear was torn out of the man, and his gun crashed. A dog snarled, and the gun crashed again. There was the sound of the dog scratching the floor in death agonies, but there were three other dogs. They were pit bred animals, accustomed to attacking in the face of death. Their claws made a faint scratching as they charged!

Gust screamed. He turned and fled wildly across the room, with the racing dogs in his wake. The *Spider* saw him clearly against the bluish light of the open window. He saw the slinking forms of the dogs as they closed in upon the man. Even then, Gust had played shrewdly. He had his back to the light so that he could see the eyes of the dogs. He fired once, twice, a third time. One of the dogs was killed, but the other two went toward him in a concerted rush.

164

The crash of the gun dropped another in mid-leap, but the last dog struck against the chest of Donaldson Gust! The man screamed. He teetered backward out the window—and suddenly, he was no longer in sight! The thin, terrified howl of a dog lifted, faded out downward into the cold and bitter night. The man's screams stayed; it lifted, died, started again—but it did not fade out with distance as do the screams of a falling man!

The *Spider* darted across the room and peered out the window. What he saw made him a little sick. In falling, Donaldson Gust had tangled his foot in the silken web which was looped over the outstretched, blessing arms of the Man whom Donaldson Gust, in his power lust, had mocked. And the wind was whipping Gust's slight body wildly out into space. He swayed out, and then he slammed against the stainless steel body of the statue. His scream was driven out of him wildly!

The *Spider* cast about for some means of reaching the man, but even as he did so, the wind and the web took command. They would not be denied. Far, far out into darkness the slight body of the master killer swayed. Then the wind let go, and Donaldson Gust swept back toward the unyielding steel which he had built to protect himself. As he swung nearer and nearer, his speed increased—and his scream mounted higher! He knew he was doomed.

He flung out an arm, and when it struck the steel wall, it crumpled like a burnt match. His head struck next with a crack like a snapping whip. Thereafter, Donaldson Gust did not scream, and there was a dark stain on the stainless garment of steel. And even then, the wind was not satisfied. It whirled and smashed, whirled and smashed that dangling figure again and again against the steel.

When police came into the World Brotherhood Building, they found doors opened everywhere. They found elevators hidden in what had seemed solid foundations, and they found every cubbyhole that had housed a watchful gunman deserted; even Easy Street was abandoned. The rats had fled the scuttled ship.

And, eventually, the police found the way up to the elaborate dwelling that was encased inside the statue of stainless steel; and they found a room where the crimson seal of the *Spider* glistened on the wall beside a window. When they found what thrashed against the wall outside, they could not put a name to it, except to say that it had been a man. It was better that way. Donaldson Gust was a name that men loved throughout the world, for he had built his "front" so well that people did not know it was a front. Let men not lose the faith his name had built; he would need their prayers.

It was on the sidewalk outside the place that Commissioner Kirkpatrick met Richard Wentworth. He was standing, hands on the head of his cane nonchalantly, head tipped back to admire the statue high above.

"Very dramatic," he murmured at Kirkpatrick. "Very. Lovely night. You've made the deuce of a row all night, old man, with your sirens shrieking like seventeen devils through the street. . . ."

Kirkpatrick said sharply, "Why *seventeen?*"

Wentworth looked at him with lifted eyebrows. "Dashed if I know, old man. Seemed sort of appropriate."

Kirkpatrick had a dour smile at his mouth corners. "Very," he said dryly. "And by the way, Dick, I'm turning loose that Sikh devil of yours. It seems he was framed. I have it on excellent authority from one who helped frame him, a girl. There doesn't seem to be much reason to hold her either. Just one of those girls who get tangled up with crime, because they think it's glamorous—the poor fools.''

Kirkpatrick was startled by a woman's voice behind him, and turned to see Nita.

"We poor fools," she said, shaking her head. "Thinking that crime is glamorous!"

She took Wentworth's arm in both of her hands.

Kirkpatrick looked from one to the other of them. He swore shortly and didn't apologize.

The Spider and
the Pain Master

CHAPTER ONE

The Spider's on the Way!

In a room on the ninth floor of the Mallard Hotel, overlooking Times Square, a frightened man sat tense and watchful. He was facing the door, and his eyes seemed to be glued to the knob, waiting for it to turn.

There were beads of sweat on his forehead. Every few minutes he would run a hairy hand over his heavy jowls. But it was always his left hand. The right never moved, for it kept a heavy automatic pistol trained unwaveringly upon the door.

On the floor were two cowhide bags, all packed and ready for him to check out. A tan overcoat and a tan fedora lay on the bed. The coat was an expensive one, and so was the hat. The man's suit was of the best, and the cowhide bags were the finest that money could buy.

Yet their owner was not happy. He was frightened. His fear was apparent in the close-set, smallish eyes, and in the occasional twitch of his thick lips. His eyes never left the door knob. He sat there that way for perhaps fifteen minutes, and then the telephone rang.

The frightened man uttered a gasp of relief. But he did not remove his gaze from the door. He reached over without shifting position, and picked up the telephone handset on the night table alongside the bed.

"Yes?" he said into the instrument, almost in a whisper.

"Sabin?" a cold, unemotional voice asked.

"Yes. This is Sabin."

"Are you ready?"

"Yes, I'm ready."

"Very well. Wait exactly fifteen minutes. It will then be nine-fifteen. Call a bell boy and have your bags taken downstairs. Pay your bill. That should take ten minutes, bringing it to nine-twenty-five. After you pay your bill, stop and buy cigarettes or a newspaper. You will then walk out of the front entrance at exactly nine-thirty by the clock in the hotel lobby. The doorman will offer to get you a cab, but you will refuse. At exactly that moment, an Onyx taxicab will cruise past. You will flag that cab and get into it with your bags. Do you understand?"

"Yes. I understand."

"All right. Set your watch at nine-ten, when you hear the signal. Good-bye—"

"Wait!" Sabin exclaimed hoarsely. "There's—there's something I have to tell you!"

"Well?" demanded the unemotional voice at the other end. "Speak quickly. Otherwise you will upset the schedule."

"It—it's about the—the *Spider!*"

"What!" The cold voice lost a little of its evenness. "What about the *Spider?*"

"He—he called up. He said he knew who I was.

He said I'll never leave the country alive. He said he's coming here to get me. I tell you—'' Sabin's voice rose to a shrill, high-pitched key *''—he's on his way here!''*

There was a momentary pause at the other end. Then the voice said, ''I see. It is good that you have told me this. Everything shall be taken care of. You will proceed according to schedule. *We* will handle the *Spider!*''

''But—but can you get here in time? He may be already in the hotel!''

''Have no fear, Sabin. My men are there now. They will see to it that the *Spider* ceases to annoy us!''

There was a click. The phone went dead.

Sabin hung up. His face was broken out in perspiration. But all during the talk he had never removed his gaze from the door, nor had his gun wavered.

He licked his lips, and kept on watching the knob. . . .

Nine floors below, in the lobby of the Mallard Hotel, a man in a black overcoat and a black fedora sat in one of the public phone booths. He was not using the phone, however. He was watching all who came and went in the lobby—and he was waiting for a call.

When the phone rang, he snatched the receiver off the hook quickly. Strangely, the phone did not ring very loud. It made only a faint tinkle which was barely audible beyond the booth. The man in the black fedora put his lips to the mouthpiece and said, ''Thirteen.''

A cold, unhurried voice at the other end said, ''Seven.''

The man in the black hat whispered, "Twenty-six. This is Loder."

"Emergency!" rapped the voice at the other end. "The *Spider* is coming for Sabin. He will try to enter the hotel, or he is already there. Take all precautions to prevent his reaching Sabin. Cover all exits. *The Spider must not escape! That is all.*"

The phone clicked dead.

Loder swore softly under his breath. He replaced the receiver, and hurried out of the phone booth. A thin man with a flat nose was sitting in the lobby, facing the desk and reading a newspaper. Loder passed close to this man, and stopped to light a cigarette. Out of the corner of his mouth he said, "Emergency. *Spider* coming—or already here. See that the back entrance is covered."

The man with the flat nose only rustled his paper in response. He waited until Loder had passed on, then he got up and walked to the rear of the lobby. There was a side street entrance here. He stepped out into the street and walked ten paces in the shadow of the building. He stopped alongside the alley between the hotel and the theatre next door. There was apparently no one in that alley. But the man with the flat nose spoke as if he were talking to thin air.

"Thirteen," he said.

From somewhere in the alley came the response: "Seven."

"Emergency," said the man with the flat nose. "The *Spider* is coming—or is already here. Cover this exit. Spread the word to all men posted here. We'll trap the *Spider* tonight."

He did not wait for a reply. He turned and re-entered the hotel, resuming his chair in the lobby. He opened up his paper, and held it in front of him with his left hand, as if he were reading. With his right he took a revolver from a shoulder holster, and held it in his lap, concealed by the newspaper. He looked across to the telephone booth. Loder was inside it again. He nodded to Loder, who nodded imperceptibly in reply.

The phone in the booth rang again. Once more Loder picked it up and said, "Thirteen."

Once more that cold, unemotional voice said, "Seven."

"Twenty-six," said Loder. "Loder speaking again. All arrangements made. Bragg has just passed the word. If the *Spider* comes, it will be impossible for him to escape."

"Very good," said the cold voice. "Sabin is leaving on schedule. Have you seen anyone enter who might be the *Spider?*"

"No," Loder said. "I have my eye on the entrance. The only one who came in was that Wentworth fellow—you know, the rich polo player. He had his fiancée with him. Nita van Sloan. Their pictures are always on the society page. Wentworth and the van Sloan girl went into the cocktail lounge."

"Wentworth, eh!" said the voice, speculatively. "He is a friend of Commissioner Kirkpatrick. I wonder . . . perhaps you had better check on him, Loder. See if he's still in there."

"Right," said Loder.

He hung up and left the booth. He started across the lobby, and when he came abreast of the chair in which the flat-nosed man was sitting, he looked down at his feet and frowned. He stooped, and went through the motions of tying his shoelace. He spoke out of the corner of his mouth.

"Go in the cocktail lounge," he said. "Richard Wentworth is in there, with Nita van Sloan. Keep your eye on Wentworth. Red Feather has an idea he may be the *Spider.*"

"Right," said the flat-nosed man.

Loder fixed his shoe-lace, got up and returned to the phone booth. The flat-nosed man put his gun in his side coat pocket, folded the newspaper, and arose. He strolled casually toward the cocktail lounge. . . .

In the cocktail lounge, Richard Wentworth and Nita van Sloan were sipping dry Martinis, and reading a newspaper which was spread out on the bar in front of them. It was the same edition that the flat-nosed man in the lobby had been holding. The headline was black, and still damp:

RED FEATHER STRIKES AGAIN! LAURA BURGESS BURNED TO DEATH BY GHASTLY FLAME-THROWERS AS SHE STEPS FROM TAXICAB!

Heron's Feather, Dyed in Human Blood is Left Beside Charred and Blackened Body of Famous Actress!

Nita van Sloan's beautifully chiselled, patrician face was white with emotion. Her long, slender hands were clenched in her lap.

"Lord, Dick!" she breathed through pallid lips, "I knew Laura Burgess!" She closed her eyes as if to shut out a terrible vision. "Laura—burned to death! She was so beautiful and so talented! Who—who could have wanted to destroy her—and *why?*"

Richard Wentworth's eyes were grim. "The man who calls himself Red Feather; the man who leaves the grisly token beside the bodies of his victims—a feather dipped in human blood! Red Feather is like an octopus who has spread his tentacles out to tear at the nerves of people in all walks of life!"

Wentworth's voice dropped an octave, and his eyes took on that faraway look which Nita knew so well. "Red Feather has a terrible advantage over any other criminal I have ever encountered. He is absolutely without a sense of mercy. In some secret way he has managed to batter down the resistance of good and decent people to the point where he can force them to do vile things. *He must be stopped!*"

Nita, seeing the faraway look in his eyes, and hearing his words, drew in her breath sharply. "Dick! You—you're going to—"

She sighed, seeing the grim resolve upon his face.

"Yes, darling," he said slowly. "The *Spider* is going to walk again tonight! Before morning, I hope to learn the identity of Red Feather!"

"You've been holding out on me, Dick!" she said breathlessly. "You had a purpose in coming here?"

"Yes, darling. A little private information." His finger slid down the page, indicating a small item at the bottom:

ARNOLD METZ STILL MISSING

Alleged Absconder Believed to be in Hiding Somewhere in New York

It was discovered today that Arnold Metz, missing bank president, was two hundred thousand dollars short in his accounts. It is believed. . . .

"Arnold Metz," he told her, "is right here in the Mallard Hotel. He's registered under the name of Sabin."

Nita frowned, looking at the news item. "But I don't understand. What has Metz to do with Red Feather?"

"For some reason which I haven't yet discovered, Metz stole that money to give to Red Feather. He's to turn it over tonight, and Red Feather will help him to leave the country. I've made arrangements to—er—pay a little call on Metz before he leaves. He has already been warned that the *Spider* is coming for him!"

Nita's eyes opened wide with consternation. "Then Red Feather knows it, too! He'll trap you—"

Wentworth smiled tightly. "I am hoping he will make the attempt!"

From his pocket he took a small vial which he slipped into her hand. "If there should be trouble, you know what to do with this. I'm going now. If anyone follows me out of here, try to detain him for three or four minutes. That is all the time I'll need for a start."

He arose from his chair, and looked at his wrist watch. Then, raising his voice for the benefit of anyone who might be listening: "I'll just go around and pick up those opera tickets for tomorrow, Nita. It's only around the corner. I shan't be gone long—" and under his breath he added "—*I hope!*"

She smiled the smile that meant much more than: "Good luck, Dick."

She turned around in her chair, and watched Wentworth's lithe and powerful figure as he moved toward the green entrance of the cocktail lounge. At the same moment, she saw a man enter the lounge from the hotel lobby. He was a burly man, with a flat nose which looked as if it had been smashed at one time, by a battering-ram.

Nita's glance flicked over this man, and she noted that his gaze was on Wentworth. When he saw that Dick was going out into the street, he immediately swerved and turned to follow him.

*　　*　　*

Nita van Sloan grew tense. Wentworth must not be followed now. Within the next few moments he was going to transform himself into the *Spider*. He must be left free and unobserved.

Desperately, Nita sought some means to keep the flat-nosed man there.

Wentworth was already through the doorway, and the man was halfway along the bar, toward the door. Nita's eyes glinted. She got off the chair, holding her cocktail glass.

"Mr. Smith!" she called out sharply.

Nita van Sloan might have given the average observer the impression that she was a carefree society girl with plenty of looks and plenty of sex appeal, but not too much brains. That impression would have been highly erroneous. For behind those warm violet eyes there ticked a brain which was a match for that of the cleverest of men. Less than that would have failed to make her a fitting mate for Richard Wentworth. Her native intelligence and quick-witted grasp of the most abstruse problems had been augmented by the things Wentworth had taught her. Among them was a sound knowledge of practical psychology, gleaned not only from the works of worldrenowned experts, but also from actual experiments in the finely equipped psychological laboratory maintained by Wentworth. One of the experiments they had tried was that of calling a common name in a high, sharp voice. Tests had proved conclusively that forty-eight people out of fifty will turn around involuntarily, even though their own name has not been called, because curiosity is one of the strongest of human instincts.

This time, the flat-nosed man reacted true to form.

His eyes had been glued to Wentworth's back. But when Nita sang out: *"Mr. Smith!"* he turned around.

Nita hurried over to him, carrying her cocktail, and smiling with apparent pleasure.

"Why, Mr. Smith!" she exclaimed, extending her hand, which he could not help taking. "Imagine meeting you here! I thought you would be in Monte Carlo at this time of the year!"

The flat-nosed man frowned. "I'm afraid you've made a mistake, madame. My name is not Smith—"

"What!" Nita's face fell, in a beautiful registration of amazement. "You're not Lorenzo Smith, the painter?"

"I'm sorry, madam, but that is not my name. If you will excuse me—"

"Oh," she said contritely. "I'm so sorry. I was sure you were Lorenzo Smith. Do you know, you would very easily pass for his double!"

"Very interesting, I'm sure," the man said. "And now, if you will excuse me, I'm in a bit of a hurry—"

He tried to release his hand from hers, but she clung to it.

"You know," she said, "I very seldom forget a face. Are you sure you weren't in Monte Carlo three years ago?"

"I have never been in Monte Carlo in my life, madam!" he said bitingly. "And my name is not Smith. Good-bye, madam!"

Reluctantly, Nita released his hand. "Well, good-by and—oh, I'm so sorry!" She made a deliberately awkward gesture, and spilled the contents of her Martini glass down the front of his coat.

Flat-nose jumped back, with his face twisted in a scowl.

Nita uttered a little gasp of dismay. "Oh, how stupid of me!"

180

She put down her glass, and snatched the handkerchief which Flat-nose had taken from his pocket. "Let me dry it for you."

"It's all right," he said hastily, but still scowling. "It'll dry by itself. I have to be going—"

"Oh, I wouldn't think of letting you go like that! It was all my fault. Here, it will only take a moment."

She held on to his coat, and dabbed at the stain.

Mr. Flat-nose growled. "I told you I was in a hurry!" He yanked the handkerchief out of her hand, glared at her, and hurried into the street.

Nita van Sloan watched him go, with a little secret smile. She had held him up long enough for Wentworth to lose him. She turned and winked to the bartender. "Another Martini, Thomas. I really don't know *how* I could have been so awkward!"

CHAPTER TWO

The Spider Rides the Web

Up on the ninth floor, the man who was registered as Mr. Sabin was still in his chair facing the door, with the black automatic in his hand. He kept looking constantly at his watch. There were still seven minutes to go before he could call for a bell boy.

That door—it was the only way the *Spider* could reach him. The window behind him was locked, and the shade was drawn all the way down. There were no fire escapes, and no terraces on this fireproof hotel. Not even a fly could walk nine floors up the smooth face of the building. Neither could a fly walk down eleven floors from the roof.

But maybe . . . maybe . . . they told strange tales about the *Spider,* how he appeared from nowhere. . . .

Suddenly Sabin jerked up out of his chair and swivelled around in a half crouch. The hand that held the gun started to shake as he stared at the shaded window. His whole body broke out in a cold sweat.

Distinctly he had heard it—somebody had tapped upon the window pane!

"God!" he muttered. "It—it *can't* be!"

He had to know. He had to be sure. Perhaps, in his overwrought condition, he had allowed his ears to deceive him. He must look. He must look out there and make sure it wasn't the *Spider* who had tapped.

A cunning look came into his eyes. He backed over to the dresser and pushed it squarely in front of the door. That would keep anyone from entering that way. Then he reached out and flicked off the light switch. The room became utterly dark.

In the blackness, Sabin stole across the room, fingered the shade. He pulled it aside an inch, so that he could peer out.

He saw nothing.

Rendered a little bolder now, he pulled the shade all the way up, and opened the window. Still with his gun in his fist, he leaned out, peered above and below, and to both sides. There was nothing on the wall of the building. But some one had certainly tapped on the window-pane. To the right, the window of his own bathroom adjoining his room, was dark. So was the window to the left of his room.

He shrugged. His nerves were going. He'd better get out of here. Probably almost time to call for a bell boy, anyway. He pulled in his head and closed the window, then pulled down the shade once more. Then he felt his way along the wall to the light switch and flicked it on. He still kept his gun gripped tightly, with finger on trigger, as the light sprang on. He blinked, and looked at the dresser. It was in place. No one had entered that way. . . .

His eyes swivelled across the room to the bathroom doorway—and he uttered a shrill and terrible scream.

An utterly frightful figure was coming slowly out of the bathroom. Sabin recognized that low-brimmed slouch hat, the voluminous black cape, the grisly death's head of a face which men had come to know as the fighting face of—the *Spider!* And in each of the *Spider's* hands was a long-barreled revolver. Slowly, with dreadful, inexorable steps, the *Spider* came toward him. And words came from those grim and frightful lips.

"Sabin, I have come for you—as promised. If you wish to live throw down your gun!"

Sabin's fright was that of a cornered rat. He stood tensed and crouched, with the automatic thrust out at arm's length, his finger taut on the trigger.

"Damn you, *Spider,*" he spat out, "don't come near me."

A queer and ominous laugh came from the cloaked figure. Slowly, the *Spider* advanced into the room. The two guns were at his hips, held low, but pointing at Sabin. And with each step he took, Sabin's fear increased.

"Well, Sabin," he said mockingly, "why don't you shoot? All you have to do is pull the trigger. Think of it, Sabin. You can pull that trigger, and shoot the *Spider!* Surely you would like to kill the *Spider!*"

Sabin's hand began to shake. He knew why the *Spider* was mocking him. Of course he could shoot and kill the *Spider.* But he knew that the moment he pulled his own trigger, those two deadly guns in the *Spider's* hands would belch and vomit death. The *Spider* might die—but he, Sabin, would also die.

He backed away from the terrible, cloaked figure until he touched the wall. He could retreat no farther. The *Spider* was four feet away—three feet—two feet—then. . . .

Sabin screamed in fright and rage, and fired!

184

But it was as if the ominous cloaked figure had read his mind, had timed his reactions to the last split-second of infinity. For just before Sabin pulled that trigger, the *Spider's* right gun flashed up and down with the speed of light. The long barrel cracked down hard upon Sabin's wrist, and the automatic exploded into the floor.

The gun blasted loudly in the close confines of the suite, and the thud it made when it dropped to the carpet from his numbed hand was drowned by the echoing reverberations of the shot.

Sabin cowered, defenseless, before the grim man whom the underworld feared more than the law— even more than death itself.

"Talk quickly, Sabin," the *Spider* said. "Who is helping you to escape from the country?"

"I—I'll talk, *Spider*. Red Feather—it's Red Feather who's helping me—"

"I know that. *Who is Red Feather?*"

"God help me, I don't know."

"Why did you steal from your bank? You didn't need the money."

"Red Feather made me do it."

"He forced you?"

"Yes."

"How?"

Sabin's lips trembled. "For the love of God, *Spider*, don't make me tell that. You don't know what you're doing—"

The *Spider* motioned impatiently. "Where is the money you stole?"

"In these two bags."

"How were you going to escape?"

"I'm to go downstairs and take an Onyx cab. That's all I know—except that they will get me out of the country by plane."

There was the sound of hurrying feet in the corridor. Men were coming to investigate the revolver shot.

"Sorry to do this, Metz. It's necessary!" One of the black-gloved fists stabbed upward to Metz's chin, with the speed of a flying meteor. There was a thud, and Metz collapsed.

The cloaked figure of the *Spider* stooped and seemed to envelop him in the folds of the voluminous, purple-lined cape. He was lifted bodily, apparently with the greatest of ease. The light-switch was clicked off. In the abrupt darkness, a vague shadow moved through the room.

Somewhere near by, a church bell tolled the quarter-hour. It was nine-fifteen—the time when the man who was known as Sabin should have called for a bell boy. But no call came down from Room Nine-thirteen. . . .

While men continued to pound ineffectually at the door, the ephemeral shadow moved in the darkness with its burden, over to the window. The shade rasped as it was pulled upward. The window slid open, propelled by an almost invisible hand.

The darkness outside was only a little less opaque than within the room. Lightwaves from electric signs in the street below cast an eerie incandescence upon the side of the hotel. The window faced west, away from Broadway, over a low, three-story building next door. Beyond the low building was a taller structure —an old apartment house which had been converted to accommodate roomers. And from a window in that building, level with the tenth floor of the Mallard Hotel, a thin gossamer thread seemed to be stretched.

The shadowy figure of the *Spider* leaned out with its burden. There was another gossamer line hanging down from the tenth floor window, directly in front of the room Metz had engaged. The *Spider* grasped this line, and tied it around the body of the unconscious man. Then, while those in the corridor pounded at the door and shouted for it to be opened, the *Spider* picked up the two cowhide bags, and tied them also, with an extra loop, to the body of Metz.

So thin and frail did that line look that it seemed impossible that it could lift the combined weight of Metz and his two bags. Yet, when the *Spider* leaned out and uttered a low, peculiarly pitched whistle, the line began to rise, dragging the weight up from the floor and over the window sill. Slowly, surely, it swung out. For a moment Metz's unconscious figure dangled precariously in the air, with a drop of at least six flights to the roof below. The line tautened, but did not give.

This was the *Spider's* Web—a line of cleverly fabricated silken rope, cunningly made and treated with chemicals so that its tensile strength was as great as that of a ship's hawser.

As it started to rise, pulled slowly up by someone in the tenth floor window, the *Spider* seized it just above where it was tied around Metz's drooping body, and pushed himself out of the window. He wound his arm once around the line, leaving his other hand free, and hung, with his legs dangling in space. To anyone who might have looked in this direction from an adjoining building, little would have been visible except a vague mass swaying in the air, for the great black cape of the *Spider* covered Metz and the bags with a mantle of dark camouflage.

The *Spider* reached over and lowered the window, thus muffling the shouts of the men in the corridor outside the door. Then, while still hanging thus, he took from his pocket a long, thin, flexible tool with two prongs at one end. He inserted it in the crack between the upper and lower frames of the window, then manipulated the prongs by means of a lever at the other end. This lever actuated the prongs through the medium of a powerful spring, so that they caught the window catch just like two human fingers. In a moment the window was locked. Now, those who entered the room would be faced with a puzzling problem. How had the *Spider* taken Metz out of there, with the doors and windows locked?

On entering through the bathroom, the *Spider* had previously locked the window. So that now there was no apparent way by which he could possibly have left the suite.

With the window locked, the *Spider* slipped the pronged tool out and put it away. Then he gripped the Web with both hands and whistled once more. Immediately the line began to rise.

From Metz's room came the sounds of breaking wood as those in the hall began to smash down the door.

The door was giving very fast now, and once they had it open, the dresser in front of it would present no obstacle. When those men entered the room, their first concern would be the window. They would surely see the great black shadow on the line outside, and then their guns would speak. It would be the end of the *Spider*.

But no matter what the urgency, the Web could not move any faster. The *Spider* did not whistle again, for he knew that the one man up there on the tenth floor was exerting every ounce of his strength to pull him up. There was no use trying to hurry him.

Grimly, the *Spider* brought out one of his automatics. To trap him like this would indeed be a triumph for Red Feather's agents. But at least one of them would go to his death with the shadowy nemesis of crime!

Inch by inch the Web moved upward. Wood was splintering, inside the room, under the powerful blows of a fire axe. And suddenly, with a tremendous crash, the door gave inward. From where he hung on the line, the *Spider* could hear the dresser scraping along the floor as it was pushed back. Then he heard the rush of men into the room, and saw light stream through the window as they clicked on the switch.

The *Spider* was almost within reach of the upper window now. He put away the automatic, and stretched his free hand up toward the sill. But there was still a good six inches between the tips of his straining fingers and the safety of that ledge.

Below him, he heard the astounded shouts of men as they found room 913 empty.

"The window!" some one shouted. "He must have gone out the window—"

And another voice: "Nuts! How could he? The window's locked!"

While they were arguing, the Web moved up another few inches. The *Spider* tried to help the man above, by bracing his feet against the wall. He could feel the tautness of the straining line, which was stretched rigid by the combined weight of himself, Metz and the two cowhide bags.

"What the devil!" some one in the room below was shouting. "We know he didn't come out through the door. So it *must* be the window. Let's look, anyway!"

The sash was raised, and a head poked out.

And just then, the *Spider* came within reach of the upper sill!

But it was too late. Looking down, he could see

that the man at the window was peering toward the roof below. In a moment he would look up. That moment would seal the *Spider's* fate, for the man at the window down there was the house detective, and he had a gun in his hand.

The thought reactions of the *Spider* were lightning-swift. Too many criminals had found that out to their sorrow. And now he was to demonstrate that speed of thought once more.

With the resourcefulness of one who has taught himself by rigid training to meet the swiftest emergency with swift action, he drew one of his automatics. But he did not fire it at the man below. That would not only have meant the killing of one who was probably an innocent party to the murderous designs of Red Feather—it would also have meant that those other men in the room would swarm to the window and send a blasting barrage of lead upward. And it would also have meant the failure of the *Spider's* plan to spirit Metz out from under the noses of Red Feather's organization.

So instead of shooting, the *Spider* sent his automatic spinning out through the darkness toward the roof below. He threw it just two seconds before the house detective began to turn his head upward, so that the man did not catch the flash of metal as it sped downward at a wide angle, over to the *left*. The *Spider* had seen the gun in the man's right hand. Knowing then that the detective was right-handed, he was able to tell which way he would turn his head when he was ready to look up. Long and interesting tests in the New York Laboratory of Psychological Research, endowed indirectly by the *Spider,* were constantly being conducted to ascertain and catalogue the normal reactions of human beings under any given set of circumstances. And one of those tests had proved conclusively that a right-handed man will turn his head to the right, while a left-handed man will turn his head to the left, when he looks around.

Thus, when the *Spider* threw that gun out toward the *left,* it was just at the moment when the house detective in the window below was turning his head toward the right, in order to look upward. So he did not notice the hurtling automatic. A second-and-a-half later, the weapon struck the roof below. Wentworth had slipped off the safety catch before hurling it, so that when it hit, the gun exploded thunderously.

The *Spider's* timing was uncannily accurate. Just at the moment when the detective's head was half way around, the gun blasted below him. At once, he jerked his head back, peering down in the direction of the shot.

"Down there!" he yelled. "Someone's down there! I can't see him—"

He yanked his head in, and shouted to the others in Metz's room, "He must have climbed down a rope ladder. He's on that lower roof! Come on! Let's go!"

In a moment those men were trooping out of the room, eager to be in the chase. And against the wall just above room 913, the *Spider* laughed harshly and gripped the sill above him. In a moment he had climbed over, and into the room.

A sturdy man with a military bearing was straining every muscle of his body as he hauled at the Web. He had his feet braced against the wall, and the coils of the line wrapped around his forearms, which were encased in leather cuffs. It was he who had been pulling that heavy load up to the tenth floor.

"Thank God, major!" the man gasped as the *Spider* vaulted into the room beside him. "I heard those men below. I never thought I'd get you in time!"

The *Spider* wasted no words. He swung to his feet, reached over the sill, and hauled at the unconscious body of Metz, which was still dangling outside. In a moment he had both Metz and the bags in the room.

"Good work, Jackson!" he complimented.

"Thank you, sir. What next?"

It was typical of this man that he engaged in no long-winded talk about the situation or its dangers, or about the almost superhuman strength he had been compelled to exert for those few minutes when he hauled four hundred pounds of freight up one floor along the hotel wall.

That was just like Jackson. Those who saw him in normal life never gave him a second look. For his ostensible position was that of chauffeur to a wealthy polo player and sportsman by the name of Richard Wentworth. Few people knew that Jackson had served as sergeant under Major Wentworth through long years of adventurous warfare in all parts of the world. And *none* knew that Jackson was the *Spider's* trusted aide at such times as these, when the *Spider's* life hung literally by a thread.

"We have less than six minutes, Jackson!" the *Spider* said as he lowered Metz to the floor. "It'll take them that long to get downstairs and around the corner. We will proceed as planned!"

As he talked, he leaned out of the window and tested the second Web line, which was looped around the steam radiator and went straight out across the low roof intervening, to the ninth floor window of the rooming house beyond. The line was taut. The *Spider* had come across on that only a few minutes ago, and now he was about to make the return journey with extra weight—and as Richard Wentworth, sportsman and millionaire. He removed the *Spider* costume and consigned it to Jackson.

192

Jackson was already ripping open the cowhide bags, using a keen-edged knife. Money tumbled out of those bags—fives, tens, fifties, hundreds; bright crisp United States bank notes, and old wrinkled ones, all neatly banded, with the number of bills in each package plainly stamped on the bands. At a quick estimate there might have been two hundred thousand dollars in those two bags.

All this money, Jackson stuffed into a capacious black rubber sack. And while he did this, Wentworth was hooking a safety belt about his own waist. It was such a belt as a window washer might use on skyscrapers, but constructed of leather much wider and thicker. There was a hook at the side, and Wentworth stooped and lifted Metz's body and hooked it to the belt by the line of Web which was tied around Metz's waist. The inert body dangled, doubled over, as Wentworth straightened.

There was no lost motion on the part of either of those two men now. Jackson handed him the rubber bag, which he fastened to his belt thus leaving both hands free.

Jackson was now holding a stop watch which had been on the floor. He glanced at it and said briefly, "One minute elapsed, sir."

Richard Wentworth nodded. "Five minutes left to get across! See you later, Jackson!"

"Good-bye, sir, and—good luck!"

The lithe figure put a leg over the window sill, gripped the taut line in gloved hands, and swung free, hanging by his two hands. Then, swinging his body in bold, rhythmic strokes, he began to travel along the line, with the weight of Metz's inert body dragging at his belt.

The Web bowed under the weight, like a bow-

193

string, but Wentworth never faltered. Hand over hand, he crossed, high above the low roof, toward the window of the rooming house beyond.

And behind him, Jackson hurried to a closet, coming back at once with a long Enfield sniper's rifle equipped with telescopic sights. Jackson knelt at the window, the rifle at his shoulder, his eyes fixed upon the roof above which his master was crossing. If anyone should emerge upon that roof while Wentworth was engaged in that aerial journey, and attempt to shoot him down, Jackson knew what to do.

Wentworth never once looked below him. His confidence in Jackson was supreme. He bent all his energies to reaching that other window within the allotted span of five minutes. The going was hard, even for the superb muscles of Dick Wentworth. The strain upon him was terrific. But he did not flounder, or stop. Grimly, purposefully, he made his way across. It was only three and a half minutes by Jackson's stop-watch when he finally climbed over the sill of the rooming-house window, and deposited his burden on the floor.

At once he signalled across, and Jackson loosened the loop of the Web from the radiator, allowing it to drop. At the other end Wentworth reeled in swiftly. Then Jackson took the two cowhide bags and heaved them out of the window. They landed with a crash on the roof below, and a moment later a skylight down there was thrust open. The house detective from the hotel pushed up on to the roof, and stopped to scratch his head over the two bags. Looking up, he saw no tell-tale sign of what had transpired. There was no light in that tenth floor window of the hotel, nor was there a light in the room into which Wentworth had disappeared.

Intently Wentworth leaned over Metz, whose unconscious body he had placed on the bed. The absconder was beginning to stir. Wentworth produced a small hypodermic. He drew off Metz's coat, and rolled up the sleeve of his shirt. Then he thrust the hypo needle into the man's arm, and pressed the plunger home. That hypo contained a dose of anaesthetic which would keep Metz unconscious for at least seven hours.

The sack of money was stuffed into a laundry bag in the closet. Then, satisfied that everything was in order, Wentworth let himself out and took the self-service elevator down to the street floor. As he emerged from the hotel, he noted the crowd gathered at the entrance of the small building next door. But he passed right by them without displaying any interest, and re-entered the Mallard Hotel through the street entrance. . . .

CHAPTER THREE

The Spider Gas

In the cocktail lounge, Nita van Sloan tried to appear cool. She nibbled at the olive from her Martini and engaged the barman in light conversation, designed to hide her anxiety. Constantly, her eyes kept flicking to her wrist watch. The time was dragging. It seemed to be hours—yet it was only six minutes since Wentworth had left.

A tall, extremely slender man entered the bar from the street entrance. His appearance immediately struck her like a blow in the face. She had never seen eyes so pitch-black, nor lips so thin and bloodless. The man's face was gaunt, almost skeletal. Yet there was an evil sort of attraction about him, which caught and held her fascinated attention.

The man came up to the bar, and the bartender greeted him with a sort of breathless respect.

"Good evening, Baron Crispi."

The man acknowledged the greeting negligently.

"Grand Marnier brandy, Thomas," he said. "With a drop of vermouth." His voice was cold, and absolutely expressionless. Nita shuddered at the thought that this was an automaton speaking, and not a human being.

The Baron sipped his brandy-and-vermouth without even looking at her. Four minutes passed. There was a slight commotion out in the lobby, and the house detective came hurrying past. He stopped for a moment and whispered to Thomas at the end of the bar, and then went quickly to the elevator.

When Thomas came down and wiped her end of the bar, Nita asked him, "Anything wrong?"

"No, Miss van Sloan," he said. "I don't think so. One of the guests phoned down from the ninth floor that she thought she had heard a revolver shot. But so many people mistake backfire for gunshots—especially out-of-towners."

Nita strove to hide her anxiety. She gripped the stem of her glass, but did not move. Baron Crispi finished off his brandy quickly. There was still no expression in his face, as he hastily laid down a dollar bill. "Keep the change," he said, and went out into the lobby. He crossed to one of a row of phone booths. Loder was still sitting in the end one.

A moment after Baron Crispi had entered the middle one, Loder's phone rang with a musical tinkle. He took off the receiver, and said, "Thirteen."

"You fool!" said the cold, emotionless voice, dispensing this time with the balance of the identification code. "Where are all your men? The *Spider* has reached Sabin—under your very noses!"

"Impossible!" Loder said. "I have a man on the eighth floor, and a man on the tenth. No one could reach the ninth by the stairs. And I've got my eye on the elevators all the time. No cage has stopped at the ninth since you called."

"Never mind. The *Spider* has outwitted you somehow. But he's still in the hotel. He must not be allowed to escape. Are you sure every exit is covered?"

"Absolutely. We have twenty men operating here."

"Very well. Wentworth is your man. He has left the cocktail lounge. The van Sloan girl is alone in there. Spread the word to watch for Wentworth. He is to be burned on sight."

"But—but supposing you're wrong? Suppose Wentworth is not the *Spider?*"

"That," the cold voice said, "is too bad for Mr. Wentworth. We shall give *ourselves* the benefit of the doubt. Good-bye!" The phone clicked dead, and Loder hung up. He left the booth just as the flat-nosed Blagg came into the lobby from the street.

"Pardon me," Loder said. "Have you got a light?"

Blagg took out a book of matches and struck a light. The first match didn't take, and it required another. This gave them extra time to exchange information.

"Did you check on Wentworth?" Loder asked, scarcely moving his lips.

"No, damn him! That van Sloan girl was too clever. She detained me for almost four minutes. When I got out to the street, he was gone. I've been snooping around the building, making sure that all the men are posted, and inquiring if they saw him."

"Did they see him?"

"No."

Loder finally got his light. "Red Feather just called. He's sure that Wentworth is the *Spider*. Orders are to kill Wentworth. Use two vacuum cleaners."

"Check," said Blagg. He left Loder, and crossed the lobby, disappearing out through the side street exit.

Loder returned to his phone booth. The one which

198

had been occupied by Baron Crispi was once more vacant. The Baron was back in the lounge, sipping another brandy-and-vermouth.

Nita van Sloan was fiddling with her cocktail glass and consulting her watch constantly. She couldn't stand it any longer. The blood was pounding in her veins. Wentworth had been away for sixteen minutes now. She didn't know what was happening up there in Sabin's room. Dick might be dead up there. He might be in a trap and need help. She had all she could do to keep herself from running out of the lounge and taking the elevator upstairs.

And suddenly, she choked back a sob of relief. In the mirror over the bar, she saw Wentworth come into the hotel lobby from the street. His clothes were immaculate, his bearing was easy and nonchalant.

He stopped for a moment just inside the revolving doors, and scanned the occupants of the lobby. He saw Blagg come in from the side street entrance, followed by two other men, each carrying a vacuum-cleaner. The two men were attired as porters. They bent over the cleaners, plugging them into sockets as if they were about to start cleaning. Blagg walked steadily across the lobby, and when he passed Loder's phone booth, he nodded.

Almost at once, Baron Crispi, who had finished his drink, arose and threw down another dollar bill. "Keep the change, Thomas," he said again, as he hurried out into the street.

Wentworth was apparently unaware that he was being watched by Loder and Blagg. He coolly lit a cigarette, and sauntered across the lobby, *but not toward the cocktail lounge.*

Out of the corner of his eye he saw Nita leaving her seat at the bar to join him, and he shook his head almost imperceptibly.

199

Nita saw the look in his face, and she froze where she stood. She knew her Dick like a book. She had seen that look in the past. No ordinary observer would have been able to read anything in it. But she knew that Richard Wentworth was taut and poised. She knew he was expecting attack.

She understood also, that he was making for the door instead of coming to rejoin her, because he didn't want her at his side when the attack was launched.

Swiftly, her eyes swept over the lobby, seeking the possible source of danger. Her glance flicked past Blagg, past Loder, and centered on the two porters. They were apparently engaged in the very innocent occupation of hooking up two vacuum cleaners. Their bodies hid the instruments from the view of anyone in the lobby. But when they straightened up, she gasped. Keyed up as she was to notice little things, she saw at once that there was something wrong with these two machines. The porters were straddling the long bars of the cleaners, which they were pointing in Wentworth's direction. And at the end of those long handles there was a gaping black hole exactly like the muzzle of a machine-gun!

Even as Nita looked, she saw the porters flick down the switches, and in response to that motion *flame lanced from the black muzzles!* Two long, licking tongues of flame stretched forth red, blazing fingers directly at Richard Wentworth's broad back.

Nita screamed, "Dick! Behind you—"

But Wentworth must have had eyes in the back of his head. For at that exact moment—even before Nita screamed—he spun on his heel.

Two guns, one in each hand, blasted simultaneously.

The deafening thunder of those guns filled the

lobby as the long, stabbing arrows of flame licked out toward him. He fired only once with each weapon. Each shot rendered one attacker helpless. They hurtled backward, dragging their flame-throwers with them. The flames were deflected from Wentworth almost as the fiery tips were about to touch him. The hot blast of those twin chutes of fire nearly seared his face. And then they were carried upward, scorching the ceiling as the nozzles were dragged backward by the collapsing porters.

The two jets of fire hissed upward, and flame began to curl around the ceiling. The heat brought the sprinkler system into operation, and water surged downward upon the suddenly panic-stricken, shouting patrons in the lobby. Men and women began to stream for the exits, fighting and jostling one another.

Wentworth swung about lithely, knowing that the fire would soon be extinguished by the efficient sprinkler system. He knew that Red Feather had not finished. Surely, he had other threats in reserve. Wentworth looked for more enemies. And sure enough, they came!

Men suddenly filled the main entrance, and the doorway from the side street. Others surged up from the lobby. A dozen guns were trained on him from as many directions.

Grimly, he faced the onslaught, but he held his fire, as did the men who approached him. Evidently the order was now to take him alive. More men kept streaming into the lobby from both entrances, and each man aimed a gun at Richard Wentworth.

Nita understood the extreme seriousness of the situation. And what she was about to do was done instinctively—with the instinct of a woman who has learned well how to be the fighting mate of a fighting man: The vial Wentworth had given her was in her hand. As the attackers closed in, she raised it high in the air, and hurled it into the center of the lobby, directly in front of Wentworth.

The glass shattered on the floor, and immediately a white, opaque cloud of steam arose in vast, billowing folds to spread out through the lobby. It rose higher and higher, and it seemed to nurture itself, for the higher it rose the wider it spread, until it almost filled the entire room.

Wentworth dropped into a crouching position, and ran straight toward the spot where Nita had been standing. He whispered, "Nita!"

"Dick!" she murmured.

Their hands met, and then they were hurrying through the dense white fog, feeling their way with arms outstretched. They passed into the bar, and felt their way along the wall to the street door.

Inside, Red Feather's men started shooting, angered at the realization that they had been tricked.

Out in the street, four men were standing at the curb, guns in their hands. They were the rear guard, posted in case Wentworth should break through. As they saw Nita and her tall escort leaving the hotel they immediately opened fire.

Wentworth thrust her behind him, and blasted back at them, standing spraddle-legged, so that she would not be hit. He fired each gun once, and two of the men fell wounded. And now pedestrians gathered across the street, and Wentworth dared not fire again. The remaining two, realizing their advantage, came running forward, triggering their guns. They were bent on closing up the space between them and Wentworth, so that they would be sure not to miss.

But they had not taken two steps, when a long, powerful Daimler roared up and spilled them backward as it braked to a stop directly in front of Dick and Nita. A bearded Sikh chauffeur sat at the wheel, his black, glittering eyes filled with a fierce joy.

"Shall I kill the dogs, Master!" he said in fluent Punjabi.

"Not this time, Ram Singh," Wentworth said grimly. "I want to get Miss Nita away from here. Then I must return.

He helped Nita into the car and they turned into the traffic of the avenue.

Behind them, white opaque smoke was beginning to eddy from the hotel out into the street. That was the gas from Nita's vial. It was a secret gas whose formula was known only to Wentworth and to a certain man in the War Department of the United States of America. Wentworth had developed it and had given the formula to the government, and it was being used for smoke-screens. Its swift expansive property made it ideal for such a purpose. Having donated the formula anonymously, he had taken the grimly humorous opportunity to select the name by which it was referred to in the records of the War Department—*Spider Gas!*

Times Square was shrilly alive as the white fumes of the gas came pouring out of the hotel, and fire engines clanged near by. Police patrol cars were racing toward them from every direction, while sirens cut the air keenly. Pedestrians were keeping their distance, but watching with avid curiosity.

The Daimler was halted in a traffic jam, only a half block from the hotel. Wentworth said, "Darling, I want you to go home with Ram Singh. I must—"

Nita's eyes flashed rebelliously. "You're cutting me out of it, Dick! You promised—"

"I'm sorry, Nita. But now it's war—war between

203

the *Spider* and Red Feather. And I don't want your precious safety to complicate things for me.''

She sighed, realizing how right he was. "Dick," she breathed, "I'm afraid—afraid of Red Feather's mind—his devil's mind! He used fire—it was real *fire* that spouted out of those vacuum cleaners. And when that failed, Dick, he had his regular killers ready."

"I know," Wentworth said, glancing back toward the hotel. "Don't worry, I'll be on my guard every minute—"

Suddenly he stiffened, and his voice caught a whip-lash of urgency: "Ram Singh! Maneuver to follow that cab! *It's part of Red Feather's underground escape system!*"

He was pointing rigidly at a taxicab which had pulled past the hotel without stopping. It had threaded its way through the frantically excited throngs of pedestrians and had swung past the Daimler on the wrong side of the street. It was now turning into a side street. The cab was almost at the end of the block, and speeding up. Upon its side was lettered the name: ONYX TAXICAB SYSTEM.

Metz had said that much—that he was to have escaped in an Onyx Taxicab. Undoubtedly this cab was the one that was to have picked him up; but seeing the excitement, the driver had kept going.

Ram Singh needed no more order than that. His long experience in Wentworth's service had taught him to swing into action at the instant of command. It was that split-second timing which had more than once saved the lives of both the fighting Sikh and his fighting master. Almost before Wentworth finished talking, the Daimler was backing and weaving through traffic like a bloodhound on the scent.

"Report at home!" Wentworth flung out, and leaped to the curb.

Nita waved acknowledgment, and the car was gone.

The last glimpse Wentworth had of her, was her beautiful face flushed with the thrill of this new and dangerous game. And then both the Onyx cab and the Daimler were lost to sight as they rounded the corner.

CHAPTER FOUR

Death Comes In Sixteen Cylinders

Wentworth himself could not go. He must remain to explain to the police; to answer countless questions. He walked back to the hotel and at once he was surrounded by uniformed men, pressing through the entrance. The lobby was already becoming free of smoke, for the volatile *Spider Gas* was swiftly rising toward the ceiling, and disintegrating into small swirling eddies resembling midget banks of fog on a misty morning.

Something had happened to the electric light system, and the two vacuum cleaners, hooked up to the hotel current, had ceased to spurt flame. The fire was already out, due to the swift operation of the sprinkler outlets.

When the police surged into the lobby, they found it in utter darkness. Their flashlights etched out the forms of the two wounded porters, now conscious. Otherwise, the place was deserted. Red Feather's killers had fled.

Wentworth found himself besieged by questioners, from a local precinct captain up to an Inspector of

Homicide. He explained very sparingly, saying only that he had been suddenly attacked by the flame-throwers, and had defended himself. As to the reasons for the attack, he only shrugged his shoulders.

"Perhaps they mistook me for someone else," he said.

"For instance—" a voice broke in ironically behind him—*"for the Spider?"*

Wentworth whirled, as the captain and the inspector stiffened, and saluted respectfully.

The new arrival was a ruddy-complexioned, stockily built man, who carried himself with an air of quiet but efficient authority. Stanley Kirkpatrick, Commissioner of Police of the City of New York, was without question the outstanding police executive in the country. Beloved by the entire force, he also enjoyed the complete respect and confidence of the civilian public.

For many years now, Kirkpatrick had waged relentless war against the *Spider,* while being at the same time a close friend of Richard Wentworth. Commissioner Kirkpatrick was a sworn servant of the Law and hated with all his soul the unorthodox methods which the *Spider* employed against the underworld. And in spite of the warm friendship between the two men, Wentworth understood clearly that if ever the Commissioner should obtain definite proof that Richard Wentworth was the *Spider*—then their friendship would be superseded by Kirkpatrick's devotion to the Law.

Many times in the past, the Commissioner had had reason to believe that his friend was really the *Spider*. But Wentworth had clearly managed to nullify that suspicion.

Now however, it was coming once more to the fore.

Kirkpatrick gazed bleakly around the lobby, eyeing the wounded men. The police were already questioning them, while they were being treated by police surgeons. But they maintained a stubborn silence, refusing to answer all questions.

The Commissioner swore softly under his breath. "They're like all the other agents of Red Feather. They won't talk. One would think they were more afraid of Red Feather than of the electric chair!"

"There are worse things than the electric chair!" Wentworth said softly.

Kirkpatrick swung on him, grey eyes glinting shrewdly. "It was you they were after, wasn't it, Dick?"

"Yes," said Wentworth. "They were after me."

"Why?" rapped Kirkpatrick.

"I haven't the faintest notion, Kirk."

"Do you mean those men attacked you without provocation?"

"Yes."

"That's ridiculous on the face of it, Dick, and you know it. I demand to know why they attacked you!"

"Permit me to suggest, Kirk, that you ask these men. They are the proper ones to answer such a question. Since when have the police begun to give the third degree to the *victims* of crime?"

Kirkpatrick scowled. "Damn it, Dick—"

He broke off as a uniformed patrolman entered the lobby and approached him. "Pardon, sir. There's a lady outside asking to see Mr. Wentworth. A Mrs. Blount, she says. She claims Mr. Wentworth knows her."

"Of course," said Dick. "Will you pardon me, Kirk?"

"I'll go out with you," the Commissioner grumbled. "I'm not through asking you questions. And I don't want you walking away on me."

Wentworth shrugged, and led the way outside. The police were keeping a cleared space in front of the hotel, and the crowd of curiosity-seekers was pressing in for a close view of the wounded as they were carried to the ambulance.

A few feet away from the curb, a sixteen-cylinder car was idling. A woman of about forty was at the wheel. She was beautiful in a stately, aristocratic sort of way, and she was attired in the most becoming clothes money could buy. Mrs. Irene Blount, widow of the airplane manufacturer, Norton Blount, moved only in exclusive social circles.

Only two weeks ago she had spent twenty thousand dollars for the début of her daughter, Ellen, whom she idolized. Wentworth had met both mother and daughter in many of the homes of the Long Island social set, but he couldn't imagine why Mrs. Blount should be driving her own car here—or why she should come expressly to see him.

He let Kirkpatrick wait at the curb and stepped out alongside the limousine.

"How do you do, Mrs. Blount. Is there anything I can do for you? How is Ellen?"

Irene Blount seemed to be under some sort of terrific nervous tension. Her hands were in her lap, but her breasts were rising and falling swiftly, and the color that suffused her cheeks was almost hectic. She looked at Wentworth queerly.

"God forgive me, Mr. Wentworth, I have come here to do a terrible thing!" She shuddered. "What am I saying! Never in this life, or the next, will I earn forgiveness for—for what I am about to do now!"

Wentworth frowned. "Surely you can't be as wicked

as that, Mrs. Blount. What is it that you're going to do?''

"This!" she cried. Her hand came up from her lap, gripping a small twenty-two calibre pistol.

"Richard Wentworth, I'm going to kill you!"

The look in her face was a terrible one. To Wentworth it seemed that all the instincts of refinement and culture and humanity with which he knew her to be endowed, were being consumed within her breast by a raging inferno of pain and agony—a pain and agony not of the body, but of her very soul.

He knew in a single instant that Mrs. Irene was doing this at the order of Red Feather. Somehow, Red Feather had means of compelling this beautiful aristocrat to do a thing which shattered the very fibre of her soul.

Her hand was clamped around the butt of the pistol, and her finger was taut upon the trigger. The horrible agony in her eyes leaped across the small intervening space between herself and Wentworth with a look that seemed to beg forgiveness and understanding, even as she killed him.

Someone shouted hoarsely behind him, and Wentworth knew it was Kirkpatrick, who had been watching the whole procedure.

But there was nothing the Commissioner could do to save him. There was only one thing Wentworth could do to save himself. He'd had ample warning as Irene Blount brought the gun up over the window ledge of the limousine. More than once had he faced drawn guns in the hands of dangerous men; and more than once had the legerdemain of his swiftly-moving hands beaten those gunmen to the kill. Men with guns in their hands, facing an apparently unarmed *Spider*, had died with faces frozen into stupefaction,

210

not knowing even in death whence had come the blasting automatics which had suddenly appeared in the grip of that sinister, cloaked figure.

So, Richard Wentworth could easily have drawn and fired before Irene Blount brought her gun into position. But the only part of her that was exposed to a bullet was her face and throat, and the lovely curve of her breast. Anywhere he hit her with the powerful driving force of his heavy automatics, would mean death for this woman. And knowing that she was doing this hideous thing because of some terrible compulsion, he could no more have brought himself to kill her than to kill a new-born baby.

The startled shout of Commissioner Kirkpatrick was still ringing in his ears as Irene Blount pointed the gun at his heart.

And he did not move.

Perhaps if he had leaped toward her in an effort to deflect the gun, or if he had attempted to turn and run, she might have pulled the trigger. But as she saw him standing there, cool and collected, perhaps the sight of his manifest courage did something that nothing else could have accomplished. Perhaps it lit within her once more the torch of decency which was her birthright, and which must have been smothered under the terrible compulsion which was driving her to this crime.

She stared at him, with her finger taut against the trigger. And she did not shoot. Instead, a strange and hungry light came into her eyes, as if she were seeing a new and unimagined thing which might yet be her salvation.

"Don't—aren't you—afraid to die?" she faltered.

Wentworth smiled. "There are many things that are worse than death," he said gently.

Of a sudden, a great trembling seized her body. A choked cry of misery escaped from her throat.

"Yes, yes!" she gasped. "Much worse than death!"

Suddenly, a great light of resolve came into her eyes.

"Richard Wentworth," she said in a voice grown strong and resolute, "you have shown me the way out. Thank God!"

And without warning she turned the pistol upon her breast and pulled the trigger!

Wentworth had no chance to stop her. The bullet plowed through the white, quivering flesh just above the heart. She jerked spasmodically, and slumped over the wheel.

CHAPTER FIVE

"Follow Richard Wentworth!"

"**B**y the Lord Harry!" Commissioner Kirkpatrick exploded, "I'll have a straight answer out of you, Dick Wentworth, if I have to choke it out of you!"

Wentworth shrugged. "I'm sorry, Kirk. I've told you everything I can."

It was almost an hour after Irene Blount's dramatic suicide. Kirkpatrick and Wentworth were in the office of the manager of the Mallard Hotel. Scores of detectives were still investigating throughout the great hostelry, piecing together the actions of Red Feather's agents previous to the moment they had unleashed the flame-throwers upon Wentworth.

And Kirkpatrick was still doggedly at it.

"Dick," he said tightly, "I want to know why Irene Blount tried to shoot you, and then turned the gun upon herself."

"I've told you every word we both said." Wentworth sighed wearily. "I've repeated the story a dozen times. There's nothing more."

"All right, then. Let's get to something else. What were you doing in the hotel?"

"I was just having a Martini with Nita."

"You had no other purpose in coming here?"

"What other purpose would I have?"

"Maybe you were trying to get Red Feather?"

Abruptly, Wentworth arose. "I'm sorry, Kirk. I can't submit to this quizzing any longer. I have many things to do. With your permission, I'll be leaving—unless you want to arrest me formally."

The Commissioner sighed, and stood up. "Look here, Dick," he said. "Why won't you cooperate with me? I need all the help I can get. Red Feather has some terrible power over men and women, a power that forces them to commit stupendous crimes. Metz didn't need the money he stole. Irene Blount surely had no motive for attempting to kill you. Yet they both were driven by an evil genius they couldn't resist. Laura Burgess tried to defy him—and she died horribly under the fire of a flame-thrower."

"I know all that, Kirk," Wentworth said harshly. "And believe me, I shall help you all I can."

Kirkpatrick shook his head. "Let's talk plainly for once, Dick. The *Spider* came here tonight to fight Red Feather in the *Spider's* usual way. Wouldn't it have been better if the *Spider* had turned over his information to the police?"

"No," said Wentworth.

"Damn it, Dick, *why not?*"

Wentworth stared at him uncompromisingly. "If I were the *Spider*, Kirk—as you insinuate—I would do just what the *Spider* did tonight. I would go after Red Feather with the same kind of weapons Red Feather uses, swift and merciless death." As he continued his voice became hard, fraught with subdued passion.

"You—the police—are hampered. Your hands are tied because you must produce evidence that will stand up in court. And Red Feather is too clever ever to allow you to obtain such evidence. But the *Spider* is not hampered. If the *Spider* finds Red Feather, then Red Feather will not live to beat the case!"

Kirkpatrick's scowl became deeper as Wentworth concluded. "All right, Dick, if that's the way you look at it—I wash my hands. You and I don't see eye to eye. If you persist—"

"Wait!" Wentworth raised a hand. "You're assuming that *I* am the *Spider?*"

The Commissioner waved a hand impatiently. "Let's do away with pretense, Dick, for this once. Yes, I'm sure you're the *Spider*. And if I had evidence, I'd arrest you and see that you were convicted. I'm sworn to uphold the Law, and by God I'll uphold it, even if it means the end of our friendship!"

Wentworth nodded brusquely. "So be it, Kirk!"

He turned toward the door, moving very slowly. He put his hand on the knob, but before turning it, he looked back. Kirkpatrick was watching him, and there was the shadow of pain in the Commissioner's eyes.

A slow smile illuminated Wentworth's features. He extended his hand. "Let's shake—just this once more, Kirk!"

Kirkpatrick choked back a lightness in his throat as he accepted the proffered hand.

Silently, the two men stood there.

Then, without saying another word, Richard Wentworth turned and went out of the room. He walked through the lobby with a set and expressionless face.

Commissioner Kirkpatrick came out after him. His lips were tight, and he was holding himself rigid. His eyes followed Wentworth's broad back to the revolving doors.

"Murdoch!" he snapped to one of the detectives in the lobby. "Follow that man! Take as many plainclothes officers as you need. *I want Richard Wentworth shadowed every minute of the day and night!*"

CHAPTER SIX

The Numbers Game

As Richard Wentworth strode away, he did not look to the right or left.

Murdoch had signalled to two other plainclothesmen, and whispered to them swiftly. One of the detectives remained with him and followed Wentworth on foot, while the third got into a police squad car and crawled along behind them. In this way, none of the trailers would be left flat-footed by any sudden moves of the quarry.

None of the detectives noted, however, that there were still others who were interested in the movements of Richard Wentworth. They did not see the flat-nosed man, or the man in the black fedora, who moved inconspicuously through the crowds in his wake.

Loder kept about twenty feet behind the detectives, and Blagg hailed a taxicab.

"Follow that man in the black fedora," he ordered, indicating Loder.

Thus, Wentworth seemed to be the unconscious head of a shadow-parade up Broadway. None of his actions indicated that he was in any way cognizant of these attentions. He walked swiftly and purposefully to the corner, and swung west. He entered a cigar store in the middle of the block and dialed the number of his penthouse apartment on East End Avenue. Since the destruction of his previous great, fortress-like retreat, he had decided to make his headquarters in no one certain place, where he would be the focus of attack for any enemy who guessed his association with the *Spider*.

In conformity with his policy, he now had four apartments in various parts of the city, in addition to four or five furnished rooms and hotel rooms in easily accessible spots. Thus, he was never far from sanctuary if he should be hard-pressed. But he had worked out a code with Ram Singh and Nita, so that when he said: *"Report at home!"* they had known by the word *home* that he meant the East End Avenue apartment. Had he said, *"At the apartment,"* it would have designated a private house in Greenwich Village, which he had leased for ten years. He had various designations for each location, which had been committed to memory.

He now waited while the dial tone buzzed six times. He clicked the hook down on the sixth note, waited a moment, then lifted it again. The interruption had not been long enough to kill the connection entirely, so that the dial tone was immediately resumed. He let it buzz six times more, disconnected for another moment, then allowed it to ring on. That was his identification signal. Ram Singh would know it was he who was calling. In this way, it would not be necessary to answer any calls except those from Wentworth.

Now however, as he held the receiver to his ear, a

sudden foreboding of evil swept over him. There was no answer to his call.

There had been plenty of time for Ram Singh and Nita to tail the Onyx cab and return to the East End Avenue address.

Wentworth held the receiver to his ear for a full minute, while he turned in such a way as to look out of the phone booth without seeming to do so. His eyes glinted as he noted a police squad car cruising slowly past the store, and a detective standing directly across the street. Wentworth's camera eye had recorded the face of that detective as having been among those in the Mallard Hotel lobby. It was clear to him that Kirkpatrick intended to keep close tabs upon him.

This did not bother him as much as the silence from the East End apartment. He started to hang up, when he suddenly noticed something else that brought a frown to his face. A man strolling past the cigar store stopped just outside the window and casually lit a cigarette. That man, too, Wentworth recognized, though he had caught only a flashing glimpse of him in the Hotel Mallard lobby just before he was attacked.

It was the flat-nosed Blagg.

He did not know the man's name, of course, nor did he know that Blagg had attempted to follow him from the cocktail lounge, and had been out-maneuvered by Nita. For there had been no time for her to tell him about that in the Daimler. But he did know two things: First, that the flat-nosed man had been in the Mallard lobby; second, that he was here now. They added up to a single conclusion—the flat-nosed man was an agent of Red Feather.

Wentworth's decision was quickly made. He hung up and stepped purposefully from the store. He did

219

not look at Blagg directly, but out of the corner of his eye he saw the man signal to someone in a taxicab which was parked farther down the street. Blagg had changed places with Loder, so that the quarry would not notice that he was being followed by any particular man.

Wentworth continued down the block, apparently oblivious of any trailers. He turned the corner and went north on Eighth Avenue until he arrived at the West View Hotel, a small, cheap hostelry which catered to transients, but which rented a few rooms on a permanent basis. Boldly, he entered the lobby and stepped up to the desk.

"I want a room for tonight," he said.

"Any baggage?" the clerk asked.

"No."

"That'll be two-fifty, sir, in advance."

Wentworth paid, and signed the register. Since he had no luggage, the clerk gave him the key, dispensing with a bell boy, and Wentworth took the elevator up to the sixth floor. His room was 612.

The operator said, "Six-twelve is to your right— the end of the hall, right near the stairs."

"Thanks," Wentworth said, and started down the corridor. He knew very well where 612 was located. In fact, he had asked the clerk to give him a room with western exposure, because he wanted one near the stairs.

He inserted the key in the lock, and pushed the door open. The operator waited only to see that he found his room, then he shut the gate and sent the cage down.

Immediately, Wentworth took the key out of the lock, without even opening the door. Two strides brought him to the stairway, and he raced down to the fifth floor. He stopped before the door of Room

514 and brought out a small, compact key container. Each key had a numbered tag which was treated with phosphorus so that it would show up in the dark. He selected key number eight and inserted it in the lock. In a moment he was inside. As he closed the door, he noticed the elevator indicator advance upward and stop at six. He smiled grimly. His pursuers were already bottling him up. A police detective, or one of Red Feather's men had also taken a room on the sixth floor. There would be others covering the hotel exits, in case he should slip past the watchful gaze of the sixth floor sentries.

Once inside, he set quickly to work. Before he was halfway across the room, he had stripped off his overcoat, jacket and vest. He removed his tie, shirt and trousers, and seated himself before the dresser, clad only in his underwear.

From the top drawer of the dresser he took a black lacquered box which opened only when he pressed two sides simultaneously in certain places. The cover slid open, revealing a complete make-up kit, together with a spare automatic and two extra clips.

This was one of the rooms Wentworth maintained under a completely different identity. The clerk downstairs knew only that the tenant of 514 was one Joseph Moulton. He knew vaguely that Moulton was connected with one of the large Manhattan gambling syndicates, and that he traveled extensively, handling large bets. Therefore, his room might be unused for weeks at a time. But the rent was always paid three months in advance, so no one in the hotel ever worried about Joe Moulton's actions.

Seated before the mirror, Wentworth's swift fingers worked surely and skillfully upon his countenance, employing materials from the make-up box.

In a small frame on the dresser he had a photograph of himself made up as Joe Moulton, and he used this picture as a guide.

A little plastic material transformed his face from the lean hard features of Richard Wentworth to the somewhat puffy face of Joe Moulton. A touch of shadow-dye under the eyes gave the effect of deep hollows, indicative of dissipation. Paper-thin aluminum plates inserted in the nostril's broadened the nose; and false tooth-bridges changed Wentworth's own perfectly white and even teeth into a mouthful of crooked bicuspids and molars liberally furnished with gold caps. A wig of dun-colored hair completed the change, and Richard Wentworth gazed with satisfaction into the mirror which revealed the personality of Joe Moulton, gambler.

Satisfied that he had omitted no detail which might betray him, he locked the make-up box and put it away. From a trunk in the closet he took a new tan suit, a tan shirt with tie to match, tan shoes and overcoat. He put these on, and inserted in his tie a huge two-carat diamond stick-pin. He carefully packed the discarded clothes away, once more locking the trunk.

As he paced up and down the room two or three times, it was amazing to see how the characteristic mannerisms and walk of Richard Wentworth had disappeared to give way to those of Joe Moulton. The only garment Wentworth retained of his old belongings was a thin rubber cape with a purple back, of such fine texture that it could be rolled to fit in his back pocket. And there was a black slouch hat of the same material, together with a small flat make-up case—only such essentials as would be necessary to use should he suddenly have occasion to appear as the *Spider*.

222

With a last glance about the room to make sure that he had left nothing incriminating in view, he snapped the switch lights and went out.

When the cage stopped at the floor in answer to his ring, the operator said, "Hello, Mr. Moulton. I didn't know you were in. You been away?"

"Yeah," Wentworth said in a nasal voice. "I been in Chi. Got in this morning. Guess you were off. Anything new around this dump?"

"Nothing much, Mr. Moulton. Except some guy just checked in on the sixth floor, and it looks like the cops is after him. One of the cops took a room on the same floor, and there's another one parked in the lobby. And just now another bozo takes a room on the sixth floor, and slips me a sawbuck not to mention it to the cop downstairs."

"Is that so?" Wentworth said. "What rooms did these three guys take? Maybe if we combine the numbers, we can hit a winner in the numbers."

"Say, that's an idea!" the operator exclaimed. "This guy Wentworth has six-twelve. The cop took six-fourteen, next door, and the other guy—he's registered under the name of Max Loder—took six-eleven, right across the hall."

"Six-eleven, six-twelve and six-fourteen, huh," Wentworth repeated. "Lemme think about them. When I come back I'll tell you if I figured a good combination."

As he got out of the cage, he saw Detective Murdoch seated near the front door, reading a newspaper. Blagg, the flat-nosed man, was at the cigar counter, kibitzing with the sales girl. Both Murdoch and Blagg gave Wentworth the once-over, and immediately lost interest in him.

Wentworth smiled grimly. He had been sure his

disguise would pass muster. He waved to the night-clerk, and crossed the lobby to the small office at the rear where the switchboard was located.

"Hello, Mamie," he said to the operator.

"Why, hello, Mr. Moulton!" she said. "Gee, I haven't seen you for a month. I never got a chance to thank you for the ten dollars you left me for Christmas."

"That's all right, Mamie," Wentworth said, making sure that the door of the switchboard room was closed so that neither Murdoch nor Blagg could see what was going on. He leaned over the board and lowered his voice.

"Would you like to make twenty bucks?"

"You don't have to ask, Mr. Moulton!"

"Okay. There's a guy in six-eleven who's got some inside dope on the horses at Tropical Park. If he should make any calls. . . ."

"Sure," Mamie said. "I get you."

He slipped two ten dollar bills over the top of the board.

"Just wait in the lobby," Mamie told him. "If six-eleven gets any calls, or makes any, I'll hold up the connection and page you. You take the desk phone, and I'll leave the board open so you can hear the conversation."

"Right," said Wentworth.

He returned to the lobby and entered the public phone booth. Once more he dialed the East End Avenue apartment, and once more he got a no answer signal. His lips tightened.

He went over to the cigar counter and bought a package of chewing gum and a copy of *Ace G-Man Magazine*. Then he sat down in a chair next to Detective Murdoch.

"Kinda cold today, ain't it?" he said in his newly-assumed nasal voice.

224

Murdoch grunted, but did not reply.

Blagg had left the cigar counter and was now playing a pin-ball game at the other side of the lobby.

It was a tribute to Richard Wentworth's self-control that he could sit and read a magazine with such an attitude of cool unconcern, when he knew that Nita and Ram Singh must have fallen into some position of unknown danger as a result of following the Onyx cab. Otherwise, one of them would surely have managed to return to the East End Avenue address to report when he called.

And he, Wentworth, could do nothing but sit here and wait. . . .

It was only ten minutes, but it seemed an hour, before the phone on the desk rang, and the clerk answered it, then called out:

"Mr. Moulton—phone call!"

Wentworth arose and hurried over to the desk. He knew that the eyes of both Murdoch and Blagg were on him, if for no other reason than curiosity. But he knew that their curiosity would swiftly be turned to suspicion if they saw him merely holding the receiver without speaking. On the other hand, he could not speak into the phone without warning the man in 611 that someone was listening to his conversation.

Wentworth had foreseen this difficulty, and prepared for it. He had surreptitiously torn a piece of the back cover of his magazine, and had folded it in several thicknesses to fit into the telephone mouthpiece. And as he picked up the receiver, his right hand slipped up over the phone and stuffed the heavy folded paper into the cup. He pressed it far in against the diaphragm. Now, he could speak into it and his voice would merely rebound from the paper without being transmitted through the open line.

He had the receiver at his ear, and caught the following conversation:

"Thirteen."

"Seven."

"Twenty-six. Loder speaking. I have that man under observation. He's across the hall from me."

To give the appearance of carrying on a conversation Wentworth spoke into the transmitter, repeating the words that were being said over the line. In this way he was also better able to memorize them. The cold voice at the other end was speaking.

"How do you know he can't get out some other way than through the hall?"

"He can't. It's a sixth floor window facing on the street. Blagg is in the lobby. He's paying a newsboy to watch that window. I'm sure our man is safe."

"Very well. We will make certain that nothing slips up this time. I am sending Kranz and four men to assist you. It is highly important that the person we are speaking of be liquidated at once. As soon as you have finished there, you will proceed immediately to take charge of the covering force at the Mandalay operation. That is all!"

The cold voice stopped and Wentworth heard the disconnecting click. As he hung up, his eyes were filled with swift speculation. He had learned two things: First, that killers were coming here at once; second, that Red Feather was planning another crime— *the Mandalay operation*. Those three words puzzled him. Red Feather couldn't, of course, have referred to the city of Mandalay. . . .

Wentworth pushed that puzzle to the back of his mind under the pressure of the more immediate danger. Those killers coming here must be stopped, and stopped swiftly before they made a shambles of this place, as they had done of the Mallard. He hurried across to the public phone booth. If he could reach Commissioner Kirkpatrick, it might be possible to get police reserves on the spot.

He was halfway across the lobby when he suddenly broke his stride, his lips narrowing into a thin, tight line.

Through the glass door of the hotel he saw a small truck pulling up squarely in front of the entrance. The driver remained at the wheel, but five men emerged from the tonneau and advanced to the hotel in a close-knit, compact group. Three of them were carrying bulky objects, loosely covered by oilskin sheets.

In a flash, Wentworth realized that he had underestimated Red Feather.

Red Feather had taken into account the fact that someone might overhear that conversation with Loder. Therefore, he had dispatched these killers, *before* calling, thereby timing their arrival in order to preclude any leeway of warning the police.

Wentworth turned on his heel. Instead of making for the phone booth, he headed swiftly for the men's room at the rear of the lobby. The first of that compact group of killers was coming through the revolving doors as Wentworth disappeared.

One by one they entered. Their leader, a stocky, bullet-headed man in a tight-fitting Chesterfield and black derby, was carrying one of the oilskin-covered objects. He crossed to the clerk's desk and said, "Take it easy, punk!"

The others advanced into the lobby spreading out as they came in, and throwing the oilskin covers off their packages, to reveal shiny machine guns!

The leader, Kranz, looked over toward Blagg, who had stopped playing the pin-game. Blagg nodded almost imperceptibly toward Detective Murdoch, who was coming out of his chair and clawing at his gun. Blagg did not wait. He hurried out past the gunmen, and disappeared into the street.

Kranz grinned and raised the machine gun, covering Murdoch. "Hold it, copper!" he grated.

The other men headed for the elevator, and one of them pushed the button violently to summon the cage.

Murdoch was no coward. He kept going for his gun.

Kranz's lips curled. "Okay, copper. Take it!"

His finger was on the trip, when suddenly, from the rear of the lobby near the men's room, came the queer, blood-curdling sound of laughter!

Every eye in the lobby was turned toward that sound. With guns suspended in mid-air, those men looked to see who was laughing at such a time.

And they beheld a grim, cloaked figure whose hideous face was almost covered by a black slouch hat. From under the cape, two hands were thrust. And each hand held a heavy black automatic!

"The Spider!" shouted one of the killers.

And then all hell broke loose in that lobby.

CHAPTER SEVEN

Joe Moulton Keeps an Appointment

The greatest soldier of all time, Napoleon Bonaparte, owed most of his military successes to the element of surprise. Time and again he defeated vastly superior enemies by striking unexpectedly. He generally attacked one flank of the opposing army, the strongest, and destroyed it, thus rendering the enemy impotent.

Thus did the *Spider* fight tonight.

The odds were one against five. But the *Spider* had two powerful allies—surprise and accuracy.

Those two automatics, peeping out from under the black cloak, thundered into action in a thrilling threnody of rhythmic doom as they blasted their messages of death into the bodies of Red Feather's paid killers. Their machine guns, lumbering into action, sprayed lead all around the dreadful cloaked figure which stood there, fearless and scornful of cover.

Detective Murdoch was forgotten as these gunmen swung their weapons to blast at the *Spider*. Flame and lead belched from the muzzles. But even as they rattled their staccato patter, their bursts went wild, stabbing zig-zag lines of steel-jacketed bullets into the walls on all sides—for the machine guns were held by dead hands.

The *Spider's* twin automatics had turned first upon those men who held the Thompsons, for they were the most dangerous. The two by the elevator door were dropped by the *Spider's* first two shots, and Kranz by the third. All three of them had pulled the trips of their guns, but they had fired too quickly, before lining the sights upon the black-cloaked enemy. They never fired a second burst, because they were dead before the thunder of their first shots ceased to re-echo back from the ceiling.

And the two remaining killers, who were armed only with revolvers, turned and ran for dear life, heading wildly and frantically back toward the street door where their truck was waiting.

But now, Detective Murdoch had his gun out of its holster, and he covered the fleeing gunmen, shouting to them to halt. The killers turned to snap shots at him, and Murdoch fired twice, swiftly, hitting both men at close range.

Then, with eyes glittering, the detective swung toward the rear of the lobby, bringing his smoking service revolver around.

"You, too, *Spider*—"

He stopped, with mouth agape, for he was talking to thin air.

The *Spider* had disappeared!

Neither the hotel clerk nor the girl at the cigar counter were in sight. They had both taken refuge by dropping to the floor, and there they remained, shivering with fright.

Detective Murdoch uttered an angry oath and sprang across the lobby, jumping over the bodies of Kranz and the other dead machine-gunners. He wrenched open the door of the men's room, and stared grimly at the window opposite—a window wide open in mute testimony as to the *Spider's* path of escape.

On the floor near the washbasin, the puffy-faced Joe Moulton was staggering to his feet, one hand at his head. He wobbled a bit and muttered hoarsely, "The *Spider*—knocked me out!"

Detective Murdoch swore harshly, and leaped across the room to the window. He threw a leg over, and jumped out into the alley in wild pursuit of his quarry. But the representative of law and order was greatly disappointed to find, when he came out on the street that the *Spider* had vanished.

Back in the washroom, Joe Moulton seemed to revive from his state of apparent collapse the moment Detective Murdoch climbed out of the window.

In fact, his revival was so swift that it would have seemed suspicious to anyone watching him.

He was, however, unobserved as he slipped out of the washroom and hurried through the lobby. Somewhere in the distance, a police car siren was shrieking. The lobby was deserted except for the dead bodies of Kranz and the other gunmen. The desk clerk and the cigar counter girl were both keeping out of sight.

Joe Moulton did not at once depart. He stopped in the lobby and did a peculiar thing. From his pocket he drew a chormium cigar lighter. A flip of his finger opened it at the bottom, and with this instrument in his hand he hastened from one body to another, pressing the bottom of the lighter to the forehead of each of the dead gunmen who had died under the *Spider's* guns. Only when he had finished that task did Moulton straighten up and walk out through the front door. Behind him, on the floor of the lobby, the stark dead men now bore peculiar marks on their foreheads. On each one was a glowing red reproduction of a spider.

The dead men lay there for all to see—and to know they had died by the hand of the *Spider*.

Moulton mingled with the excited crowd that was thronging close to the hotel entrance to see what had happened. Questions were flung at him, and he answered them all by saying that there had been a shooting inside.

"Better not stick around!" he shouted. "I think the killers are coming back!"

In the confusion, he made his way down the street, and was gone before the first police car arrived.

There was no satisfaction in his eyes as he hurried away. For, although he had succeeded in thwarting the agents of Red Feather in this instance, he knew very well that he had not crippled the vicious organization of which that sinister person was the head. Somewhere in the city another stupendous crime was in preparation—one which even now might be progressing to a bloody climax. The words he had overheard on the phone were etched in his mind—*the Mandalay operation!* If he could only guess what that phrase referred to, he would know where Red Feather was going to strike next!

Wentworth's ruse in assuming the character of Joe Moulton had not been entirely for the purpose of evading his shadowers. Under the name of Moulton he had established many connections in the sporting world. Joe Moulton was known as a man who could handle a bet of any size, and who could be trusted with the details of confidential transactions. Thus, he was often called upon as a go-between when delicate negotiations were in progress. None of the people with whom he dealt knew the origin of the substantial funds which seemed to be always at his command.

And it was this financial stability which supported the fiction of the huge syndicate supposedly backing him. In all transactions he was careful to keep his own name in the background as far as the public was concerned. He sought no publicity. It was not strange, therefore, that neither the public nor the newspapers were aware of the fact that Joe Moulton had been largely instrumental in arranging the last three heavyweight matches, as well as a number of other sporting events which might otherwise have been unsuccessful.

So he had not been unduly surprised when he received word that morning that Carl Webster, the horse-racing magnate, wanted to see him. All calls for Joe Moulton came to the West View Hotel, and were then relayed by Mamie to a certain address which he had given her, supposedly that of a brother. When he received the message he had at once phoned Carl Webster.

"I've got to see you tonight without fail, Joe!" Webster had said thickly. "It—it's damned important!"

"I may be busy tonight, Mr. Webster. How about tomorrow morning?"

"No, no, Joe. For God's sake, don't fail me. Cancel any other plans you may have for tonight. Come to see me at eleven o'clock. It—it's a matter of life and death, Joe!"

"Life and death? What do you mean, Mr. Webster?"

Webster's voice had dropped almost to a whisper. "You've heard of—*Red Feather?*"

Wentworth's pulse had begun to race.

"What about Red Feather?"

"I can't tell you any more over the phone, Joe.

But you've got to come at eleven o'clock tonight. Promise!''

"All right," Wentworth had promised.

And now, in spite of the fact that he was worried about Nita and Ram Singh, he must keep his word and go to see Carl Webster.

Webster's office was only a few blocks north, opposite Madison Square Garden. As Wentworth walked swiftly in that direction, police radio cars whizzed past, going south toward the West View Hotel. He smiled grimly. Twice tonight he had balked the undertakings of Red Feather's hirelings, with serious loss to them. But he knew well that Red Feather must have many such men at his command. And there was still the puzzle of the *Mandalay operation*. Whether his visit to Carl Webster would yield any concrete clue to the identity of Red Feather, he could not tell. But he must follow up every slightest possibility—for he realized that in this war between himself and Red Feather, he—Wentworth—was at a distinct disadvantage, for Red Feather had guessed the identity of the *Spider*.

From now on, all the resources of this brilliant criminal's vicious organization would be devoted to the destruction of Richard Wentworth. For himself, Wentworth did not mind such attention. In fact, he would have welcomed further attempts against himself, for each attempt gave him renewed opportunity to seek contact with Red Feather. It was for Nita, however, that he experienced anxiety. Knowing that Wentworth was the *Spider,* what better means could Red Feather find for striking against him than through Nita van Sloan?

A block from Carl Webster's office, Wentworth entered a drug store and once more phoned the East

End Avenue apartment. Still there was no answer. Now, his premonition was reduced almost to a certainty. Somehow, Nita and Ram Singh had met with disaster!

Impatiently, he hurried toward the Webster Building. It was five minutes to eleven by his wrist watch, and he hoped to finish quickly whatever business Carl Webster had in mind, so that he would lose no time in locating Nita.

As he approached the entrance of the building, he saw little Tommy Tildon, the newsboy who always sold the sporting extras in front of Madison Square Garden as the crowds came out. Tommy's left leg was a half inch shorter than his right, as a result of a hit-and-run accident six years ago. Everybody bought papers from him, because they knew he was saving money to have an operation. Wentworth had several times offered to advance the money, but Tommy wouldn't take it, insisting that he must be able to see his way clear to repaying it before he could accept such a loan. Wentworth admired the boy's guts, and he had found a good job for Tommy's pretty, older sister, Lillian, as secretary to Carl Webster.

Ordinarily, Tommy's thin, almost elfin face, would be bright and smiling, in spite of the constant pain of his left leg. And his cheerful voice could be heard above the rumble of traffic, calling out the latest extra. But tonight, as Wentworth neared him, he saw that the boy's face was set and unsmiling.

Tommy was standing close to the curb, watching the traffic swirl past. He was not crying out his wares. His papers were bundled under his left arm, and his right hand was fumbling with something hidden under the threadbare coat.

Richard Wentworth was still perhaps thirty feet away when he saw what Tommy Tildon was watching. A black town car with license plates numbered W-2 was swinging to the curb. That would be Carl Webster's car. The racing magnate was just arriving in time for his appointment with Joe Moulton. Wentworth recognized Mike Stockly, Webster's chauffeur, as he climbed out from behind the wheel to hold the door open for his employer.

And then, things began to happen with gruesome swiftness.

Carl Webster was stepping out of the town car; one foot was on the running-board, and the other on the sidewalk. Less than six feet away from him, little Tommy Tildon suddenly let the newspapers drop to the ground. From beneath his coat he brought a small automatic pistol and pointed it at the racing magnate.

For an instant, Carl Webster thought it was some sort of boyish prank. His kindly eyes twinkled.

"What is it, Tommy?" he asked, smiling. "A new kind of water-pistol?"

Tommy didn't answer. His hand shook as he kept the gun pointed; his finger curled around the trigger. Even though he was unsteady, he couldn't miss at that distance.

Too late, Carl Webster realized that it was not a water-pistol Tommy was holding, nor was he playing a childish prank. His face tightened into cold, fatalistic lines.

"I know why you're doing it, Tommy," he whispered. "May God forgive you—"

Mike Stockly, the chauffeur, had not even been looking at the little newsboy. But, at his master's words, he swung around, staring at the frail lad with the gun.

Tommy's finger was beginning to contract on the trigger. His thin face was taut with emotion, and real

236

hatred flared in his eyes—hatred which was inexplicable because Webster had always been more than kind to Tommy and his sister.

"Damn you! Damn you!" he screamed. And he pressed the trigger.

No one was close enough to stop the boy. No one was close enough to save Carl Webster from the death which would spit from the black muzzle of that pistol. Not even Richard Wentworth, who was still almost fifteen feet away!

Wentworth saw the whole thing as if it were a scene from a motion picture being filmed in the street. When the papers dropped from Tommy's hand, and the gun came out, Wentworth knew that this was no prank. Trained as he was to judge human beings by their attitude, to read a man's intentions from little movements like the hunching of a shoulder or the clenching of a hand, he knew with sure instinct that Tommy Tildon intended to kill Carl Webster.

The average man would have been so astounded by the realization of the boy's intention as to be frozen into immobility—as Mike Stockly had been. But not Wentworth. His uncannily accurate ability for measuring space and time in an emergency, to the hair's-breadth of an inch, told him that he could not reach Tommy before the boy would shoot.

But beside him on the sidewalk there was a tall, wire-meshed trash-basket, such as the city provides for rubbish. Wentworth seized this basket and whirled it with a swift, powerful motion which sent the refuse-can skidding along the sidewalk to smash against Tommy Tildon's back at the very instant he pulled the trigger.

Tommy was thrown forward by the impact of the basket. He went stumbling toward the town car, and the gun in his hand exploded harmlessly, as the slug thudded into the running-board.

The boy caught his balance and twisted around, raising the gun once more, grimly resolved to kill this man. But now Wentworth had reached him. He struck down with the edge of his hand upon Tommy's wrist, knocking the gun from the lad's hand. The weapon struck the running-board, and Wentworth swooped and snatched it up.

Mike Stockly now sprang forward, aiming a terrific blow at Tommy's face. But Wentworth blocked the punch, pushing the chauffeur aside. He seized Tommy about the waist and effortlessly lifted his frail, struggling body from the ground.

"Lemme go!" Tommy panted. "Lemme kill him—"

Carl Webster's face was ghostly-white—the whiteness of one whose cheek has just been fanned by the breath of Death. But he maintained his poise.

"Moulton!" he exclaimed. "You saved my life! Why in God's name does the boy want to kill me?"

Wentworth grimly thrust him aside and forced the still struggling newsboy into the car.

"Get in here, Webster!" he ordered harshly, "before the police come. We don't want Tommy going to jail!"

Webster obeyed. He could not do less for the one who had just pushed Death's hand aside from him.

At a nod from Webster, Mike Stockly got behind the wheel and tooled the big car away from the curb. The small crowd which had already begun to gather was left gaping on the sidewalk, not even understanding what had happened in those few fleet moments of swift action. To the patrolman, who came running over from his post across the street, in front of the Garden, they told confusing and conflicting stories. One man maintained that a newsboy had been kidnapped in the car; another said that a man in a brown suit had fired at the car, which had then jumped the curb and struck the trash can; a third maintained that five gangsters in the car had dragged a passing man into it and were taking him for a ride. The cop scratched his head in confusion. He had recognized Carl Webster's town car, and hesitated to turn in an alarm for it. So he compromised by phoning in to his precinct house and asking the desk sergeant's instructions.

In the meantime at Joe Moulton's direction, the town car was driven swiftly across the Park to Carl Webster's home just off Fifth Avenue. They hustled Tommy Tildon into the palatial house, while Mike Stockly took the car back to the garage.

CHAPTER EIGHT

Blonde Omen

In Webster's library, the newsboy suddenly broke down. He burst into tears, his thin little body was wracked by violent sobs as he clung to Wentworth, trying to blink back the tears.

Wentworth gently eased him into a chair, while Carl Webster poured a double Scotch and downed it neat.

"Phew!" he said. "I needed that! Here, Moulton, I poured one for you—"

Wentworth wanted no liquor tonight. The coming battle with Red Feather would provide all the stimulation he needed. But he took the glass and placed it to Tommy's lips, allowing the lad to sip a few drops.

"There," he said in kindly fashion. "Do you feel better now, sonny?"

Tommy Tildon looked up at him out of tear-filled eyes. There was no longer any hate in them—only deep contrition. He did not recognize Richard Wentworth in his disguise.

"Thanks, mister, for what you did," he whispered

hoarsely. "I—I would have been a murderer if you hadn't stopped me!"

"But why—" demanded Carl Webster "—why in the world did you want to kill me, Tommy?"

The lad shuddered. "You know why!" he said.

Out of his pocket he pulled a crushed and crinkled envelope. Wentworth took it, and saw that there was no stamp on it, but that it carried a superscription scrawled in pencil:

"Finder, please deliver at once to:
Tom Tildon, 890 East 49th Street"

"Read the letter!" Tommy said hoarsely.

Wentworth glanced quickly at Carl Webster, then extracted the single sheet which the envelope contained. It bore a short message which had evidently been written in frantic haste; perhaps in the dark, for the lines went off at all angles, and crossed each other twice, making it very difficult to decipher.

As Wentworth looked at it, Tommy, sitting with clenched hands as if trying to restrain himself, said, "That's from Lillian. She hasn't been home for two days. When I asked Mr. Webster where she was, he said he hadn't seen her, that she hadn't come to work— "

"That's right," Carl Webster broke in. "Lillian didn't show up at the office yesterday, or the day before—"

"And tonight," Tommy interrupted, "a man left this note at the house, with our landlady. The man said he'd found it in the gutter on Riverside Drive. Read it. Read it and you'll see why I tried—to kill him!" Once more there was a terrible light of hatred in the lad's eyes as he looked at Carl Webster.

Wentworth hastily put a hand on the boy's shoulder, and held the note up so that both he and Webster could read it. With difficulty they were able to understand the scrawled writing:

> *"Tommy dear—Red Feather has me. I've been a prisoner for two days and they've kept my eyes taped, and I'm writing this without seeing it. One of the men gave me paper and pencil because I begged him, and now they're going to take me in a car somewhere, and I hope to drop this out as we ride. Oh, Tommy, Red Feather has tortured me, and he's going to kill me. The pain all over my body is dreadful and I daren't even tell you what they've done to me. I'll never see you again, Tommy, in this world, but I must tell you what I heard the men saying—Red Feather is—Carl Webster! Don't tell the police, Red Feather will get you if you do. But watch out and be careful. I don't know why they've done this to me, I haven't any money or anything they want, and they might do it to you. For God's sake, Tommy, try to save yourself. Go away. Or try to contact the* Spider. *I heard the men saying that the* Spider *was the only one whom Red Feather feared. God forgive me, I can't believe it, but I'm sure I heard it—that Carl Webster is Red Feather . . ."*

The writing trailed off as if she had been abruptly interrupted. There was no signature.

"That's Lillian's writing!" Tommy gulped. "I'd know it anywhere. And she says—she says—" his voice rose hysterically as his eyes lanced burning hatred at Carl Webster "—she says that *you* are Red Feather. *You* tortured her. You're going to kill her—or you've done it already!"

242

Carl Webster's face grew pallid as he stepped back from the lad's vitriolic outburst.

"No!" he exclaimed. "God, you mustn't believe that, Tommy! I loved Lillian as if she were my own daughter. I had great plans for her—and for you. I would never harm her." He turned pleadingly to Wentworth. "Moulton! You don't believe I'm Red Feather, do you?"

Wentworth's face was grave and puzzled. "I don't know what to believe," he said slowly. His glance dropped once more to the letter, then switched to Tommy Tildon.

"Where did you get the gun, Tommy?"

"It—it used to belong to my brother, Joe. We kept his gun and his badge after he was killed, preventing that holdup. We also have the police medal he got—"

"If Joe were alive, Tommy, he wouldn't like to think of you as a murderer."

The boy covered his face with his hands, and gave way to unrestrained sobbing. Wentworth nodded sympathetically and took Carl Webster by the arm. He led him over to the window, so that the boy couldn't hear what he had to say.

"I tell you, Moulton," Webster began in a hoarse whisper, "there's something fiendish going on. Poor Lillian was tortured, and then deliberately led to believe that I was Red Feather, so that she'd write that note. They even gave her a chance to write it and think that she was unobserved. Then one of Red Feather's own men must have delivered it to Tommy's home. God, what a plot—and all for the purpose of getting me killed!"

"How do you know that was the purpose?" Wentworth asked.

For answer, Carl Webster took another letter from

his pocket. This one was post-marked, and addressed to Webster at his office, and had a Special Delivery stamp.

"Here," he said. "This speaks for itself."

Slowly, Wentworth took the enclosure from the envelope, and unfolded it. He stiffened as he saw the carefully drawn reproduction of a heron's feather at the top of the note. It was drawn in red ink, and looked just like the feathers that had been found beside the bodies of Red Feather's victims. The note read:

> "Carl Webster:
> You have the unfortunate honor to be on my list of contributors, voluntary or otherwise. The sum assigned to you is $150,000. This is little enough, considering the value of your life, and your financial resources. Your secretary, under my artful persuasion, has already given me full information as to your bank balances. She was a brave girl, and refused to talk in spite of great physical pain, so I employed a little trick, making her think that I was you. In the conversation that followed, she unwittingly divulged all the information I needed. I tell you this so that you won't think her a traitor to yourself, because I want you to remember that if you go to the police with this note, Lillian Tildon will die in a far more terrible way than planned for her. What I want you to do is to withdraw $150,000 in cash in any denominations you wish. Select an intermediary, but tell him nothing of what he must do until eleven o'clock tonight. At that time you will give him the cash and tell him to go to Riverside Drive and One Hundred and Tenth Street, with the money in a paper parcel.

*My men will handle the rest. Meet this interme-
diary at your office at eleven o'clock sharp, and
let him start out at ten minutes after eleven. In
the event that you do not meet this demand,
Lillian Tildon will be painfully killed, and you
will die before midnight. Believe me, sir, to be
earnestly yours,*

RED FEATHER."

"I see," breathed Wentworth, raising his glance to
meet that of Carl Webster. "And you were going to
use me as the intermediary?"

"Yes, Moulton. I knew I could trust you for the
job. I have the money in the car, all wrapped and
ready. But I don't understand why they set Tommy
onto me before the money was paid over."

"That's easy," Wentworth said bitterly. "Red
Feather intended to kill you anyway—whether you
paid or not. But something must have gone wrong
with his timing. Tommy got the letter from his sister
before he was supposed to."

It was then the phone rang. Tommy did not move,
but sat with his head in his hands, though his sobs
had abated somewhat. Carl Webster almost jumped
at the sound of the bell. He seized the instrument and
said hoarsely, "Well?"

He held the receiver well away from his ear, so
that Wentworth could hear what was said at the other
end.

"How do you do, Mr. Webster?" said that same
cold, emotionless voice which he had heard only a
little while ago over the switchboard in the West
View Hotel. "I am sorry that my arrangements went
a little wild. That letter should have been delivered to

Tommy Tildon, *only* if you failed to pay up tonight. My agent made a mistake. Believe me, he shall be well punished. As for you, are you still ready to pay the sum specified?''

"Why, you—you—" Carl Webster's face became red and mottled with anger. "You murderous fiend! I'll pay no—"

He stopped short as Wentworth tugged at his sleeve. "Tell him you'll pay! Let me go with the money!"

Webster hesitated, then a gleam came into his eyes. He put his mouth to the phone. "Wait, Red Feather. I've changed my mind—"

He broke off, and gave Wentworth a despairing look. "He's hung up!"

"Damn!" Wentworth whispered under his breath. This was another chance lost to contact Red Feather.

"I'm sorry," said Webster. "I should have thought faster. By God, now Red Feather will try to kill me again."

A loud, persistent horn began to blast in the street, just outside the window.

Webster frowned, and ran to the window, but Wentworth pulled him back. "Don't show yourself!" he cried. "Red Feather works fast. That may be his man—"

He pulled the curtain aside and peered out. As he did so Tommy came out of his chair and stood next to Wentworth, looking out of the window. They saw a car, without headlights, at the curb directly in front of the house. The street lamp illuminated eerily the faces of the three brown men inside—one at the wheel, and two in the back. As Wentworth and Tommy watched, the door of the sedan opened, and a body was thrust out to the sidewalk. It fell with a thud, and lay still upon its back. It was the body of a blonde-haired girl, and it was entirely naked; long,

246

bloody wounds covered the white skin. The eyes were open, staring upward under the street lamp, and the face was contorted into a frozen death mask of unutterable agony.

"Oh, God!" Tommy Tildon screamed. "It's Lillian!" His voice ended in a gurgling, choked cry as he flung himself headlong through the window pane, crashing through it to land on his knees on the turf just outside. He sprang up and ran awkwardly with his crippled gait, shaking his fists at the sedan. Blood stained his face and hands where he had been cut by broken glass, and he looked like a puny but terrible figure of vengeance as he went straight for the black sedan.

Wentworth uttered a low-voiced oath. His hand streaked up and down from his armpit, coming out with a gun. He started to put a leg over the sill to go after Tommy, when he felt his coat seized from behind. He was dragged back by Carl Webster, who shouted, "No, no! You'll be killed. See the machine-gun—"

Wentworth pushed him violently away and started over the sill once more. But he was too late. It was not a machine-gun which Webster had seen in the window of the sedan, but one those same flame-throwers which Red Feather used to such horribly effective purpose. Flame streaked from the sedan and engulfed Tommy Tildon. He threw up his hands and screamed once, terribly, and then he fell to the ground.

Wentworth, his lips drawn into a hard line, emptied his gun at the sedan. But it was already in motion, and the bullets ricocheted harmlessly from the bullet-proof metal and glass. He lowered his sights and sent the last two shots at the tires, but he knew at once that it was useless. He hit the rubber with both shots. But there was no *pop*. The sedan was riding on solid tires!

In a moment the car, with its little, grinning brown men, was out of sight around the corner. And by the time Wentworth and Carl Webster got out the window, Tommy Tildon was dead. They beat out the fire in his clothes, but his frail little body was charred and black. He lay less than ten feet from the hideously mangled body of his sister, Lillian—two innocent victims of the most brilliantly vicious criminal against whom Wentworth had ever waged battle!

For a long, timeless minute, Richard Wentworth stood above the piteous body of the newsboy, forgetting that he was supposed to be Joe Moulton, forgetting everything except the burned thing at his feet.

"Tommy Tildon," he said in a voice that was strange and frightening, "I swear that you have not died in vain!"

CHAPTER NINE

Battle in the Cage

Fifteen minutes later a grim, tight-lipped man entered a drug store two blocks from Carl Webster's house, and dialed a number. People who knew Joe Moulton would have been startled to see the grimness in his face now. He had left Webster's house before the police arrived, because now less than ever did he want interference or help from Kirkpatrick or his men. He was determined to come to grips personally with the man who called himself Red Feather.

In the tragedy of the last few minutes, he had forgotten about Nita and Ram Singh. But now, after seeing a sample of Red Feather's merciless ruthlessness, he felt as if a vise were clamping at his heart as he dialed for the fourth time tonight the number of the East End Avenue apartment where he had told Nita to report.

There were now only two thin threads by which he could hope to reach contact with Red Feather: One was the cab which Nita and Ram Singh had followed from the Mallard Hotel, the other was the riddle of the *Mandalay operation*, which he had heard Red Feather mention over the phone.

He completed dialing the code, and suddenly his blood raced as he heard the click at the other end, denoting that someone was lifting the receiver.

So Nita and Ram Singh had finally returned!

"Greeting, Master!" It was the voice of Ram Singh. "I have but just returned. Allah be praised that you called so soon—"

"Ram Singh!" Wentworth rapped. "Where is Miss Nita?"

"We followed the Onyx taxicab, Master. The cab picked up a passenger whom we do not know, and took him to a night club on Fifty-Ninth Street. Miss Nita followed this man into the club, and sent me hither to await your call."

"Fifty-Ninth Street? Quick, Ram Singh—the name of this club?"

"It is that club which is on the roof-top of the newly erected Steel Building, Master—"

"The Mandalay Gardens!" Wentworth barked.

"Yes, Master. Miss Nita awaits you there—"

"Ram Singh! There is great danger to Miss Nita. Red Feather plans to strike there tonight! Go there at once, Ram Singh. I will meet you in front of the building!"

"By Allah!" the Sikh growled. "Perhaps we shall have some good fighting! I go, Master!"

Wentworth hung up, and raced out of the booth. He hailed a cab and rapped out, "Mandalay Gardens!"

Grimly, as the cab rolled northward, he inserted a pair of clips in his automatics. He wanted to stop and change his appearance back to that of Richard Wentworth. But there was no time for that. He must go as Joe Moulton, gambler.

The Mandalay Gardens! Why hadn't he thought of

that when he overheard Red Feather's orders? The place was the most exclusive night club in New York. Atop a sixty-story skyscraper, it was the focal point of all wealthiest and most socially elect of the city. To the Mandalay Gardens each night, came men of power, influence and wealth; and here too came women of rare beauty and great talent—actresses, wives and mistresses of statesmen and millionaires. What a profusion of jewels and wealth there would be for the taking in such a place, by such a man as Red Feather! And when he struck, it would be with the thoroughness and the ruthless cruelty for which he had already made himself feared.

And Nita—Nita was among those gay and innocent patrons who were slated to die tonight!

"Faster, driver. Faster!" Wentworth urged.

When they reached Columbus Circle, he threw a bill to the cabby, and leaped out of the taxi while it was still moving. Directly in front of him was the towering bulk of the huge Steel Industries Building, reaching sixty floors toward the sky. All along the curb were parked the glittering, expensive limousines of New York's Four Hundred, whose owners were enjoying the lavish entertainment and exquisite food of the Mandalay Gardens far up on the roof of the giant structure.

Short-lived indeed would be their enjoyment, for they did not know that tonight they were to receive the attentions of—Red Feather!

As Wentworth leaped from the cab, he saw his own Daimler swinging around the corner from Central Park South, with Ram Singh at the wheel. The Sikh gave no sign of recognizing Wentworth in his disguise as Joe Moulton, but merely pulled the car in to the curb in a vacant space alongside a fire plug.

Wentworth, who had already left his cab, slowed up for a moment as he passed the Daimler's open window. His swift, all-embracing glance spotted a number of cars distributed at various points around Columbus Circle, which were apparently merely parked there. But in each sat a silent man as if awaiting a signal. It was a strange thing that all of them should have chosen Columbus Circle in which to park their cars and have a quiet smoke.

"There are many who watch, Ram Singh," Wentworth said in Punjabi. "You will come up with me, but you will not appear to know me—"

"They will not let me in, Master," the Sikh said hurriedly. "Only those with cards—"

"Make some pretext, then. Say that you have brought Miss Nita's gloves—"

"And if they still refuse, Master? Shall I crack their skulls—"

"Use any means you can think of—*but be sure to come up*. Once upstairs, your task will be to locate Miss Nita, and remain at her side every instant. It is you, Ram Singh, who must protect her tonight. I shall have work . . ."

As he spoke he was already past the Daimler, moving into the lobby of the Steel Industries Building. An observer would not have thought that any words had passed between the flashily dressed gambler and the Sikh chauffeur in the Daimler. But almost at once, Ram Singh got out of the limousine and went swiftly into the building. He passed Wentworth, who was purposely walking more slowly, and headed straight for the special elevator which served the Mandalay Gardens. Wentworth turned aside to a phone booth, while Ram Singh entered the elevator. He could hear the Sikh arguing in a loud and belligerent voice with the Hindu doorman and with the elevator operator.

All the employees of the Mandalay Gardens were native Hindus, imported by the management for the express purpose of lending Oriental color to the night club. Each attendant was dressed in white turban and white burnoose, and carried a wide-bladed, curved scimitar in his waistband. The scimitars, of course, were not made of steel, but of thin, shellacked wood, polished to such a high degree that they fooled many of the patrons.

It was with two of these attendants that Ram Singh had to argue in order to be permitted to go upstairs to the roof garden. The doorman tried to stop him from entering the elevator, but the huge Sikh merely pushed him to one side and stepped into the cage. The elevator operator motioned to him to get out.

"You may not go up, chauffeur. Step out—"

"Bismillah!" thundered Ram Singh. "You son of a dog! Will you speak to me so? I go up!" He brandished a huge roll of bills in one hand. "My mistress has sent me to fetch money for her, so that she may try her fortune at the gaming table in your Mandalay Gardens. I must bring it to her!"

The doorman came in and took him by one arm, while the elevator operator seized him by the other.

"Come now, chauffeur, get out. We will not take you up. Give us the money and we will send it to your mistress."

Ram Singh laughed deep in his chest, and with a single powerful lunge he sent both turbaned attendants staggering through the elevator door.

"What! Trust you jackals with my mistress's money? Never!"

* * *

It was at that moment that Wentworth emerged from the phone booth. He had made a single quick call to Commissioner Kirkpatrick.

His message was short. With the deep, metallic voice he knew so well how to use, he had said, "Kirkpatrick, this is the *Spider!* Wait! Say nothing, but listen closely, for there is no time. Men and women are going to die at any moment. You have often said that the *Spider* should cooperate with the police. Well, this is my answer. Send men—many men, quickly, to the Mandalay Gardens. Red Feather plans a raid!"

"When?" Kirkpatrick rapped.

"I don't know. Perhaps in an hour, perhaps in five minutes, perhaps in one minute. God grant your men come in time. I shall be there—in case they are late!"

"Wait, Spider!" Kirkpatrick's voice came harsh and unyielding over the wire. "If your tip is authentic, then I thank you. If through your information we are enabled to capture Red Feather it will be a great boon to the city. But—I warn you—there is no reprieve for you. You are still wanted. If you are at the Mandalay Gardens when I arrive, you shall be captured—dead or alive. I want that clearly understood!"

"I ask no favors of you, Kirkpatrick!" Wentworth said coldly.

And with that, without giving Kirkpatrick a chance to ask another question, Wentworth hung up and hurried out to the elevator cage. He was just in time to see the doorman and the operator come hurtling out onto the lacquered floor, propelled there by Ram Singh's powerful thrust.

Before the two turbaned men could recover their

footing, Wentworth seized each by the scruff of the neck and thrust them violently back into the cage.

Another party of men and women in evening clothes was just entering, and Wentworth closed the door of the cage before these new arrivals could catch a glimpse of what was going on. Then he pushed over the lever and sent the cage shooting upward.

The two turbaned men were scrambling to their feet, the make-believe scimitars having fallen from their waist-bands. But weapons suddenly appeared in their hands—gleaming knives, with which they leaped upon Wentworth and Ram Singh!

For a long second the elevator cage shot upward without a guiding hand as Wentworth turned to defend himself against the onslaught. He caught his man's descending knife-hand, twisted the wrist in a quick, deft jiu-jitsu maneuver, and the blade went flying out of the man's grip accompanied by a screech of pain.

Ram Singh handled his man with less finesse but with just as much efficiency. He uttered a roar of glee, and charged directly into the attacker.

In the close quarters of the elevator cage, they were all thrust against each other, and Ram Singh's attacker backed away from the Sikh's bull lunge, only to bump into his companion, who was still screeching with the pain of his twisted wrist.

Ram Singh shouted in Punjabi: *"Bismillah!* I kill jackals!'

His huge, hairy hands flicked out, fingers wrapping themselves around each man's throat. Then, with hardly a sign of exertion on his part, he brought the two of them together with a crash. Their heads met with pile-driver force, and the two men went limp. Ram Singh dropped them carelessly to the floor.

"Wah!" he grunted. "Pigs like these should not seek a quarrel with fighting men!"

Wentworth was already back at the controls, his forehead was wrinkled.

"I don't like it, Ram Singh. These two are no ordinary attendants. Otherwise they would not have knives."

Ram Singh spat contemptuously. "I hope that this Red Feather will give us worthier foemen than these before the night is over!"

"I'm afraid," Wentworth said soberly, "that your wish will be granted!"

CHAPTER TEN

Red Feather Demonstrates

Their car was an express elevator, and there was no stop before the sixtieth floor. Blank walls faced them all the way up. But when the indicator showed "60," strains of exotic music filtered through. "Prelude to Terror" might have been an appropriate title for the selection, Wentworth thought, as the cage came to rest at the top floor. He opened the sliding door and motioned to Ram Singh, who stepped out quickly. Wentworth followed, deftly closing the door behind him so that those on the floor might not see the two unconscious men in the cage.

The entire top floor of the building was devoted to service space for the Mandalay Gardens on the roof above. The foyer into which Wentworth and Ram Singh stepped had no doubt cost many thousands of dollars to furnish. Rich Baluchistan rugs cushioned the sound of their footsteps, and oriental drapes of untold value hung from ceiling to floor on all the walls. There was a great curving staircase which led from here up to a mezzanine, from which in turn, a smaller flight took the patrons out into the roof garden.

Down here on this floor were the kitchens and the bar, as well as dressing rooms for the patrons. Also, at one end of the floor, and well-protected from the casual approach of any but the initiated, was the gambling hall where men and women of the élite could play for stakes as high as fifty thousand dollars.

Everywhere there was bustle and activity. Waiters hurried back and forth, and beautiful women in evening clothes emerged from the dressing rooms to meet their escorts who were waiting for them at the foot of the grand staircase.

Wentworth had never been able to discover just who owned the Mandalay Gardens. But whoever it was must surely have a fortune at his disposal, for the lavish furnishings and the expensive service and cuisine represented an overhead expenditure that the owner couldn't possibly hope to get back out of the patrons. For no matter how much they charged for a bottle of champagne or a caviar sandwich, it was manifestly impossible to make a profit. The exclusive social set who frequented the Mandalay Gardens assumed that it was supported *sub rosa,* by one of their own set, who probably had nothing to do with his money but amuse himself.

All the waiters were swarthy men, attired in white turbans, but instead of the burnoose, they wore pantaloons and tight-fitting, sleeveless jackets of embroidered cloth. The attendant who was charged with the duty of welcoming guests as they came off the elevator was a tall, dark-skinned girl, who wore nothing but a tight-fitting, spangled band about her breasts, and a pair of diaphanous silk pantaloons. At the head of the stairs, leading out into the Mandalay Gardens itself, stood the head-waiter, who was attired like an Indian Rajah.

The hostess in the silk pantaloons frowned at Ram Singh and Wentworth. "All guests must wear evening clothes!"

Ram Singh pushed past her and started for the staircase. "I will stay but a minute, sweet girl," he grinned at her, showing two rows of gorgeously white teeth through his beard. "I must see my mistress for a moment. The one who guards the door down below has not stopped me, as you see."

The girl shrugged, and let him pass. After all, it was none of her business. If the doorman had allowed this chauffeur up, then it must be all right. She turned to Wentworth, and frowned again. For he was no longer there!

The soft, indirect lighting left the whole place in a sort of semi-darkness, which was conducive to the atmosphere of eastern luxury with which the place was imbued. But it was also conducive to the swift and unperceived movements of the dark, shadowy figure in the black cloak and hat, who seemed to blend with the shadows as he disappeared into the alcoved recesses of the rest rooms. . . .

The dark-skinned hostess wrinkled her forehead. "I wonder where that man in the tan suit went—"

She very quickly forgot about the man in the tan suit, for her attention was attracted to the head of the grand staircase where a vehement argument had begun between the bearded Sikh in the chauffeur's uniform, and the head-waiter in the robes of a rajah.

"Impossible!" The head-waiter was gesticulating wildly. "You cannot go in there. It would be sacrilege! Imagine—a chauffeur entering the dining room of the Mandalay Gardens!"

"Nevertheless," Ram Singh said silkily, "that is where I go, my pig!"

259

He pushed past the head-waiter, who snatched at the jacket of Ram Singh's uniform, and shouted for help.

Half a dozen turbaned attendants came running up the stairs to his aid. And strangely enough, they drew those scimitars of theirs, which they carried in their waist bands. As they came up they brandished them. And the blades glittered as no wood ever glitters, no matter how highly it is polished or shellacked. Those scimitars were real, deadly weapons, made of steel. And these turbaned men were no mere attendants, but Hindu killers!

In a glance Ram Singh realized all this, and he suddenly laughed deep in his throat. The head-waiter was still clutching at his coat when he whirled around in a single lithe motion, and picked up the head-waiter as if he had been no more than a child. Then, with the superb ease of smooth and powerful muscles trained to perform any task asked of them, Ram Singh hurled his assailant directly straight at the advancing Hindus!

The man screeched, and his arms flailed the air wildly. His body struck the group of Hindus with the force of an avalanche, and sent them all rolling back down the grand staircase like a batch of nine-pins.

At the top of the stairs Ram Singh threw out his chest, and, showing both rows of white, even teeth, laughed loudly. He waved a hand ironically to the red-faced head-waiter who was getting to his feet, but was all tangled up in the folds of his rajah's robe.

"*Allah, akbar!*" he sang out to the sweating group below, speaking to them in Hindustani. "Ye are no true Moslems. Ye are carrion, and pig-eaters. When I return, ye carrion, I will show you how a true Believer fights!"

260

And so saying, Ram Singh turned on his heel and went through the door at the head of the stairs, which led out to the Mandalay Gardens.

The orchestra was playing a soft and slumbrous Oriental melody, and a girl upon a raised dais was dancing a sensuous eastern dance whose every movement was calculated to arouse the passions of men. The dancer wore no single bit of clothing. Her body was oiled from head to foot, so that she glistened in the amber spotlight. Her hair was black in two great braids behind her. Fingernails and toenails were painted a vivid red so that they shone like scars against the background of her brown and oily skin. And every eye in the room was turned upon her in unhealthy fascination.

It was exhibitions such as these which brought the blasé social set to the Mandalay Gardens. They had thought that nothing could thrill them any more—till they came and witnessed the exotic numbers presented here. Upon the tables food and drink lay unnoticed while all followed the strange and provoking dance.

Ram Singh's eyes only flickered to the dancer. A second they lingered upon her, appreciatively. And then the Sikh was all business again. For him there was a time and a place for everything. Now was not the time for pleasures of the flesh.

His glance darted all over the room, and finally centered upon Nita van Sloan, sitting alone at a table near the edge of the roof garden. He looked behind him to make sure that the Hindus were not pursuing him, and grinned when he saw the head-waiter eyeing him murderously from the doorway. They would not dare to come after him out here, for the slightest disturbance would break the spell of that voluptuous dance.

261

He crossed the floor toward his mistress, and no one even noticed him or his chauffeur's uniform—so rapt was their attention upon the dancer silhouetted in the amber spotlight.

But Nita saw him. Perhaps she alone of all that gay throng had eyes for anything else. She was sitting tense and watchful, though none but the Sikh could have noticed anything unusual about her.

As soon as he was at her table, she raised her eyes to his, questioningly.

"Master Dick?"

Ram Singh smiled, and nodded. "He is here, Mistress Nita."

Her body relaxed, and a little sigh of relief escaped from her lips.

Ram Singh went through the motions of handing her the money which he was supposed to be bringing her. Under his breath he said, "Be careful, Mistress Nita. There are many who watch us. And here comes one whom I like not!"

Nita turned slightly to look at the tall man with the gaunt, skeletal face, whom she remembered having seen last, in the cocktail lounge of the Mallard Hotel.

He threw a quick look of distaste at Ram Singh, then turned to Nita and bowed from the hips. "Permit me, mademoiselle. I have the honor to present myself—Baron Cornelius Crispi. It is my privilege to be a friend of the management here. They have asked me to speak with you. This chauffeur of yours—it is impossible to allow him to remain. You understand—the other patrons. . . ."

"Of course," said Nita. She looked up at Ram Singh. "You had better go now—"

The Sikh moved deliberately around the table until he was standing behind the chair which faced her.

His back was now to the dais upon which the dancer was performing. He drew himself up to his full height, and folded his arms over his chest.

"It is my great sorrow that I must disobey, Mistress Nita. I have my orders. The Master has ordered that I remain at your side until you arrive home. I must stay."

Nita frowned. She looked up at Baron Crispi with a little helpless gesture. "You see, Baron, it is quite impossible for me to order him to leave. He won't go."

Crispi's face was utterly expressionless. For a long minute he stared at Ram Singh. Then he looked down at Nita.

"It is too bad," he said. Then he bowed once more from the hips, turned on his heel, and strode away.

Nita glanced up at the Sikh. "Watch where he goes, Ram Singh!"

"I watch, Mistress," he said, in Punjabi. "It is he whom we followed here. I have the thought that he is one who can be a dangerous enemy!"

Nita said, "Ram Singh! I am afraid of that man. He—he looks like Death itself."

The Sikh smiled. "Have no fear, Mistress. The Master is close by. And while I am beside thee, they must kill *me* before they can touch thee—" Something whined past Nita's ear, like the low hum of a distant bee. And Ram Singh ceased speaking, with a dreadful, appalling suddenness.

His body stiffened as that same something which had whined in the air, struck him in the chest. Blood spurted from a wound high above his heart, and the bone handle of a long-bladed, glittering knife vibrated in the wound. Some one had thrown the knife from the shadows, and it had struck true to the mark.

                    *   *   *

Ram Singh's teeth tightened upon his lower lip, and he slowly raised both hands to the knife handle. He wavered on his feet, and his forehead became bathed in perspiration. Slowly, painfully, he tried to pull the knife out. His great body seemed to heave in a mighty, titanic struggle against the wicked wound.

"Mistress Nita!" he gasped. "Guard thyself! Thy unworthy servant—has—failed thee!"

And he toppled over with a crash.

As if that had been a signal, the music suddenly ceased. Dead silence fell upon the Mandalay Gardens. The dancer came to a rigid stop, poised with her arms in the air. For a full two seconds, it seemed as if nobody breathed.

And then, a shrill whistle pierced the night air. The dancer bent low in a sort of crouch, and ran from the dais through the curtains at the rear, her brown, oiled flanks glistening under the amber light.

And then the spotlight went out. For an instant, the roof garden was plunged in utter darkness.

Nita van Sloan was on her knees, cradling the head of Ram Singh, who was bleeding on the floor. When the light went out, she could not see his bearded, pain-wracked face any more. But she heard his gurgling voice: *"Go Mistress. Go quickly. Guard yourself. Leave me—"*

"No, Ram Singh!" There were tears in her eyes, and her words choked in her throat. "I—I'll stay with you."

She felt the Sikh's head jerk against her breast, as from somewhere in the darkness, a cold, emotionless voice began to speak. The voice was coming from a concealed loud-speaker, and it dominated that whole roof garden with a sort of fiendish malevolence.

"Listen, all of you! You are hearing the words of Red Feather! Many of you have heard from me privately. You have been ordered to do certain things. *I will show you now what happens to those who disobey!"*

Abruptly, the amber spotlight went on once more, flooding the dais. Upon the platform there was a wooden rack, some six feet high and five feet wide. Spread-eagled within the frame of that rack was the body of a girl. Wrists and ankles were stretched taut by ropes tied to the framework. Her head hung limp upon her breast, but her face was etched by the spotlight, as was the rest of her body. A great gasp went up from all those who were sitting, paralyzed by fright, at the tables. They all knew that dead girl.

"Ellen Blount!" the name whipped around the garden, from table to table.

Every eye was fixed upon that pitiful victim. And it was easy to see what had been done to her. For it was apparent that there was not a whole bone left in the body. While she was stretched taut upon the rack, she had been struck repeatedly with a hammer or a heavy bar, each blow breaking another bone. How long that inhuman torture had lasted while she yet lived, no one could tell.

Women began to scream hysterically; men cursed in low, subdued voices. Nita van Sloan, with Ram Singh's bearded head against her breast, gasped with horror. And as suddenly as the amber spot had gone on, it now went out.

A hush spread over the garden.

At once, Red Feather's voice came again, "The girl you just saw was the daughter of Irene Blount. I ordered Irene Blount to perform a certain task. She thought to cheat me, by killing herself instead of doing the thing I ordered. She thought that if she were dead, I would spare her daughter. Well, you have all seen how wrong she was. I promised Irene Blount that her daughter would be broken bone by bone until dead, unless my will was done. And that has happened. Remember, all of you—you cannot escape the will of Red Feather, even by destroying yourselves!''

CHAPTER ELEVEN

Trap for the Spider!

While that cold and heartless voice was proceeding, a shadow which was darker than all the other shadows upon the roof seemed to move around behind the dais like an oozing puddle of blackness. This shadowy figure seemed to be interested not in the voice, nor in the dais, nor even in any of those present. It seemed to be tracing wires. Could anyone have noticed that dark blotch in the night, it would have appeared to be nothing more than the shadow of one of the palms. In reality, it was a man; a man whose features were hidden by the night and by the brim of a black slouch hat; whose deft hands were covered by black gloves, and whose entire form was enveloped by a cloak darker than the night.

This figure at last seemed to find what it sought, for it bent and touched a wire which ran along one side of the roof, up against the trellised coping. Swiftly it followed that wire toward the rear. This was the cable connecting the loud-speaker with the microphone into which Red Feather was talking. The loud-speaker was hidden under the dais. And by following the wire, the black-cloaked figure would come to the microphone.

The voice of Red Feather continued.

"And now you shall all of you contribute to the war chest of Red Feather. When the lights go on, my men will circulate among you. You will strip yourselves of your jewels, your diamonds, your money. Put everything into the sacks my men carry. I warn you, hold nothing back. My eyes will be on you. Whoever holds back will die on the instant!"

With the last word, the lights went on all over the place.

The body of the dead girl, Ellen Blount, still hung upon the rack, gruesome reminder of the heartless cruelty of Red Feather.

And from all sides, came small brown men. Like the attendants and the waiters, they were clad in white turbans and burnooses. Each had a scimitar at his belt, and an open sack in his hand. For each man with an open sack, there was another at his side with a queer, bell-shaped gun, whose stock resembled a bellows.

The brown men began to circulate among the tables. They spoke no single word, but merely stood with the yawning sacks while a roomful of trembling men and women poured jewels and money into them.

The shadowy figure had faded back against the trellised coping along the side of the roof garden. From under the low hat brim, glittering eyes stabbed in all directions, seeking, seeking, seeking. . . . Somewhere here, Red Feather was hidden. He had said that he could see everything. Therefore he himself must be within sight.

And suddenly, that vague shadow seemed to stiffen. The glittering eyes were fixed upon the water tower, high above the roof. A wire ran down from that structure, to be lost in the thick climbing ivy of the trellis-work. It ran to the top of the water-tower, where there was a small cupola, apparently placed there for decoration, but which was large enough to hold a man comfortably.

The little brown men were making the rounds methodically. Two of them came to the table where Nita van Sloan had been sitting. She was on the floor, still cradling Ram Singh's head against her breast. She stared up defiantly at the two small brown men.

Just then a scream sounded from the other end of the garden. It diverted their attention from Nita. Over at the end from which the scream had come, a woman in evening clothes was cowering away from one of the turbaned killers.

The brown man had ripped away the front of the dress, and was pointing to a string of pearls which she had tried to hide from him.

And from above came the cold voice of Red Feather. "Woman, I warned you. You must pay the penalty!"

At once, one of the brown men with the bellows-gun turned it upon the unfortunate woman. Before he could squeeze the bellows, however, a single shot blasted from somewhere in the darkness. The man screamed, and toppled backward, dropping the bellows-gun. At once, all the other brown men turned in the direction from which the shot had come. They beheld a figure of vengeance rising out of the shadows. Cloaked and terrible, it belched flame from two thundering guns, and as they blasted, brown men fell everywhere.

But there were many of them, and new ones came, with bellows-guns. They squeezed, and flame lanced out across the garden toward the cloaked figure. Long, brilliant fingers of flame licked at his cloak.

And then he was no longer there, and the flames were licking at empty space.

The whole garden was thrown into a vast pandemonium of panic and fire. Men and women ran in wild fright, to escape the lancing flame from those bellows-guns, which the brown men were turning in every direction in a vicious effort once more to locate the *Spider*.

Had they thought of looking up at the water tower, they would have found their man. He was already up the ladder, and climbing on the far side of the tower, toward the cupola.

Somewhere down in the bowels of the building a police whistle was shrilling as Kirkpatrick's police arrived on the scene.

Fire set by the bellows-gun was breaking out in half a dozen places. A woman's dress caught fire, and she raised her voice in piercing, inhuman shrieks. A man in evening clothes attempted to leap to her aid and put the fire out, but one of the brown men turned a jet of fire on him, too, and flames burst from his clothes. Now, all those wealthy patrons were milling about in stark terror, and the brown men ran among them snatching jewels, rings, necklaces. They did not seem to be worried or hurried by the approach of the police.

Far up on the top of the water tower, a desperate, deadly battle to the death was going on.

The *Spider* had managed to reach the top, by using the ladder which ran up along the side. And just as he put his hand on the top rung, a man emerged from the cupola. One single glance at the face of this man, which was illuminated by the flames from below, told the *Spider* that he had failed once more to run Red Feather to earth.

This man was not Red Feather. It was the flat-nosed Blagg.

Bitterly, the *Spider* understood that Red Feather had been too clever and too cautious to endanger himself up there in the water tower cupola. He had sent another to make his speech, imitating that cold, hard voice.

But there was no time for regrets. Blagg bent over the top of the water tower, his flat-nosed face peering down at the caped figure of the *Spider*. A gleam of vicious triumph entered his eyes. No doubt he saw here a golden opportunity to earn a rich reward from his master by ending the career of the *Spider*.

His hand, gripping a gun, pushed over the edge of the water tower, point-blank in the *Spider's* face. But before he could pull the trigger, the *Spider's* free hand had reached up and caught his ankle, yanking hard.

Blagg went over backward, uttering a wild shout. The gun flew from his hand as he hit the roof of the water tower. He scrambled to his knees, swung around—and came face to face with the *Spider,* who had vaulted up alongside him.

Blagg shouted hoarsely, and leapt at the cloaked figure. His courage was that of a cornered rat. There was no retreat from the top of the water tower except by jumping. And to jump from this side was to drop sixty floors out into space. So, with the rat-like bravery of a beast that had been run to earth, he bared his teeth and threw himself upon the *Spider*.

The two men grappled there on the water tower roof sixty floors above *terra firma,* and their bodies strained as they strove to break each other's grips.

Blagg had one hand about the *Spider's* throat, and with the other he was gouging for his eyes.

The *Spider* reached up with both hands and seized the one arm of Blagg, then turned swiftly with his back to the flat-nosed man. Too late, Blagg understood the maneuver. He tried desperately to break that hold, and screamed shrilly when he failed. The next moment, the *Spider* had heaved him over his caped back, and Blagg went flying through space—hands clawing at thin air. The sound that issued from his lips was like that of nothing human. And then his body went hurtling into the vast darkness beyond the building—out, out into space, turning over and over on itself until it disappeared from view.

For a long minute the *Spider* stood very still, waiting to hear the thud of the falling body against one of the set-backs below. But there was no thud. Evidently he had thrown the man far enough out so that he fell clear of the building, all the way down to the ground.

Swiftly now, the *Spider* reloaded his two automatics and went to the edge of the tower. He frowned as he looked down. Fire was raging in half a dozen places. Men and women were milling around, trampling each other in attempts to escape. But of the little brown men with the bellows-guns, there was not a sign. They had made good their escape. But how? Surely, not down through the building, for the police were on their way up.

Anxiously, the Spider's gaze scanned that throng, seeking Nita. Ram Singh was there, lying on his back by the table, with the blood soaking into his tunic. But Nita was not beside him. And the *Spider* knew her well enough to know that she would not have deserted the wounded Sikh of her own free will!

With reckless speed, the cloaked figure descended the ladder and sped through the hysterical crowd to the side of Ram Singh. People made way for him with awe and fear—albeit, they had seen him espouse their cause against the little brown men. They let him pass without touching him, and he stooped quickly alongside the Sikh.

"Ram Singh!" he said with a catch in his throat. "They got you, my friend!"

A tired smile showed through the Sikh's bearded lips. "No, no, Master, do not think of me, who am an unworthy servant. They have taken Mistress Nita. Go. Go quickly and take her back from them. *Allah*— they will break her bones upon the rack—like that other one. . . ."

Ram Singh's voice died away, and his head drooped, almost touching the bone handle of the knife still protruding from his chest.

The *Spider* bent his head close to Ram Singh's mouth, and felt a slight puff of breath. The faithful Sikh was still alive. If he could be gotten to a hospital. . . .

The *Spider* laid the bearded head gently on the floor, and came erect.

And at the same instant a stream of police came storming up the grand staircase and into the garden!

At their head was Commissioner Stanley Kirkpatrick, with a gun in his hand.

Kirkpatrick saw the charred bodies of the man and the woman whose clothes had caught fire, and who were now still, after their agony. He saw the terrible, broken body of Ellen Blount upon the rack on the dais. He saw the dead brown men whom the *Spider* had shot, and he saw the flames licking at the trellis-walls and the furniture. But his glance remained on none of those things for more than the space of a second. He had eyes only for one thing in that whole dreadful scene—the figure of the *Spider!*

Of a sudden, his face had become ten years older, and there was a gray look of agony in his fine eyes. This was the moment for which Stanley Kirkpatrick had hoped for many years. But it was also a moment which he dreaded more than anything else in life. His one tireless objective always was to catch the *Spider*. And here was the *Spider,* trapped on a roof top, with no means of escape except a jump to his death. Kirkpatrick should have been satisfied. Yet he dreaded the moment when that hideous disguise would be stripped from the face of the *Spider* to reveal—he feared—the face of his dearest friend, Richard Wentworth.

CHAPTER TWELVE

Wentworth's First Master

Slowly, almost as if he were doing it against his will, Stanley Kirkpatrick moved forward, his gun centered on the cloaked figure.

"*Spider*," he said in a hoarse voice, "you are under arrest. I call on you to surrender!"

The *Spider* moved carefully away from the inert form of Ram Singh, so that if there should be any shooting, the Sikh would not be hit. He brought his gloved hands out from under the cloak, and extended them, with the fists clenched.

"Handcuffs?" he asked ironically.

Kirkpatrick kept him covered, never removing his eyes from the *Spider's* face.

"Cole!" he ordered one of his detectives. "Put the bracelets on that man!"

Flames were licking here and there fitfully, and bodies lay upon the floor. Frightened men and women herded together, watching this tense scene of drama, knowing they were witnessing what had hitherto been dreamed impossible—the capture of the *Spider*.

A woman in the crowd moaned. "Oh, how terrible. And he helped us. He saved us all from being burned by those brown men!''

Kirkpatrick's face was gray and drawn. He watched Detective Cole approach the *Spider* with the glittering steel of handcuffs. The *Spider's* wrists were still extended. Cole approached gingerly, reaching for one of the extended wrists.

And it was then that the *Spider* opened his clenched left hand. It contained a small vial. He flipped the vial with his thumb, straight past Detective Cole, toward Commissioner Kirkpatrick. At the same time he opened his right hand and flipped another vial at Cole.

Both Kirkpatrick and Cole ducked instinctively. And then the vials struck the floor and shattered in a hundred pieces.

A dozen policemen fired simultaneously at the spot where the *Spider* had been. But the black-cloaked figure was already in motion, and the slugs ploughed through empty air.

The detectives never had a chance for another shot, because the dense, opaque clouds of *Spider* Gas rose in such thick, billowy waves that they lost sight of him behind that smoke-screen.

Kirkpatrick's voice rose in an angry shout: "Cover the door! Surround the roof! Spread out! Don't let him get away!"

A rush of heavy feet thundered across the roof as the police hastened to obey staccato orders. But they were running about blindly, unable to see through the thick screen of smoke that enveloped them. They barged into each other, grappled with each other thinking they had the *Spider*, and swore luridly when they found they were struggling with a brother officer.

276

And already the *Spider* was at the edge of the roof. With swift, deft fingers, he unwound a length of the Web from under his cloak. Working swiftly, yet with no lost motion, he tied the free end of the Web to one of the struts of the water tower. Then, with the rest of the line still wound around his body, he climbed over the roof coping, and let himself drop. He hung suspended in air thus, sixty floors above the ground, while the blinded police raced about the roof in frantic search for him. Slowly then, with both hands gripping the line, he paid it out, rolling over and over in the air so as to unwind it from around his body. His hands gripped that line tightly. If he let go for an instant, his body would go catapulting into space, whirling around as the Web unwound, just like a spool of thread that had been dropped. But the marvelous reserve power which he could always call upon in emergency enabled him to keep a firm grip on the line, paying it out foot by foot.

Slowly he moved lower in space, passing the top floor window, then coming abreast of a window in the fifty-ninth floor. Here he stopped. He pulled back his right foot and kicked, smashing the glass in the window. Then he let go the line with one hand, and caught hold of the frame. He pulled himself in through the window, and dropped to the floor of the office.

Swiftly now he produced a small knife. One of the blades was a small, fine-toothed saw. He used this to saw through the Web, for there was no means of releasing the upper end which was tied to the water tower strut. He would have to leave that much for the police to find. And nothing but that saw-toothed blade would have been sufficient to cut through the Web.

As he sped swiftly through the closed and deserted office to the corridor, he could hear the clamor from above as the police still searched for him up there.

Upstairs, he had left Ram Singh, perhaps dying of a chest wound. Somewhere in the city, Nita was in the hands of Red Feather—facing the ghastly prospect of being broken on the rack, like poor Ellen Blount. And with it all, there was the problem of how Red Feather and his little brown men had been able to leave that roof and escape from the police!

That last question was answered almost at once as he rounded a bend in the dimly-lit and deserted corridor. The bank of elevators serving these floors was here, and opposite them the fire-stairs. The safety door to the fire-stairs was open. And straight across the tiled floor from that open safety door to the closed door of one of the elevator shafts, there was a fresh trail of blood!

This was undoubtedly the way the killers had come!

Perhaps one of the little brown men, who had been wounded in the fight upstairs, had escaped this way with the others. Mentally measuring the corridor, Wentworth decided that the fire-stairs were directly in line with the kitchen on the sixtieth floor. From that kitchen up there, serving elevators would run up to the roof, so that waiters could come and go for the orders. It must have been by those serving elevators that the brown men and Red Feather had escaped. Then, while the police were rushing up to the roof, the killers had come down the fire-stairs and gone all the way down in an elevator previously left at this floor. Looking at the indicator on the elevator shaft before which the blood-stain lay, Wentworth saw that it showed the cage to be down at the second sub-

278

basement. In these huge buildings there were four or five basements and sub-cellars, and often there were exits from them into the subway and sewage systems. Thus, the killers could easily have escaped under the very noses of the police.

And Nita must have been brought this way, too.

Grimly, Wentworth nodded as he understood why Nita had not been killed up there on the spot. Alive and a hostage, she was far more valuable to Red Feather than dead. Red Feather had forced Irene Blount to do his will by threatening the torture of her daughter. No doubt he had compelled many others to commit criminal acts by the same threat. Perhaps Arnold Metz had been forced to take those funds from his bank for the same reason.

And by the same token, Red Feather would be certain that the *Spider* could be brought under this thumb through Nita. The devilish part of it was that it was entirely true. Wentworth could never allow the things to be done to Nita, which had been done to Ellen Blount. Much sooner would he offer up his own life in exchange.

The whole grisly picture was clear to Wentworth in a flash as he stripped off the cloak, hat and gloves of the *Spider*, and stood once more in the personality of Joe Moulton.

Swiftly he sought some way of leaving the building. There was one tenuous thread by which he might still pull back onto the trail of Red Feather. That thread was Arnold Metz. The man must be questioned, forced to talk. Perhaps—even though he himself knew little about Red Feather—something he might say would give Wentworth the needed clue.

But to leave the building now was no simple matter. Even as Joe Moulton, he would most certainly be stopped if he were seen. Without doubt the police would hold and question every man and woman found in the building. If he could get an elevator up here, he might be able to shoot down to one of the sub-basements and escape that way, into the subway. But all the cages were downstairs. . . .

With a start, Wentworth whirled, and a gun appeared in his hand as if by magic. From the open safety door behind him had come the unmistakable sound of a quickly indrawn breath!

His eyes probed into the darkness of the landing beyond the door, but he saw nothing. He took a quick step forward, and sprang through the doorway, then stopped short, sucking in his breath.

A girl was crouching there. She was naked, and her body glistened with oil. Her little hands were up pathetically before her breasts, and she looked at Wentworth with a strange and curious terror in her dark and frightened eyes. It was the dancer who had been performing under the amber spotlight when Red Feather interrupted the proceedings.

"You poor thing!" Wentworth said gently.

From an inner pocket he once more took the rubber *Spider's* cape. He turned it inside out, with the purple lining outward, and put it across her shoulders. She shivered and pulled it together, looking up at him gratefully.

Wentworth put out a hand and helped her to her feet. She was shivering as if with fever, and sobbing with short, jerking sobs. He put an arm around her shoulders, and she suddenly broke down and buried her dark head against his chest. Now the sobs came unrestrainedly, wracking her lithe young body.

Time was growing too short. At any moment the

police would discover the fire-stairs, and come barging down. Yet Wentworth let her sob without restraint for a full minute before he spoke.

"Tell me about it," he said, lifting up her chin with a finger. "You look so young. Too young to have been doing a dance like that. Were you forced to do it?"

"Y-yes," she said. "Red Feather kidnapped me. He—he told Father that he'd impale me on a bed of spikes if Father didn't raise two hundred thousand dollars. Father didn't have the money, so he stole it from the bank."

"You're Arnold Metz's daughter?" Wentworth asked gently.

She nodded. "I'm Susan—Metz."

"But why the dance?" Wentworth asked. "How did Red Feather force you to dance?"

The girl's voice broke a little, but she went on. "When Father stole the money, the police went after him. Red Feather told me he knew where Father was hiding out. He said he'd betray him to the police if I didn't dance here. I—I consented. Father had made himself a thief for my sake. Could I do less for him?"

"Brave girl!" said Wentworth. His eyes were grim and bleak. "So Red Father used the daughter to ruin the father, and the father to ruin the daughter! That's how he managed to get such sensational entertainment for the Mandalay Gardens!" His voice took on an edge of intensity. "Tell me, Susan—*do you know who Red Feather is?*"

"No," she breathed. "There are several managers, and they keep changing all the time. I—I was frightened, I hid when they showed poor Ellen Blount's

281

body on the rack. And they forgot me when they made their escape. I followed them down, hoping I could escape—''

"*Wait!*" Wentworth clapped a hand suddenly over her mouth, and jerked her back through the doorway onto the landing. He had noticed just in time, that one of the elevator cages was shooting up from the main floor. And the indicator stopped with startling suddenness at fifty-nine—the floor they were on!

He had barely managed to get Susan back out of sight when the shaft door slid open, and two plain-clothes detectives stepped out with guns in their hands.

Susan Metz started to tremble violently in Wentworth's arms.

"They know we're here!" she whispered. "They've come for us!"

Again he put a hand over her mouth, dragged her back farther into the shadows.

In a moment however, they were reassured by the conversation of the two detectives. For it was apparent from what they said that they were merely making a routine search of every floor in the building. Apparently other cages were taking other detectives to all the floors.

"I'll take this end, Mike, and you take the other," one of them said. "Shoot if you see anything. The boss says if you see the *Spider,* plug him!"

"Okay, Sam," Mike replied.

Wentworth and Susan heard Mike's footsteps moving away toward the end of the hall, while Sam went in the other direction.

Abruptly, Sam's footsteps stopped, close to the fire-door.

Wentworth grew taut. He knew that Sam had spotted the bloodstains on the floor. He pushed Susan behind him, and stepped closer to the door.

Sam began to move again. He was stepping softly, and he was moving toward the door behind which Wentworth crouched. Wentworth saw a gun push through the doorway, then an arm. Sam was taking no chances. He was coming in with his gun in front of him.

Wentworth drew a deep breath. He thrust forth both hands, and seized the detective's arms. He yanked, and Sam came tumbling forward. Wentworth brought up his right fist to connect with the detective's jaw, and Sam crumpled. Wentworth caught his sagging body, and let it down easily to the floor. His eyes were glittering as he took Susan by the arm and led her swiftly across the hall into the elevator.

He slid the door shut and sent the cage rushing downward.

The express elevator shot down like a plummet, and Susan Metz gasped for breath.

Wentworth streaked past the main floor, the arcade, the first basement and the sub-basement. He stopped at the lowest level, the second sub-cellar.

All was dark down here as he opened the door of the cage and led Susan out.

"We've got to hurry," he told her. "The detectives on the main floor will have seen the indicator drop, and they'll know some one came down here. They'll be right on our heels!"

Using his flashlight, he led her through passage after passage of damp and musty concrete. He stopped at a ventilator grating, through which the rumble of a subway train was plainly audible.

"Stand back!" he ordered.

When she was sufficiently far away, he took out one of his automatics and fired seven times in quick succession into the frame-bar of the grating where it was set in the concrete. The bullets ricocheted, and flying bits of cement struck all about him. The cellar was filled with the ear-splitting detonations which reverberated in wave after wave of deafening thunder.

But Wentworth was already pulling at the grating with all the strength he could muster. It loosened at the spot into which he had fired, and the metal frame began to come away from the concrete.

Susan came up close to him and whispered, "Hurry. I heard an elevator door slam back there. Some one is coming!"

Wentworth grasped the grating in both hands and braced his feet against the concrete. The muscles bulged against his tight-fitting coat as he pulled with all the power he could muster.

Now he could clearly hear the sound of cautious footsteps down the other end of the sub-cellar.

He clamped his teeth shut, and put every ounce of reserve into the task. And suddenly there was a crackling sound. Concrete crumbled all along the side of the frame, and the grating came away in his hands!

He seized Susan's arm and half dragged, half pushed her through the opening.

"The subway!" she exclaimed as they got out on the other side.

They were in the tunnel, and the lights of a station blinked a hundred yards away. A train was rumbling toward them, and they flattened themselves against the wall.

The train roared past like a terrible prehistoric monster, and the great rush of air in its wake almost dragged them off the ledge onto the third rail.

"Come on!" Wentworth shouted. He took her hand and began to run, with Susan hanging on behind. As the rumble of the train died away, they could hear a man in the sub-cellar they had left, shouting to them to stop.

Wentworth turned and saw a uniformed policeman leveling a gun at them.

He yanked Susan off the ledge, hurdling the third rail, just as the patrolman fired. The shot made a queer, whining sound in the subway tunnel, like the wailing of a banshee.

Wentworth pushed Susan in front of him, and kept on running, and the policeman aimed again. But just then a southbound express train came rushing toward them on the next track, and its powerful spotlight blinded the uniformed man. His shot went wild. And by the time he got the light out of his eyes and was ready to fire again, Wentworth had reached the station, and had boosted Susan up on the platform.

The ticket agent in the booth stared at them as if they were mad, as they raced through the turnstiles and up the stairs to the street. It brought them out halfway around Columbus Circle from the Steel Building, and they could see that a vast mob of people had gathered in the street to watch the raid on the Mandalay Gardens. The crowds overflowed into the gutters all around, and the press was so thick that it was difficult to get through.

But no one paid the slightest attention to the puffy-faced man in the tan suit, and the slim girl in what seemed to be a purple raincoat, who wiggled their way through the crowd toward Broadway. Once, Wentworth looked back, and saw the pursuing policeman standing at the mouth of the subway kiosk, scratching his head in perplexity. He must have realized that his quarry was lost in such a crowd.

A moment later Wentworth hailed a cab on Broadway, and they were speeding toward the East End apartment.

Nita kept a complete change of wardrobe in each of Wentworth's retreats, in the event of emergency. And from these he told Susan to select whatever clothes might fit her, though Nita was taller. Susan found a blouse and skirt which she thought would do, and she handed the cloak out to him over the dressing-screen.

Wentworth left her then, and hurried to his own room. He quickly discarded the personality and the clothes of Joe Moulton, and became once more Richard Wentworth. As he worked over his facial details, his mind flew back and forth, from possibility to possibility. He could see no way out. With Nita in the hands of Red Feather, Wentworth could do nothing but bow in defeat. He understood too well, now, how Irene Blount must have felt when she almost brought herself to commit murder to save her daughter from torture. And how Arnold Metz had felt when he deliberately made a thief of himself for Susan's sake.

What, he asked himself, would he—Wentworth—not do to preserve Nita from the fate of Ellen Blount? Suppose Red Feather demanded that he commit a crime? Could he refuse, knowing that Nita would suffer unspeakable tortures while he smugly refused to demean himself?

No! Anything that Red Feather asked, he must be prepared to do! And even as the full force of that realization struck him, the phone rang!

The phone in this East End Avenue apartment was hooked up on a party line with the phone in his officially listed residence, which was only a block away. So that when it rang there he had only to pick it up here to answer it.

For a long minute he stood over that phone, debating whether to answer it. Out of a sure instinct as well as a knowledge of how the criminal mind operates, he was certain that this was Red Feather, calling to lay down an ultimatum. If he should fail to answer it, the time of Nita's ordeal might be delayed. He might have more time to track down Red Feather and his organization.

Yet he could not bring himself to ignore that call. Within him there was a terrible turmoil and impatience. He must know the worst at once. *He must answer now!*

Before picking up the instrument, however, he took some elementary precautions. He picked up another phone and dialed the Telephone Company Emergency office. Giving his name, he requested tersely that the call coming in on the other line be traced. His connection with Commissioner Kirkpatrick was known to the company officials, and they asked no unnecessary questions. He hung up, and switched on the photo-electric recording device, which would make a record of the caller's voice, thus enabling him to analyze the tone content for future use.

The phone was still ringing when he picked it up.

"Wentworth speaking," he said curtly.

That same cold, emotionless voice snapped at his eardrums.

"You know, of course, who this is, Wentworth?"

"No."

"Then shall we say . . . Red Feather?"

A cold rage gripped Wentworth. But he kept his voice level. "What do you want, Red Feather?"

"My dear Wentworth! From you there is only one thing I want. A little service which I should like you to perform for me. I am certain that you will gladly do it—when you learn that your lovely Nita is—er—a guest of mine."

"How do I know that's true?"

As he asked the last question, a light flashed in front of the desk, indicating that there was a call on the other phone. He picked it up with his left hand, and whispered, "Wentworth talking."

"Telephone Company, Mr. Wentworth. That call is coming from a drug store pay station at Two Hundred and Forty-second Street and Broadway—"

"Police!' he said into the phone, and hung up.

At his other ear, the voice of Red Feather was speaking unctuously: ". . . so if you require proof that she is my guest, I shall be glad to send it to you. Shall we say—one of her fingers? Which finger would you prefer? The index finger is too valuable, of course. Perhaps you would like to see her thumb?"

"No," said Wentworth, restraining the rage that welled up within him. "I'll take your word for it."

"Ah, so! That is much better. Now we come to the thing which I wish you to do."

"If I do this thing, whatever it is, do you promise to set her free?"

"Hardly, Mr. Wentworth. Hardly. She is too pleasant a guest. I will only promise that life will not become—er—unbearable for her. You understand? You were at the Mandalay Gardens. You saw the body of Ellen Blount. You comprehend what I mean."

"You mean that if I do this thing, you won't torture her?"

"Exactly. And as I require other things of you, you will do them. Should you fail me, then you will

288

sentence your beautiful friend to a very hideous ordeal. In other words, you are virtually my servant."

Wentworth gripped the phone tightly—so tightly that his knuckles shone white. He wanted to keep Red Feather on the phone as long as possible. Yet he could hardly believe that the man was so foolish as to remain there long enough for the police to come.

"What is it that you want me to do?"

He tried to keep his voice steady.

"Your first task," said that implacable voice, "will be the murder of Commissioner Kirkpatrick!"

CHAPTER THIRTEEN

Susan Remembers the Sunset

Those words struck like individual hammer-blows against Richard Wentworth's brain. A cold wave of hopelessness swept over him.

The devilish coldness of Red Feather's voice had not changed by so much as a single tonal wave while he voiced that mad, inhuman order. It was so unbelievable that he might have thought Red Feather was making some macabre joke, had he not remembered the case of Irene Blount. She, too, had been ordered to murder a man in order to save her daughter. Red Feather had wanted Wentworth dead. His men had failed in the attempt at the Mallard Hotel, so he had callously ordered Irene Blount to do the job. And now that he had Wentworth under his thumb, he was going to force him to remove Kirkpatrick, who, as an efficient police commissioner, was dangerous to his fiendish operations.

Wentworth forced himself to speak in a normal tone of voice. If he could only keep that vicious devil on the phone a little longer, the police might get there and pick him up.

"What you ask," he said, "is quite impossible. Stanley Kirkpatrick is my friend—"

"You may have your choice, Wentworth," Red Feather interrupted. "Stanley Kirkpatrick, or Nita van Sloan. I assure you that Kirkpatrick's death at your hand will be a far easier one than Nita van Sloan's death—at *my* hand!"

Suddenly, a new sound came very clearly to Wentworth over the phone, as a sort of background to Red Feather's voice. It was the sound of stuttering machine guns!

Wentworth's eyes glinted, and his whole body tautened. Without doubt, those were machine guns. The police had arrived there then!

But that sudden hope died in his breast a moment later, when the unmutable voice of Red Feather spoke again.

"I see that you have had my call traced, Wentworth. It is too bad. Unfortunately for the police, only one squad car has arrived. I took the precaution of planting a number of my men in the neighborhood. Those sounds you heard were machine guns, all right. But they belong to *my* men. The police are quite dead, my dear Wentworth! I must be leaving now, before more police arrive. Good-bye, my dear Wentworth! It is now almost midnight. I give you until five o'clock in the morning to carry out my order concerning Commissioner Kirkpatrick. After five—if the Commissioner is still alive—you may pass the time imagining the screams of agony which your Nita will be uttering!"

The phone clicked in Wentworth's ear as Red Feather hung up.

White-faced, he flung away from the desk—to see little Susan Metz standing in the doorway.

She was clad in one of Nita's blouses, and a plaid

291

skirt, which she had pinned up around her waist. She was staring at him with wide, frightened eyes.

"That—that was Red Feather?"

"Yes!" he said bitterly.

"He—he wants you to kill somebody?"

"Yes."

"He's holding someone you—love?"

"Yes."

"Oh!" There was such a wealth of sympathy in her young eyes as she came running to him, that he forced a smile for her.

"I don't know who you are," she said. "But believe me, I'm sorry for you if—if your sweetheart is a victim of Red Feather."

"My name is Wentworth," he told her gently. "This is my apartment."

"But—but—" her face clouded with perplexity "—the *Spider* brought me here. I know who he is. He's a man in a brown suit—"

"The *Spider* phoned me to come here," Wentworth told her. "He said he had left you in my apartment. The *Spider* frequently makes use of my services. His orders are that I take you to your father. I know everything that has happened to you. The *Spider* instructed me to question your father, since he cannot go there himself. Perhaps your father can give us some lead to Red Feather."

She looked up trustingly at Wentworth. "If the *Spider* trusts you, then I will, too!" Then she added diffidently, "I—I hope you can save your sweetheart."

"Perhaps," Wentworth said tightly, "I shall have to do what Irene Blount did. But even that won't save Nita!"

In fifteen minutes they were at the rooming house around the corner from the Mallard Hotel, where

Wentworth had left Metz, lulled to sleep by a hypodermic needle.

They ascended in the automatic elevator, and rang the bell. Jackson opened the door. He had come over as soon as it was safe to leave the Mallard.

Jackson was in his shirt-sleeves, and he was sweating a little.

"I can't make him talk, sir," he said. "He's been conscious for an hour, but he won't open his mouth."

Wentworth motioned to Susan to remain outside, and he entered the room.

Metz was sitting up on the bed. His appearance was miserable. His clothes were rumpled, and there were deep bags under his eyes. His lips were trembling. Wentworth pulled a chair over to face him.

Metz put out a supplicating hand. "Please—have you got any news? Have there been any murders today? Any—any girls found—dead?"

"Yes," said Wentworth. He saw Metz stiffen, and a dreadful look of despair come into his face.

"Damn you all!" he shrieked. "You've murdered my daughter. If you'd let me give the money to Red Feather, she'd still be alive!"

"It wasn't your daughter, Metz. It was Ellen Blount. Susan, is safe."

"Safe?" Metz's eyes opened wide.

Wentworth got up and opened the door. "Come in, Susan," he said.

He and Jackson stepped out in the hall, so as not to witness the reunion between father and daughter. It would have been too painful for them.

While they waited out there, Wentworth swiftly told Jackson the story of the evening.

"Ram Singh is in the hospital—unconscious," he finished. "The doctors say he must have a heart of leather. The knife just scraped it. He'll be laid up for a month, but he'll live. But in the meantime, he's unconscious, and Nita's in Red Feather's hands. Whatever they know, I'll never learn from them in time to stop Red Feather. So, Jackson, I guess I'm at the end of my rope. At five o'clock in the morning, I've got to finish up—*kaput!* A shot in the brain will do it for me. But Nita—when will it end for her?''

Jackson's big hands were clenching and unclenching at his sides. ''You can't do that, major. You can't take your own life!''

He dropped his eyes before Wentworth's gaze. He knew that Wentworth could not live and remain sane, knowing the unspeakable agony which Nita would be enduring.

At last he thought of an argument. ''You must live, sir! You must live to bring that fiend to book. We'll track him down, sir—''

Once more he stopped. He could read his master's mind. With Nita gone, there would be no incentive for Wentworth to go on living—not even the incentive of vengeance; not even the *Spider's* loathing for crime.

Silently, the two men turned and reentered the room.

Susan and her father were sitting on the bed side by side, with hands entwined. Metz looked twenty years younger than he had looked fifteen minutes before. His eyes swept up to Wentworth, and they were filmed with gratitude.

''Red Feather would have killed Susan next, if the *Spider* hadn't broken up his plans. Susan tells me, Mr. Wentworth, that you are a friend of the *Spider*. If you can give the *Spider* a message, tell him that I shall return the money I stole, and take my punishment for it. I wish there was something I could do to repay the *Spider*—or *you,* who are his friend. I know that you are in trouble. If I could only help—"

Susan said, "I told Dad about—about Nita. He wants to help you. But there's so little he knows."

Wentworth's face was bleak. "There's nothing you can tell me, then?"

Metz shook his head miserably. "I never saw Red Feather. The only contact was made with me by phone, after Susan was kidnapped."

Wentworth turned to the girl. "What about you, Susan? How were you kidnapped? Did you see the men who did it?"

"I had phoned for a cab," she said. "I was going to visit a friend uptown. When the cab came to the house, I got into it. And suddenly, two of those brown men appeared from nowhere. They were dressed in street clothes. One of them put his hand over my mouth so I couldn't scream, and the other stuffed a chloroform sponge against my nose. The next thing I knew, I was alone in a little room with a barred window. The window was too high for me to look out—"

She broke off, startled, as there was a sudden rush of feet in the hall outside. Someone turned the knob and thrust the door in, violently—and Commissioner Stanley Kirkpatrick burst into the room, followed by half a dozen plainclothesmen.

Kirkpatrick's glance rested only for a second on Wentworth, then flicked over to Metz.

"Arnold Metz," he said, "you are under arrest!"

Metz sighed. "I was about to give myself up."

Kirkpatrick snorted. "And you, Dick, are also under arrest—for harboring a fugitive from justice!"

"How did you find this place?" Wentworth asked.

The Commissioner nodded toward Detective Murdoch, who had come in behind him.

"Murdoch spotted you in a cab with this young woman. He tailed you, then phoned me. I'm sorry, Dick, but I've got to lock you up. There's a little explaining you'll have to do. The *Spider* escaped from us, over at the Mandalay Gardens. I'll want to know where you've been for the last two hours."

Detectives were putting handcuffs on Metz. He was standing with squared shoulders, his head held high. "I'm not afraid any more!" he said.

Kirkpatrick nodded to Wentworth. "It's your turn, Dick—for the handcuffs." He motioned to another of the detectives.

"Wait, Kirk!" Wentworth said suddenly. "There's something I've got to tell you."

"Well?"

"Not here. In the hall."

Kirkpatrick looked at him suspiciously, then shrugged and led the way out into the hall. The door remained open so the detectives could watch them; but they couldn't hear what was said.

"All right, Dick," the Commissioner said. "What is it?"

"I have to be free now, Kirk. Nita's in trouble."

The Commissioner raised his eyebrows. "What do you mean?"

Wentworth lowered his voice. "Red Feather has her!"

"What!"

"He's going to put her to the torture at five o'clock this morning."

"By God, Dick!" exclaimed Stanley Kirkpatrick. "I can't believe it. I don't want to believe it. Has he made a demand on you?"

"Yes."

"Then do it. Do anything. But don't let the same thing happen to Nita that happened to Ellen Blount!"

Wentworth smiled wearily. "No, Kirk, I can't do what he asks."

"Well, what is it, man?" Kirkpatrick demanded. "Are you afraid to tell me?"

"Almost, Kirk. He wants me to—murder *you!*"

Kirkpatrick's face seemed to congeal. A long, low sigh escaped from his lips.

"Dick," he said slowly and distinctly, "if it's my life that will save Nita from the torture, you're welcome to it!"

Wentworth shook his head. "Just give me a chance to find her. Don't put obstacles in my way."

"All right, Dick. Whatever you say. I'll go further. If it should be necessary for the *Spider* to operate tonight, I'll give orders to my men not to molest him."

"Thanks, Kirk. If I can contact the *Spider,* I'll ask his help."

"And what's more, Dick, if the *Spider* catches up with Red Feather, I won't complain if the *Spider* takes the law into his own hands!"

The two men returned to the room, and Kirkpatrick waved aside the detective with the handcuffs. There was a look of terrible intensity in his eyes as he issued swift orders to be spread through the Department—a truce with the *Spider*—till five o'clock in the morning. Mr. Wentworth to receive full cooperation in whatever he required. . . .

Susan Metz was comforting her father. "They won't keep you in prison long, Dad. They can't. I need you. I'll be thinking of you all the time. Thinking of how you'll be looking out of the window with bars. And maybe the window will be too high for you, too, so all you can see is the mail plane as it flies north at sunset.''

Richard Wentworth suddenly uttered a hoarse, wild cry. He thrust the detectives aside, and seized Susan by the arm, swinging her around violently.

"What about the mail plane at sunset?"

Susan winced from the pain of his steel-grip on her arm. She looked up into his eyes, and suddenly she was breathless.

"The mail plane," she whispered. "I was in a cell for a week. Every night, just at sunset, it passed quite low, flying north. It had a green light on the right wing, and a red light on the left one. It was the only thing I could see from my window. The plane had a number on the wings which I made out once or twice in the twilight. It was NC451. Every night I tried to reach the window to wave my handkerchief, but it was no use. I couldn't reach the sill.''

There was a bright, dancing light in the eyes of Richard Wentworth. He seized Susan about the waist, lifted her up high, and kissed her.

"Susan," he exclaimed, "you're the most gorgeous thing in the world!"

He set her down, and swung on Kirkpatrick. "Get it, Kirk?"

The Commissioner's eyes were glittering. "Let's go!" he said. "We'll know what company owns that plane in fifteen minutes. Then we'll check every mail route the outfit operates!''

CHAPTER FOURTEEN

Red Feather's Lair!

It was a great, modern castle, set high on a cliff overlooking the Hudson River, and located just north of the boundary line of New York City. Five acres of landscaped grounds lay between the massive structure and the road. On the west there was the river. On the east, south and north there ran a tall stone wall, its upper surface encrusted with jagged bits of broken glass.

Twenty feet inside the stone wall there was a fence of barbed wire. Small, dead animals lay against the fence—animals twisted into grotesque contortions which could only have been achieved by the application of a powerful charge of electricity. In the twenty-foot wide space of no-man's land between stone wall and electrically charged wire fence, there roamed three huge mastiffs, hungry and growling. They had been taught never to touch the wire.

From the tower of the castle, two brilliant searchlights played constantly upon the grounds, rotating in opposite circles, and moving at a speed calculated to light up each sector of the grounds every four minutes.

All these things Richard Wentworth observed carefully, and noted in his memory. Six times Jackson had driven up and down the road skirting the castle property, and Wentworth had lain prone on the roof of the car with a pair of field glasses glued to his eyes. By the end of the sixth trip, there was little he did not know about the dispositions against a surprise raid on the castle.

After a feverish hour in police headquarters, checking by phone with the air lines, they had found plane NC451, and had caught one of the plane's pilots in Albany, preparing for the return trip. Without hesitation, over the phone, he had given them the exact location of the place answering their description.

Susan Metz's story had given them enough to go on. It had to be a place set on a high cliff, because she had said that the planes flew low enough to distinguish the number. And surely, the pilot couldn't have failed to note barred windows.

So now they had the place. This was Red Feather's lair. Here—and the odds were a hundred to one in favor of the supposition—was where Nita, and perhaps many others, were being held for the unspeakable tortures which Red Feather evolved for them.

The next question had been one of jurisdiction. Being just beyond the City Line, Kirkpatrick had no authority to act. It was a question of calling in the County law officers, or the State Troopers.

In either case there would have to be an application for a search warrant, and a loss of valuable time. And even if a search warrant could have been obtained without delay, Wentworth argued that Red Feather would have means to dispose of his prisoners so that no trace could ever be found of them. For a man of Red Feather's devilish ingenuity would certainly make provision for the possibility of detection and raid. Just as he had provided a means of escape for his killers from the Mandalay Gardens, and just as he had arranged for protection while he made his phone call to Richard Wentworth, so surely would he have planned for the time when the law would come down upon him.

And so it was decided that Wentworth should go alone.

Kirkpatrick, at the conference with Captain Sheffield of the State Police, had put it a little differently.

"This," he had said, "is a case for the *Spider*. He is the only man that could get in there without giving the alarm."

"Perhaps I could get in touch with the *Spider*," Wentworth had said tentatively.

And there they let it lie—except that Kirkpatrick obtained permission from Captain Sheffield to station a large squad of men on the City Line, with the understanding that if they noticed a disturbance which required their attention, they had permission to cross over. And as an added precaution, a police boat was hove to, just around the bend in the river, with a machine gun on the prow ready for action.

But it was Richard Wentworth who had to go in there.

So when all the observations had been made, the car made one more trip down the road, with all lights out. Halfway along the stone fence, it swerved in sharply, until it was almost touching the wall.

From the roof of the car, a black, cloaked figure arose. It peered over the wall, waiting until the two moving searchlights had passed that spot. Then, working swiftly, the figure grasped the end of a wide board—a two-by-eight—which some one handed up from below. Swiftly, the cloaked man swung the board over the wall, sliding it out until one end of it rested on top of the barbed-wire fence, and the near end remained on the stone wall. Thus, it made a perfect bridge over the twenty feet of no-man's land.

It took almost the full four minutes to complete that operation. Then the cloaked figure dropped back to the roof of the car, waiting till the searchlights passed once more. As soon as they were gone, the cloaked figure called down softly, "Here goes, Jackson."

"Happy landings, major!" was all that Jackson said.

And then the *Spider* was on the wall, and crawling on the eight-inch bridge over the no-man's land. He moved swiftly, yet surely. For he must avoid falling into the jaws of the vicious mastiffs below, and he must also be across before the searchlights returned.

He reached the end of the plank and jumped to the ground inside the barbed-wire fence just as the beam of the searchlight swung around to finger once more at the spot. Both beams met right at this point, which was why he had chosen it, for it gave him twice the time.

Now, as the light splashed across the ground, the *Spider* lay flat, with his black cloak billowing out about him. A watcher in the castle might note the dark splotch on the ground, and might also notice the plank. And if he should be seen, the *Spider* would have no knowledge of it until a vicious burst of machine-gun bullets cut him down, or perhaps, until one of the flame-throwers burned him to a crisp.

But it was a chance he must take. Behind him, Jackson was already pulling back the plank. It was useless as a means of escape, for it would be impossible to scale the barbed-wire fence to reach it. The *Spider's* bridges were burned behind him!

And now, as he inched forward toward the castle

across the smooth and velvety lawn, the three mastiffs in the twenty-foot enclosure became aware of his presence, and began to utter low growls.

He paid no attention to them. He knew dogs. Their growls would grow in intensity as the strange man-smell *approached* them, until they were barking loud enough to sound an alarm. But he was now moving *away* from them. Their growls would continue. But the dogs would not begin to bark.

Slowly, cautiously, he made his way across the lawn, watchful of pits or charged wires. Also, he must be careful to flatten out every four minutes, when the stark glare of the searchlights struck with their merciless light. The castle was still a hundred yards distant. He could not hope to traverse all that space without being detected. Red Feather had not worked out this elaborate system of protection without posting adequate guards. And a watchful guard could not help spotting the black blotch he made against the green grass. Yet, he must try every trick at his command. It must be time for Jackson to send up his rocket. . . .

CHAPTER FIFTEEN

Bed of Pain

Within the great castle there was an air of
watchful expectancy.

The Baron Cornelius Crispi sat in a stiff-
backed chair in a chamber on the ground floor. His
chair faced the open French windows. He had a pair
of field glasses glued to his eyes, and the glasses
were trained upon a dark blotch that moved slowly
and laboriously across the green grass.

The Baron Cornelius Crispi chuckled.

"A very ingenious fellow, this *Spider!*" he said.

On the Baron's right side stood a small brown
Hindu with an automatic rifle. On his left stood
another Hindu with a flame-thrower. Both were watching the dark splotch on the grass. But it was to
neither of these that the Baron Crispi talked. He was
addressing himself to someone in the rear of the
room.

Since the entire chamber was in darkness, it was
difficult for anyone whose eyes had not become accustomed the gloom to discern just how that rear half
was equipped.

But, as one's eyes gradually adjusted themselves, they would have widened at the ghastly sight presented to them.

The entire rear half was occupied by a sinister machine which at first sight was reminiscent of the horrible days of the Inquisition, in the dark Middle Ages when men like Torquemada devoted their lives to the scientific study of the most effective means of producing pain and suffering in the human body.

Psychologists of the abnormal in human behavior maintain that the streak of sadism—the desire to inflict pain on others—which was so pronounced in the dark eras of human history, has not been eradicated from human consciousness by the refinements of civilization, but that it is merely dormant, ready to come to the fore whenever opportunity presents.

The ghastly machine in the room behind Baron Crispi was definite proof in support of this theory.

The backbone of the machine consisted of a bed of spikes, whose points were ground to a deadly sharpness. Suspended eight inches above the spikes, was a woman. She was tied firmly by the ankles. But at the other end she had no support except that which she could furnish for herself by gripping two ropes hanging over her head. She had to support the entire weight of her body by her hold upon those ropes. Each time that she weakened, her body would drop and the deadly-sharp spikes would bite into her back. If she let go entirely, her weight would drive her body down upon those spikes and she would die slowly and agonizingly, impaled by her own weight.

Nita van Sloan was thankful that it was dark, so that the agony written upon her face could not be witnessed by Baron Cornelius Crispi. She had been suspended over that bed of spikes for twenty minutes

305

now, and the strain upon every muscle of her lithe body was almost unbearable. Already, she was tempted to let go, and give up the struggle for life. But she knew that even this would not be the end. It would take her hours and hours to die, and the Baron would sit and gloat, and watch, and keep rhythmic time to her death struggles with his tapping, patent-leather shoe.

Directly above her head there was another threat—a guillotine of spikes, sliding up and down in grooved channels. The guillotine hung in such a position that if it dropped, it would pierce her throat, but not at the jugular vein. She would bleed to death slowly and surely.

The rope that controlled this guillotine ran across the room and was tied to the arm of Baron Crispi's chair.

"This, my dear," he explained to her, "is to take care of any emergency—such as the *Spider's* unexpected arrival. Even if he should succeed in entering and overpowering my guards, I would have only to slash the ropes with this knife, and you would die before his very eyes!"

"Why do you hate him so much?" Nita gasped.

"Why?" Crispi laughed harshly. "The *Spider* has blocked me everywhere tonight—or, rather, last night. He snatched Metz from right under my nose, with two hundred thousand dollars in cash. Then he caused me a loss of almost a quarter of a million in money and jewels when he interrupted the hold-up at the Mandalay Gardens. He killed Blagg, one of my best men. And he brought Susan Metz back to her father, thus depriving me of my hold over that man!"

Crispi stopped talking, growled deep in his throat like a terrier from whom someone has taken a luscious bone. "You, my dear, are paying for the *Spider's* achievements!"

Nita had no more strength to talk. Every last dram of her strength was required to keep her from slipping down upon the pointed spikes.

Crispi was talking now, low and vehemently. "There is no one in the world today who can appreciate the monetary value of human suffering—no one but myself. Motion picture producers, actors, writers, publishers, all try to make fortunes catering to the whims and desires of the multitude. But they all forget that there is a stronger instinct in the human race than the desire for pleasure—the instinct to avoid pain!

"Look at a baby. If it is burned, it will never touch fire again. Look at the millions of invalids who spend their last penny for doctors to relieve them of pain. Therefore, I—Baron Cornelius Crispi—have devised the plan of profiting by the instinct to avoid pain. People will pay huge sums frantically, to be spared pain and torture. Even you, my dear, would give me anything I asked of you, in order to be spared this agony!"

From his chair he regarded her sardonically. "Well now, my dear, speak up. Suppose I were to release you—at the price of betraying the *Spider* into my hands. Suppose I were to lift you off at this very moment, and relieve the terrible strain upon all the muscles of your body—*would you help me trap the Spider?*"

Nita was gasping with the dreadful exertion. But she drew in a deep breath, and managed to say in a fairly even tone, "If I weren't a lady, I would tell you to go to hell!"

Crispi spat out a curse, and flung violently away from her. "A little while longer, my dear—you will

307

be pleading with me. The longest anyone has lasted over those spikes was an hour and a half! But, if I am correct in my observations, I will trap the *Spider* without your aid!''

For ten minutes the Baron watched the movements of that dark shadow on the lawn. He felt secure with his Hindu killers at his side, and the rope which controlled the guillotine tied to his chair. He was ready to slash at the rope at an instant's notice. As he watched, he took grim pleasure in telling Nita everything that he observed.

And it was more the fear for Wentworth than for herself which caused her to strain at the ropes. For she knew Dick Wentworth; she knew that he was coming here, hoping that if he couldn't free her, he might die with her. Otherwise, why would he enter so boldly?

"Ah!" Crispi was saying, with his eyes at the binoculars. "Your *Spider* is moving again! Inch by inch!''

He turned to the Hindu at his left—the one with the automatic rifle. "We shall try to capture him alive, Mali, if possible. There are some—er—experiments I should like to try upon this mighty *Spider!* Besides—he is fabulously rich.''

In silence they waited, watching the progress of that shadowy figure.

"See," said Crispi, "how clever he thinks he is! He has reached a tree. He stands erect, thinking that he is safe in its shadow—'' He broke off, uttering an exclamation of annoyance.

In the distance to the left, a rocket suddenly went soaring up to the sky. It spread into a multi-colored band of light, then dissolved high in the heavens.

Crispi watched, frowning. "Perhaps that is a sig-

308

nal, Mali. Perhaps he does not come alone after all. If police come, we must have everything ready, Mali. All the prisoners go in the underground chambers— including Miss van Sloan. Our torture machines will then be merely specimens—eh, Mali?''

He chuckled in that slimy, gloating way of his. ''We have foreseen everything, Miss van Sloan. Please give up thought of rescue. Let us see what your friend the *Spider* is doing. Perhaps that rocket had no connection with him . . .''

He swung the glasses back to the tree, and clucked with satisfaction. ''He has not moved yet. How long does he think to wait? If he knew that you, my dear, were tearing the muscles of your body to keep off those spikes, perhaps he would hurry!''

Nita was wondering how close Dick was. If she used every remaining bit of strength to shout a warning to him, would he hear it? After such a shout, she would be too weak to hold herself up. She would have to let go and drop on the spikes. She'd do it, too, if she could only be sure it would save him. But to waste that precious energy, and not have him hear her cry. . . .

Dear God! What was that shadow above her?

Was it a shadow, or were her eyes playing tricks on her? Maybe, in her weakness, she only imagined that shadowy. . . .

But no. Surely, those were eyes peering down into the room through the trapdoor which housed the guillotine frame. Yes . . . something seemed to be drifting down toward her!

Hope! Hope began to surge in her breast, and then died instantly. For Crispi, with the glasses still at his eyes, was saying, ''Your *Spider* has not moved for a long time, my dear. I think I will make you scream. That will hurry him!''

309

Crispi got up from his chair, moved over toward Nita. Mali came with him. The other Hindu remained to watch from the window. Crispi clapped his hands and a small group of white-turbaned Hindus appeared armed with gleaming scimitars.

"You will go out on the grounds," he told them. "Watch the fool who hides by that tree. When the girl screams, he will move. Then close in on him. Wound him, but do not kill him. And bring him here!"

He nodded to one of the Hindus. "Slash her across the stomach, Vodee. One slash—enough to make her scream."

Vodee licked his lips and raised the scimitar in one hand. With the other he reached to Nita's dress.

But before he could touch her, the black and sinister figure of the *Spider* hurtled down upon him from the trapdoor above, and the *Spider's* feet, lashing out, smashed the Hindu's jaw as if it had been made of china. Vodee catapulted backward, and the *Spider* swung past through the air, like a man on a trapeze.

He was swinging from a line of web, which he had tied about his waist to give him freedom of action with both hands.

The *Spider* had out-maneuvered Crispi!

He had brought an extra cloak and hat into the grounds with him. And when Jackson had released the flare, the *Spider* had taken advantage of the momentary distraction of those in the house, to drape the cloak and hat on a branch. Then he himself had stolen across the lawn and climbed the creeping ivy to the second floor window, whence he had come down into this chamber of torture.

Baron Crispi realized this in a flash, as the *Spider* swung free after smashing Vodee's jaw. He shrieked orders to his Hindus, and they came trooping back

310

from the grounds with flashing scimitars, while Mali trained his automatic rifle upon the flying figure.

But the *Spider's* guns were already belching. Mali went down with a slug through his own belly, and the other Hindu with the flame-thrower took the blasting lead from the *Spider's* gun square in his face.

Baron Crispi uttered a cry of rage and sprang across to his chair, snatching up the knife with which to cut the rope that would send the spiked guillotine down upon Nita's throat.

The *Spider,* swinging free above her, was unable to get a shot at Crispi, because of the heavy oak chair. His quick mind grasped the meaning of the rope running from the guillotine slide to the Baron's chair. He sent himself swinging back, shouting to Nita, *"Hang on, girl!"*

His foot smashed another of the Hindus out of the way, and he reached the guillotine side just as Crispi cut the rope. The spikes began to drop toward Nita's throat, and Wentworth thrust out one of his guns. As the slide dropped in the smooth grooves, he placed the muzzle against the frame and fired six times!

The impact of those heavy forty-five calibre slugs, striking with the impact-weight of a fifty-pound sledge-hammer, twisted the metal frame of the groove. The heavy blade jammed to a stop in mid-descent!

Baron Crispi screamed with rage and snatched up a revolver. The Hindus dashed in, the nearest one of them trying to slash at the ropes by which Nita was supporting herself.

One of the *Spider's* guns was empty now. He threw it away, and smashed a terrific left into the jaw of the Hindu who was trying to cut the ropes. The man went flying backward, his head cocked at an unnatural angle.

Now, lead was whining past the *Spider*, converging upon him from Crispi's gun as well as from the guns of the Hindus.

The *Spider*, in his black cloak and hat, was a poor target for them. But his own shooting was uncannily accurate. He had only one gun, and he must make every shot count. The narrow confines of that torture chamber were filled with the fumes of cordite and the thunder of heavy explosions as he blasted again and again at the advancing Hindus. Four of them fell in as many seconds, and the others had had enough. They turned and fled, leaving their dead and wounded on the floor.

Nita had managed to wind the ropes about her wrists for greater purchase. She was watching the fight with blazing eyes, forgetful of her own predicament.

She screamed. "Look out, Dick! Behind you!"

The *Spider*, still swinging from his Web, kicked away instinctively from the framework, sending his body swinging outward. It was Nita's warning and his swift action which saved his life, for Baron Crispi was kneeling on one knee and taking careful aim with a long-barrelled Luger. He fired just as Wentworth kicked away, and the bullet smashed harmlessly into the framework of the torture machine. The Baron's face became a gaunt, malevolent visage of hatred as he aimed a second time.

The *Spider's* gun was empty.

But he was not at the end of his resources. The Hindu whom he had kicked in the jaw had dropped his scimitar across Nita's stomach. The *Spider* grasped and hurled it, and the blade cut diagonally into Crispi's forehead, a fraction of a second before he fired. His shot missed the *Spider*, and he fell backward, with blood streaming from a shallow wound in his forehead. It was not fatal, but the blood blinded him momentarily.

The *Spider* acted now with the speed of a fighting man who knows that a split-second may mean the difference between life and death.

His fingers slipped to his waist, loosening the noose which he had looped about himself. With one hand he supported himself by reaching for the line of Web above him, while with the other he slipped the loosened noose down until it dropped from his legs.

He was now hanging by one arm, directly above Nita, who was showing signs of weakening. She was gasping for breath. Looking down at her Wentworth saw that her whole body was trembling with the strain.

"Another minute, Nita!" he called, and hurled himself past her body, letting go of the Web just as he acquired momentum.

Crispi had wiped the blood from his eyes and he was leveling the Luger again when Wentworth's hurtling weight struck him in the chest. The smashing impact flung him backward. His head struck the heavy back of the oak chair and he collapsed.

The *Spider* wasted not even a second glance at him. He snatched up a scimitar and slashed at the ropes binding Nita's ankles to the framework. In a moment he had her off that terrible bed of spikes. Anyone else but Nita van Sloan would have collapsed, probably gone into a fit of hysterics. But not Nita.

She came into his arms swiftly, but her first words were, "Dick! There are other prisoners in this house—fifteen of them. Women, girls, and children whose loved ones that fiend has been forcing to commit

313

hideous crimes by threatening torture to the prisoners. We must free them!''

The *Spider* nodded. "Come—"

He broke off as he glimpsed the look of horror in
Nita's eyes. Sensing the danger behind him, he thrust
her out of the way and swung to meet the vicious
attack of Baron Cornelius Crispi, who had picked up
one of the scimitars, and was coming at Wentworth
with the blade raised high for a decapitating blow!

There was a wicked glint of triumph in Crispi's
eyes. He was only three feet from the *Spider,* and the
Spider was unarmed. The scimitar was coming around
now in that vicious slash which would sever the
Spider's head from his body!

The *Spider's* laughter clashed through the room.
He dropped backward before the vicious onslaught,
hitting the floor on his back just as Crispi slashed.
The Barron's attack brought him forward at great
momentum, and the *Spider's* legs rose straight in the
air to catch Crispi in the stomach. Crispi's forward
charge carried him high up, riding on the *Spider's*
feet. He described a parabola in the air, and sailed—
straight for the bed of spikes in the torture machine!

A weird, dreadful cry pulsed from his throat. This
inhuman student of human suffering couldn't take it
when it was his turn.

The scream of fear turned to a gurgling rattle of
animal fright as his body landed on the sharp-tipped
spikes. His weight and his momentum carried him far
down upon those deadly points, and the *squoosh* of
the barbs piercing bone and flesh and muscle was
terrible to hear.

Crispi flailed about in agony for a half-minute, his
arms thrashing wildly, serving only to drive the spikes
deeper.

"Mercy! Mercy . . ." he frothed. And then the

314

finger of Mercy touched him. For one of those spikes had evidently driven to his heart. His body stiffened into dreadful rigidity. His mouth opened wide in one last attempt to scream . . . and he died!

Nita van Sloan turned her face away. And the *Spider* put an arm about her waist and led her out of that chamber of pain and terror. . . .

Twenty minutes later, Richard Wentworth—without his *Spider* makeup—led a staggering, pitiful group of women, girls and children out of that gray, grim castle to freedom. Nita van Sloan was on his arm as he greeted Commissioner Kirkpatrick who was standing with a squad of police at the gate.

"Glory be!" Kirkpatrick said. "We caught half a dozen Hindus escaping, and we came to see if you were still alive!"

Wentworth nodded soberly. "And a monster is dead."

"You killed him?" Kirkpatrick demanded. "You killed Red Feather?"

Wentworth and Nita both exchanged looks.

"Why no, Kirk," said Wentworth. "Not I. The *Spider* killed him. You know, it was the *Spider* who saved us all."

Commissioner Kirkpatrick scowled and shook his head. "The *Spider* deserves the thanks of thousands for what he did tonight, Dick. But I warn you—if the *Spider* walks again, I'll come down on him with the full force of the law! And that's a promise!"

Richard Wentworth shrugged without answering, and turned back to Nita. And she, looking into the depths of his eyes, knew that he was thinking of those who had died so terribly today, and also of those who were miraculously alive, and happy, and freed forever of the menace of Red Feather. And she

315

swallowed the lump in her throat, and her long, patrician fingers touched his sleeve.

"I'm glad, Dick—" she whispered throatily "—glad that the *Spider* walked again tonight!"

FINE WORKS OF FICTION AND NON-FICTION AVAILABLE FROM CARROLL & GRAF

☐ Amis, Kingley/THE ALTERATION   **$3.95**
☐ Brown, Harry/A WALK IN THE SUN   **$3.95**
☐ Buchan, John/JOHN MACNAB   **$3.95**
☐ Burnett, W.R./HIGH SIERRA   **$3.50**
☐ Chester, Alfred/THE EXQUISITE CORPSE   **$4.95**
☐ Cozzens, James Gould/THE LAST ADAM   **$4.95**
☐ Crichton, Robert/THE CAMERONS   **$4.95**
☐ Crichton, Robert/THE SECRET OF SANTA
  VITTORIA   **$3.95**
☐ De Quincey, Thomas/CONFESSIONS OF AN
  ENGLISH OPIUM EATER AND OTHER
  WRITINGS   **$4.95**
☐ Eastlake, William/CASTLE KEEP   **$3.95**
☐ Farrell, J.G./TROUBLES   **$4.95**
☐ Farrell, J.G./THE SIEGE OF KRISHNAPUR   **$4.95**
☐ Farrell, J.G./THE SINGAPORE GRIP   **$4.95**
☐ Garbus, Martin/READY FOR THE DEFENSE   **$4.95**
☐ Gresham, William Lindsay/NIGHTMARE
  ALLEY   **$3.50**
☐ Gurney, Jr. A.R./THE SNOW BALL   **$4.50**
☐ Higgins, George V./COGAN'S TRADE   **$3.50**
☐ Hilton, James/RANDOM HARVEST   **$4.50**
☐ Huxley, Aldous/GREY EMINENCE   **$4.95**
☐ Innes, Hammond/THE NAKED LAND   **$3.50**
☐ Innes, Hammond/ATLANTIC FURY   **$3.50**
☐ Johnson, Josephine/NOW IN NOVEMBER   **$4.50**
☐ Kipling, Rudyard/THE LIGHT THAT FAILED   **$3.95**
☐ L'Amour, Louis/LAW OF THE DESSERT BORN   **$2.95**
☐ Lewis, Norman/THE SICILIAN SPECIALIST   **$3.50**
☐ Lewis, Norman/THE MAN IN THE MIDDLE   **$3.50**
☐ Mason, A.E.W./THE FOUR FEATHERS   **$3.95**
☐ Martin, David/FINAL HARBOR   **$4.95**

☐ Masters, John/BHOWANI JUNCTION	$4.50
☐ Masters, John/THE DECEIVERS	$3.95
☐ Masters, John/NIGHTRUNNERS OF BENGAL	$4.95
☐ Mitford, Nancy/THE BLESSING	$4.95
☐ Mitford, Nancy/PIGEON PIE	$4.95
☐ Mitford, Nancy/CHRISTMAS PUDDING	$3.95
☐ O'Hara, John/FROM THE TERRACE	$5.95
☐ O'Hara, John/SERMONS AND SODA WATER	$4.95
☐ O'Hara, John/HOPE OF HEAVEN	$3.95
☐ O'Hara, John/A RAGE TO LIVE	$4.95
☐ O'Hara, John/TEN NORTH FREDERICK	$4.50
☐ Proffitt, Nicholas/GARDENS OF STONE	$4.50
☐ Purdy, James/CABOT WRIGHT BEGINS	$4.50
☐ Rechy, John/BODIES AND SOULS	$4.50
☐ Reilly, Sidney/BRITAIN'S GREATEST SPY	$3.95
☐ Scott, Paul/THE LOVE PAVILION	$4.50
☐ Scott, Paul/THE CORRIDA AT SAN FELIU	$3.95
☐ Scott, Paul/A MALE CHILD	$3.95
☐ Short, Luke/MARSHAL OF VENGEANCE	$2.95
☐ Smith, Joseph/THE DAY THE MUSIC DIED	$4.95
☐ Taylor, Peter/IN THE MIRO DISTRICT	$3.95
☐ Thirkell, Angela/THE BRANDONS	$4.95
☐ Thirkell, Angela/AUGUST FOLLY	$4.95
☐ Thirkell, Angela/CHEERFULNESS BREAKS IN	$4.95
☐ Thirkell, Angelea/MARLING HALL	$4.95
☐ Thirkell, Angela/HIGH RISING	$4.95
☐ Thirkell, Angela/POMFRET TOWERS	$4.95
☐ Thirkell, Angela/BEFORE LUNCH	$4.95

☐ Thirkell, Angela/WILD STRAWBERRIES $4.95
☐ Thompson, Earl/A GARDEN OF SAND $5.95
☐ Wharton, Williams/SCUMBLER $3.95
☐ Wilder, Thornton/THE EIGHTH DAY $4.95
☐ Wilder, Thornton/THE CABALA $3.95

Available from fine bookstores everywhere or use this coupon for ordering.

Carroll & Graf Publishers, Inc., 260 Fifth Avenue, N.Y., N.Y. 10001

Please send me the books I have checked above. I am enclosing
$_____ (please add $1.00 per title to cover postage and
handling.) Send check or money order—no cash or C.O.D.'s
please. N.Y. residents please add 8¼% sales tax.

Mr/Mrs/Ms _____

Address _____

City _____ State/Zip _____

Please allow four to six weeks for delivery.